THE KING'S SEER

BOOK 5

DREAM UNVEILED

D1519959

L.S. BETHEL

CHAPTER 1

Serenity had been sleeping soundly. Only the sounds of the soft breaths of her husband lying beside her filled the room. Kang-Dae's arm lay across her side in a comforting hold. Despite the peacefulness of it all, Serenity was unable to stay asleep. Instead, she lay awake in anticipation. 'It wouldn't be long now' she thought to herself. Only a few seconds passed before she heard it. Footsteps. They were so soft they barely made a sound. Serenity kept her eyes shut feigning sleep, but she knew it wouldn't make a difference. Shuffling feet ended at her side of the bed. Serenity didn't move, she barely breathed. The movement of the blanket shifting only startled her for a second. The weight of something crawling up her body had her trying even harder to keep her eyes shut. A tiny hand touched her cheek and Serenity could no longer keep up the ruse. With a smile, she opened her eyes and stared into identical brown orbs.

"Good morning, my blessing," Serenity spoke softly, trying not to wake Kang-Dae. Her baby girl smiled down brightly at her mother, before throwing herself into Serenity's chest with a giggle. Not even a year yet, her daughter, Blessing, had mastered the art of escaping from her crib on the other side of the room and waking her parents whenever she grew bored of waiting for them to get her.

"Shh, don't wake daddy." Serenity cooed into her curly hair. She wrapped Blessing up in her arms and sat up, holding the tiny girl in her lap. She looked back at Kang-Dae who still had not stirred. He had come to bed late in the evening exhausted after a full day of meetings with the lords, nobles, and officials in the capital. He'd been disappointed to see Blessing was already sleeping when he returned. Serenity reassured him their daughter wasn't going anywhere and would be there when he woke. She wanted him to rest but knew he would want to see them both when he woke up. Trying to keep an eleven-month-old quiet for an indeterminate amount of time was not a task she felt she could accomplish. Getting an idea, she carried Blessing over to the chest by her crip and grabbed a cloth diaper before heading to the balcony.

Serenity handed Blessing her rattle drum for her to play with. She accepted the small drum happily and played with it while Serenity changed her on the pallet on the balcony, where she and Kang-Dae would sometimes lay to do their "star writing." Once Blessing was clean and dry, she sat the girl up, but she was more interested in the toy in her hand. Satisfied that her daughter was occupied, Serenity took a moment to admire the rising sun above the grounds. It was early enough that the sky was tinted purple and orange. Birds were singing in the distance and a cool but soft breeze blew through the air. Serenity leaned back on her palms and closed her eyes, taking in the tranquility of the moment. She enjoyed these little peaceful moments before her day officially started. She had only recently jumped back into the political side of things a few months ago when she felt comfortable leaving Blessing. It had been so hard to do. Once she was born Serenity never let her out of her sight. After all she'd been through, she didn't think she could ever be more scared but the fear of a mother was something new. She had worried about her all the time. It was only after a visit and an encouraging talk from her mother that Serenity felt herself begin to relax. It helped to have complete trust in those who looked after her. Amoli was amazing with Blessing and loved her dearly, a feeling Serenity knew was mutual given how her tiny face would light up whenever she came to get her. If they did things like godparents in Xian Serenity would've made her Blessing's godmother. She'd never tell Rielle that though. Not that she had many opportunities to tell Rielle anything. Her last visit had been when Blessing was born. She had made a swift exit following that. Serenity wanted to be understanding but it had stung a bit. Rielle had been very distant the past year, and not just because they were literally worlds apart. Even when they saw each other she seemed detached, like she was waiting for the moment to end. Serenity tried bringing it up with her but she only denied anything was wrong and attributed her behavior to regular fatigue.

Serenity felt something lightly crawling down her neck. Startled, she looked down only to relax when she saw two fingers creeping their way down her collarbone. With a smile, she lifted her head to see Kang-Dae smiling mischievously at her. "Morning," she greeted.

"Morning," he returned.

"Ap, ap!" Blessing squealed noticing her father had joined them. She hadn't mastered many words as of yet but it didn't stop her from trying. She loved trying to call for her dad even if the Xian word for it never fully formed on her little lips.

"My Mi-Sung," he cooed Blessing's Xian name while taking her into his arms. The idea of giving her both a Xian name and an English one had been his idea. Serenity had been fine with the Xian one but he insisted on incorporating both their cultures. It was why they spoke both their languages to her equally.

"Will you be spending today with your appa?" he asked her. Blessing's response was only to smile down at him. Kang-Dae kissed the top of her head. Kang-Dae joined Serenity on the pallet with Blessing in his arms. Serenity snuggled into him. Blessing immediately started playing in Serenity's hair.

"You sure you can handle her all day on your own?" Serenity asked only half-jokingly. Blessing had been a handful before she was crawling, now that she was fully mobile the child was practically unstoppable. Kang-Dae chuckled.

"Our Mi-Sung is a formidable foe but I think I can manage," he said. Serenity shrugged knowing he most likely had no idea what he was in for.

"How did you sleep?" He asked the question casually but Serenity knew better. There was nothing casual about his inquiry. He was prodding, as subtly as he could while trying not to upset her.

"Good. Nothing to report," she told him and she was telling the truth. She hadn't had any dreams last night, at least not in the variety he was asking about. A small shudder went through her as the memory of the nightmare surfaced. She hoped he didn't notice it. The dream came months ago and had been so bad she woke screaming, bringing the guards in. It had taken Kang-Dae over an hour to calm her. She had been sobbing and shaking so badly. The fear of that night still haunted her but she did her best to put it to the back of her mind. As horrible and terrifying as that night had been, she could not remember any of her dream. It had never happened to her since she'd come to Xian, her forgetting a dream. For it to happen on such a clearly impactful dream angered and scared her greatly. Her frustration began to manifest in her attitude to the point where Kang-Dae had become very careful when he spoke to her trying not to set her off. Having just had Blessing her emotions were already fluctuating and the poor man couldn't seem to catch a break around her.

Serenity reached back and wound her hand in his hair. He shifted and planted a kiss on her cheek. They sat in peaceful silence watching the sun continue to rise over pink skies. A knock at the door finally interrupted their moment of tranquility. Kang-Dae let out a sigh before getting up. He helped Serenity up as well and they headed back inside. The servants set up the breakfast as they took their seats at their table. Breakfast time was their must-do tradition to make sure they always started the day as a family. Neither of them had any disillusions about their availability and duties and knew being able to spend time together regularly was a luxury. So, they made it their mission to have at least this one time during the day.

Blessing sat on Kang-Dae's knee as he bounced her while giving her a variation of mashed fruit. While Kang-Dae fed their child, Serenity took it upon herself to feed him. Whenever Blessing got distracted Serenity would sneakily reach over and slip some porridge in his mouth. Kang-Dae winked at her success. Like a typical baby, Blessing was not big on sharing which made things even more difficult when she considered every food she saw as hers. Whoever had the challenging task of feeding her resigned themselves to not being able to eat themselves or having to fight her for every bite.

The door opened unexpectedly letting them both know exactly who it was.

"Good morning, Jung-Soo," Serenity greeted without turning from her meal.

"Oo, oo," said Blessing happily. Not bothering with a greeting, Jung-Soo moved right over to Kang-Dae or rather Blessing. He took something out of his pocket and handed it to her.

She squealed, snatching the small horse figurine from him. Kang-Dae gave Jug-Soo an exasperated look.

"I believe it is the parent's duty to spoil the child," he said dryly but there was playfulness in his eyes. Jung-Soo didn't respond, only moving back and standing over them. Serenity smiled up at their friend and general.

"I hope you're getting some sleep. She doesn't need her favorite uncle keeling over from exhaustion because he spent all night carving her another toy," remarked Serenity.

As usual, Jung-Soo didn't show any outward regret for his actions. One thing Serenity could never have predicted following the birth of their daughter was Jung-Soo's immediate taking to her. Even though it was in a very Jung-Soo way. He would never be caught making silly faces or engaging in baby talk but he was their main supplier of toys and would often watch over her when she was with Amoli. He was also Blessing's favorite mode of transportation. Anytime they walked the palace and Jung-Soo was near she reached for the guard demanding he carry her for a reason no one has figured out yet.

"Will you be joining us to feed the horses today?" asked Kang-Dae, not taking his eyes off Blessing who already had her new toy in her mouth.

"Unfortunately, that is not something either of us will be able to do today," Jung-Soo said in a low voice. Kang-Dae looked at him with a frown on his face.

"What's happened?" he asked, dreading the answer.

"A situation in the outskirts of Gai has been brought to our attention and the lords requested an emergency meeting." Serenity looked at Kang-Dae with concern and sympathy. She knew how much he had been looking forward to spending time with Blessing but she also knew he would not shirk off his duties.

"I can take her," she offered. "The kids like when I bring her around." Kang-Dae shook his head.

"No, I will keep her," he stated. Both Serenity and Jung-Soo gave him apprehensive looks.

"Baby-," she began gently.

"I will take her with me," he reiterated more forcibly. Serenity knew then not to push.

"Okay," she conceded.

"You may want to bring her some more toys," Serenity said to Jung-Soo who didn't say anything but silently agreed.

CHAPTER 2

Blessing was babbling to herself as she sat on her father's lap, playing with the armrest of the throne. The gold plating fascinated her enough to keep her occupied for a time. Kang-Dae hoped to keep this meeting as brief as possible. He'd promised his daughter a day together playing with the horses. It didn't matter if she had no understanding of what he promised. He would always keep his word to her.

"The building has been placed on hold my king," Lord Wang spoke from his seat. Kang-Dae steadied Blessing as she attempted to look over the side of the throne. "After pulling some of the men to help in the north there were not enough to keep the schedule."

"I still believe the northern lords can wait. Most of their estates have been rebuilt already. It seems unwise to put off fortifying our stronghold for a few homes." This came from Lord Bai.

"The North had more damage in the war than anyone. We help rebuild to show good faith," Kang-Dae reminded the man.

"If not for so many of them falling to the enemy there may not have been as much destruction in the first place," he retorted. A couple of lords murmured among themselves at the statement.

"Lord Bai, your opinion has been noted. Let us move on," Kang-Dae said a bit of warning in his tone. Everyone knew there had been more than a few lords who had chosen to align themselves with Katsuo to save themselves. Some had repented, some claimed it was to save their people and they had no other choice. As for the others, they fled in their shame and defeat never to be heard from again. It was still a sore topic for many. The ones deemed worthy were able to keep their lands but had to give up a majority of their men to the Xian army. Some of the less worthy ones lost their titles and land. The others who'd been caught trying to flee were either forced into exile or rotting away in prison. The more egregious traitors were forced to pay the ultimate price.

Six men were on their knees before the leaders of Xian. Four of the six were appropriately anxious. The other two on the opposite sides of the line held a steady composure but from the way one of their hands slightly trembled Kang-Dae could see it was just a front.

Serenity rubbed at her pregnant belly, a habit she picked up once her stomach "popped" as her mom would say. She used to try to appear intimidating at these things but gave up, unable to muster even a smidgen of intimidation. So, she left it up to Kang-Dae. Kang-Dae was the one who could instill fear into others with just a look. She let him play to his strengths.

Satori stood to the side reading off the names of each man on the floor along with what they were accused of. The large crowd was made to stay in the back while the lords and officials sat in front of them.

"Treason, conspiracy, failure to protect those in your charge...," Satori went on and on making it clear to the accused and those in the room just how much they had done. Kang-Dae and Serenity had decided to make these trials public so there was no question of what they had done and how badly things could have gone had they succeeded. Many had shown up, some from outside the city from the looks of them.

The crowd murmured as the crimes were listed. Satori held up a hand to silence the crowd once he was done.

"The witnesses may come forward!" A line of people were led out. Serenity watched every kneeling man's face fall as the people, people they clearly recognized, were brought before them. The servants spoke first confessing to being forced to run messages between the men. An act one of the lords deemed innocent until one of his soldiers, another witness, spoke up to the contents of the letter as he had been ordered to make his men stand down to accommodate the enemy. There were more

than just subordinates there. A few noblemen had come forth as well, eager to separate themselves from the men and their plans. They claimed to have been approached to throw in with them but had supposedly declined and were imprisoned in their homes because of it, unable to warn anyone of their deceptive actions. The more the witnesses spoke the more the light of hope dimmed in the men's eyes.

"Do you have anything to say in your defense?" Kang-Dae asked once the evidence became overwhelming. The lies came out instantly. Some claimed their families' lives were threatened. Others still maintained their innocence dismissing the witnesses as liars with ulterior motives. One even tried to claim their treason was merely an act to get close to the enemy and turn against him at the right moment. Kang-Dae let out a sigh. Serenity reached for his hand and the two shared a look. They knew it was all lies. Serenity had already dreamed about each one of them. She saw them happily and greedily accept Katsuo's gold. She and Kang-Dae had already discussed the extent they

would show mercy. Kang-Dae wanted to give the highest and most appropriate punishment for their crimes. Serenity and he came to the agreement mercy would only be given if remorse were shown. Given the way they so easily lied to avoid their rightful punishment, Serenity knew that type of mercy was now off the table. The couple turned to the men, with their decision made. Kang-Dae squeezed her hand knowing that this part of their job was difficult for her. She drew on that strength to keep her neutral expression.

"You have betrayed your people, you have betrayed your families, you have betrayed your country and you have betrayed us. There is no ruling I can give that will allow you to continue to draw breath in this kingdom." The crowd whispered heavily among themselves. The men began shaking their heads in denial. "For your crimes, you will all be executed among the red rock. Your remains will be given to your families so you may have the honor you lacked in this life." The crowd exploded in shouts of approval, gasps, and more aggressive

murmurs. The men ranged from silently crying to loud sobbing as they were led away. Serenity wasn't aware she was looking at her belly rubbing even more aggressively as the men pleaded on their way out. A pull from Kang-Dae made her look toward him. He gave a look of encouragement and she took a deep breath. She had returned to accept her role as queen and though there were things that were hard for her to stomach, she knew they were now a part of her "job."

"I only meant that with the whispers of enemies still walking the lands, now would not be the time to not have the fort at our disposal," Bai kept talking.

"We have already discussed those rumors and have not found any truth to them," Lord Liu interjected.

"Yet they continue to spread," Yu spoke up for the first time. "Now we have been hearing word that Katsuo's soothsayer has resurfaced."

Kang-Dae's head shot up at that. "When was this?"

"Only a few days ago, my king. But again, nothing has been proven," Satori told him.

"Still, it's not something we should dismiss," Kahil spoke from the side by Jung-Soo.

"No, it's not," agreed Kang-Dae. Serenity's nightmare entering his thoughts. She'd told him of the soothsayer's power. While it was not as great as Serenity's it still was a threat. "We need to either substantiate these whispers or put them to rest," Kang-Dae announced.

"It is almost impossible to find the source of the rumors," said Hui.

"Not if we ask the right people," piped up Amir. The men looked to the King's current advisor. The role had sat empty since Min's dismissal until Kang-De appointed the previously youngest council member following the end of the war. Kang-Dae had been very impressed by the man's helpful strategies for rebuilding and decided to put his talents and intellect to good use. "If there is truth in these rumors, the only ones privy to it would be the enemy itself, or those who have allied themselves with them."

"You believe there are still traitors among us?"

"Only if the stories are true," Amir clarified. "For the enemy to stay hidden for so long they would need allies. If these men are under the impression that the enemy is still around it may have given them the confidence to give them aid in hopes of gaining whatever promise Katsuo made to them."

"We still don't know who they are," said Yu.

"We have our suspicions," Kahil said. There were lords and officials who were accused of being collaborators but there had been no evidence to make a judgment. In the essence of fairness, Kang-Dae chose not to persecute them. "Perhaps we should pay these men a visit," continued Kahil.

It was a delicate matter. Kang-Dae risked offending some of the oldest families in Xian if they were wrong. With the dream on his mind, Kang-Dae felt an offense was better than another war. "Kahil, you, and Amir go. Meet them in their homes, and root out any snakes you might find," ordered Kang-Dae. The men bowed.

"Yes, my King." They said in unison.

He looked at Jung-Soo. "Have some of your men check the surrounding villages as well. If the cities are compromised, they may have seen or heard something." Jung-Soo gave a nod and the meeting continued.

CHAPTER 3

Serenity stood over the young group of children as they wrote out the characters on their papers. "Very good," Serenity praised. The youngest of the four, Su-Yin, looked up and gave Serenity a smile that warmed her heart. Though she'd never say it out loud she felt more fulfilled working with the children than on her queenly duties. Maybe it was nostalgia, a reference to a less complicated life from her past. But Serenity wouldn't trade her life for anything, no matter how complicated things became. The children she taught were just a small group of orphans staying within the palace until another home for them could be built. The one she set up didn't have enough room to house the number of children that had appeared following Katsuo's campaign. Her goal was to start getting the word out to help the children find homes.

In the aftermath of the war, there weren't many people in the position to take in a child. It was one of the reasons she worked so hard with her mother-in-law to help generate more jobs and opportunities among the people. The country hadn't just taken a hit physically, but economically and it was a long road to recover what had been lost. Kah-Mah, the misty island ruled by Queen Prija, had been willing to help where they could. After word of Katsuo's demise, she had reached out to Serenity, surprising the couple. They were even more surprised when she offered to send two ships full of food, seeds, and soil in exchange for nothing. Serenity sent the soil to several of their farms around the land to hopefully increase their harvest.

"I'm hungry," one of the boys spoke out.

"After you finish, we will all have something to eat," said her co-teacher, Huifang. She was a teenager who had also been displaced by the war. Serenity found her trying to care for a group of kids on her own when she went out to help deliver supplies in the city. Serenity felt an instant need to help the girl and offered her a place in the palace helping her with the same kids she had been protecting. She had been very appreciative, swearing to pay back Serenity's kindness by working hard but Serenity had just wanted to get her off the street. Her appearance back then had been jarring. Her pale skin made her look sickly and her malnourished frame didn't help. She looked as though she could be knocked over by the wind back then. Now, she'd gained a healthy amount of weight, her skin sported a healthy tint and she smiled more often than not.

"Queen Serenity, can we play in the gardens today?" asked Su-Yun. Serenity pretended to think about it, with her head tilted and her eyes pointed toward the ceiling.

"Hmm, I don't know. It's springtime." She slowly walked over to the young girl. "All sorts of bugs flying around."

The kids looked up from their work and started giggling. "I would hate to see a bee-," she stopped behind Su-Yun who had frozen in excited anticipation. "Carry you away!" She shouted, grabbing the girl, and lifting her in her arms as she shrieked and laughed along with the other children. Serenity flew her around the room and the children chased her to "rescue" their friend. Serenity carefully put her down and immediately picked up another child, the young boy, Mu-Gin, who let out an ear-piercing shriek before giving a full belly laugh. Once she was tired, they all came to a stop. "Put your things away. We'll have some lunch and then go to the gardens," she informed them. The kids moved quickly.

"Don't go far!" Serenity called out as the children sprinted on the paths between the flowers.

"I'll keep up with them," Huifang told her. She did a slow jog behind the group as they disappeared behind the hedges.

"My Queen," someone called out behind her. Serenity turned to see one of their messengers walking up.

"I have a letter for you," he told her, holding out the rolled-up parchment.

She thanked him and accepted it. Seeing the seal, a flutter of excitement went through her. It was from Ami. The teen had only written to her a few times in the past year. She never knew when she would hear from him but always looked forward to it, wanting to know he was all right. His life had gone through such significant changes and she worried about him. After he returned to his village, he claimed to have been found by his birth mother and brought back to the Anoeka, where he had been born. The news was surprising to Serenity but it didn't matter to her. He was still Ami. According to him, he had very few memories of his life before he was taken in by Iko. Serenity had found it strange his mother had only been able to find him after the woman's untimely passing, but Ami had been willing. He didn't say much about his family or his life back in Anoeka and Serenity got the feeling there was much he wasn't saying on purpose but as long as he kept in touch, she was fine with his secrets.

She snapped the seal and began to read right then and there. The more she read the more her expression dropped.

By the time Serenity made it back to the bedroom Blessing was already sound asleep. Kang-Dae sat at the table drinking tea and playing a game similar to chess by himself. He looked deep in concentration. Serenity went behind the decorative room divider to check on Blessing. Seeing her clutching her doll as she slept made her feel slightly better. After giving her a soft kiss she went over to the table and sat down with Ami's letter in her hand.

"Despite what they say, it's clear the rumors are beginning to unsettle some of the nobles," he spoke quietly, moving a piece on the board.

"Has there been anything substantial yet?" she asked. He shook his head.

"I've sent Tae-Soo and Hai-In to check into one of the areas where the claims originated from. Perhaps the people there can put us all at ease," he said in a hopeful yet logical tone.

"It probably wouldn't hurt for us to make a few appearances ourselves, show the people we're looking into it," she offered. Kang-Dae nodded in agreement.

"It may be a good time to unveil the plans for schools," he added. It was in these moments, here together, that most of the work was done, contrary to popular belief. Even though it was not often both king and queen attended the meetings with the lords and nobles to strategize or work on the economics with the Dowager and officials, they always debriefed each other on the going ons of all kingdom issues and worked together on how to improve things. Most times any plan they presented to their respective cohorts was drawn by the other or both of them.

"I'm still not sure how that's going to go over with the nobles," Serenity said. Those people clung to their traditions like a religion. Doing something so drastically different may undo all the goodwill she managed to build with them over that last year.

"They will push back, as is their nature. Education has always been one of the things they had to consider themselves better. Giving that privilege to everyone threatens their status in their eyes."

Serenity hung her head, knowing he was right and wondering if she should hold off. "They will, however, get over it," he said suddenly, borrowing a phrase from her. Serenity let out a short laugh.

"We're doing what's best for all our people. That is what matters," he reminded her. She gave him a gracious smile, which soon fell away as she remembered the letter.

"What is it?" Kang-Dae asked, noticing the shift in her demeanor.

Serenity handed him the letter. Kang-Dae read over it carefully as Serenity watched. The boy was very vague with his wording. He spoke only about how he was feeling day to day and being unsure if he had made the right decision to return with his mother. When Kang-Dae was done, he placed it down and held his hand out to her. Serenity didn't hesitate to take it and allow him to lead her around the table and pull her into his lap.

"I'm not just being paranoid right? He's in trouble," she said.

"We can't be sure. Ami is still young. With everything he has been through he's entitled to feel a bit lost. It does not mean he is in any danger."

"We should go see him," she declared. Kang-Dae dropped his head.

"Serenity-," he began.

"He's miserable," she told him, picking up the letter for emphasis.

"But not harmed," Kang-Dae reaffirmed.

"There's something up with his mother. I know it. She abandoned him."

"We do not know the full story," he reminded her gently.

"Because he won't tell us. Probably because he knows I'd bring him right back over here," she said half to herself. Kang-Dae gave a slight smirk.

"We do not know where to even look. And if we did, we may not be welcome on their shores," he informed her. There had already been attempts to make peace with the country and their new king. They knew nothing about the new leader, whether he agreed with his predecessor's actions or condemned them, and hoped by offering an olive branch their two kingdoms could start again with peace, but every envoy they sent had been turned away. They only received a singular letter seeking the return of any living Anoekan soldiers, the remains of Katsuo, and the promise not to come to their shores again, that was signed by "King of Anoeka." Serenity didn't seem deterred by this information judging from the displeased look on her face.

"He's not ours, my neeco. His choices are his own." Serenity continued to frown, not liking the truth in his words. "However, if you would like a son of our own…" he trailed off his voice dropping an octave. Serenity rolled her eyes, pretending that she didn't get a tiny flutter in her belly.

"Don't distract me," she pouted. Kang-Dae didn't listen, in fact, he took it as a challenge. His hand snaked around her waist to bring her closer. He nuzzled the side of her neck.

"I missed you today," he whispered in her ear, giving her lobe a tiny nibble making her gasp. "Did you miss me?"

"Kang-Dae," she warned, trying to take on a commanding voice but failing miserably. He began undoing the front of her gown while he planted kisses up and down her neck.

"You'll wake her," she said in a halfhearted attempt to stop him.

"*You* will just have to be very quiet then," he smiled, capturing her lips in his. Any shred of resistance from her was gone the moment his lips met hers. Kang-Dae smiled into the kiss when she wrapped her arms around his neck. He carried her over to the bed, passing the room divider where their daughter slept in her crib. Their lips did not part once even as he lay her down. He took his time removing her dress. Their intimate time together was not as frequent as he would have liked. Between their duties to the country, the people, and their child, it was hard to take time for just themselves. When they could dig out a little bit of time, he cherished it. He could see her mind start to wander as she looked back toward the divider, most likely worried Blessing would wake. He gently brought her face back to his and kissed her softly, sensually, kissing her until all thoughts were just on them. He knew he'd succeeded when her hands went to his robes. He shrugged them off, pushing them to the floor. He removed his shirt next. Her hands went to work sliding up his torso before reaching his shoulder and pulling down for another kiss. For a while, they didn't do more than kiss. An act that they'd greatly missed as well. When they parted to breathe, he stared down at her flushed face and mimicked the soft smile she had. Her hands played in his hair as his thumb stroked her cheek.

Serenity stared up at Kang-Dae. Her heart was still pounding in anticipation but it didn't stop her from appreciating the man above her. She loved him so much and she knew he felt the same. Every day, even on days they weren't able to interact for more than a few minutes, she thanked God for him. She never regretted her choice to stay in this land because of him. He was hers and she would be his until God and only God tore them apart. She lifted her leg to slide her foot on his leg before wrapping it around his waist. Kang-Dae's grin widened and he captured her lips once more. She angled her hips at the same time he surged forward. She moaned into his mouth, completely forgetting her earlier fears of not being quiet enough. He reached for her hand and their fingers interlocked as they moved together in sync, their dance having been perfected with their now expert knowledge of the other's bodies and desires. He positioned himself in just the right way and kept their pace masterfully. He burrowed his face in her neck, never breaking their stride. She had never and would never tire of these moments. These moments when they were perfectly in sync, one in body and spirit. She felt so connected with him she believed at that moment that even their thoughts were the same. She took a breath at the same moment he did. When she whimpered, he'd moan. Just as she would pull at him to bring him closer, he was already pushing himself deeper into her. It was in these moments she knew there would never be or could have been another person for her. It was always meant to be him. She knew soon he would want to watch her come apart, wanting to watch him do the same. She would oblige like she always did.

Kang-Dae felt the familiar stirring and pulled back enough to stare into her eyes. Both had their mouths slightly parted, their soft breaths and moans filling the room. They pushed each other to the brink ready to cross that wonder plateau as one. Before either of them could scream they slammed their mouths together in a hard but passionate kiss swallowing the other's cries as they slid into euphoria. Seconds rolled into another. All concept of time was gone as they trembled together clutching at the other unable to do anything but feel. Minds blank, hearts pounding, bodies tensed as the waves continued washing over them. It had been too long, they both thought when they were able to think again.

Sweaty, exhausted, and blissful Kang-Dae kissed Serenity's glistening head and slid to her side, keeping his arm around her. Her bare chest heaving almost had him climbing back on top of her. She must've caught him looking because she scoffed before sliding the sheet up to cover herself, making him pout. She let out a tired laugh. She brought him over to lie on top of her and he was more than happy to. They didn't speak, having said all they needed to with their bodies.

CHAPTER 4

1 Month Earlier…

She ran faster than she ever had in her life, but she knew it still wasn't fast enough. Her upbringing had never prepared her for this. The branches slapped against her soft cheeks as she continued through the brush. She whimpered at the sting but did not slow her pace.

"My lady, I can't-," the young woman's voice behind her panted. She grabbed her hand and pulled her along.

"We cannot stop." The two kept running with only the light of the moon to guide their steps. She was sure they must have noticed her absence by now. They would be searching the area for her. If she shared what she knew it would endanger all their plans. If she didn't reach their destination soon it would be too late, for them and for Xian.

Only a few more miles and they'd be able to make it into the city and get a horse. From there, it would take them a couple of days to make it to the capital. She had to warn them, warn all of them.

When running became far too difficult the two women opted to walk. Still wanting to keep moving but lacking the energy to do anything more. They shuffled on, in a sluggish state, for another hour before the sight of city gates came up on the horizon. The relief the woman felt was great but not enough to make her believe their troubles were over. Making their way to the road, the light of the rising sun began to make its appearance. She could hardly believe that they had been running all night. It was probably too early to expect any assistance but if they could just make it inside, they could seek shelter at the inn for an hour or two.

The gate was in their sights only a few meters away. The sound of several galloping horses came from behind them. She turned to look and felt her heart drop. "Run!" She screamed to her companion, who looked back and paled. The two started running once more, only to be cut off by three men on horseback. The man in the middle jumped down in front of them forcing them to take several steps back. Her companion clung to her and she held on to her tightly, as tears streamed down her face.

"Please come with us my lady," the man ordered, his tone much gentler than his demeanor showed. She shook her head. Her companion was sobbing now.

"No harm will come to you. You have my word, but you must come with us now. It is too dangerous for you to be out here on your own."

'Dangerous' she scoffed to herself. They were the danger.

"You have had a long night. Let's escort you back, Lady Gi." He used her title. An empty gesture to her. That title would mean nothing soon, Jae-Hwa thought. Now that she had failed there was nothing to warn the capital of the impending threat.

CHAPTER 5

The people knew their king and queen had arrived in the city judging from the large crowd of people approaching the carriage and being kept at a distance by both their personal guards and soldiers. Kang-Dae helped her step down. Kang-Dae had brought her to show her some surprise he had for her. He wouldn't give her a hint as to where they were going or why, no matter how much she tried to beg. She even tried to use Blessing to wear him down but even their daughter's big brown eyes had no effect. When they made it to the city she wondered if this was just a special outing like they'd always planned to have but never quite got around to it. A "date night" so to speak. As they approached a less populated part of the city in front of an abandoned building, she became even more confused. Kang-Dae led her inside. Both guards stayed outside, blocking the entrance for anyone else. There weren't many windows, making the room dim. There were a few pieces of left behind furniture around but the place was mostly empty. It was a wide space, with lots of room. There was an upstairs leading to an overhead balcony that overlooked the first floor. From the looks of it, the balcony had a decent amount of space as well. Serenity looked around the empty building still unsure why he had brought her.

"Where are we?" Serenity finally asked, hoping she'd get the answer this time.

"The first of many," he said, gesturing for her to go further in, allowing her the chance to look around better. "Serenity's school for the people."

Her head snapped towards him in disbelief.

"What?" He grinned, making him look younger. He grabbed her hand and led her upstairs and Serenity froze at the top. Multiple rows of small desks were set up. A podium was placed at the front.

"This is just to show you what it can be. You are welcome to change it as you see fit. The land in the back gives you the opportunity to expand when needed, which I suspect will be soon."

"I thought we would wait until the rebuilds were finished before we started on this."

"No build was necessary for this," he explained. "It used to be a restaurant, owned by Lord Eul." Serenity immediately understood.

"As long as we are repurposing these properties, we could use them to enhance our land to make up for their actions." Serenity couldn't argue with that logic.

"We still need teachers," she said, stepping around the "classroom." She felt like she was back in her old school the summer before they reopened. She remembered how she used to dread returning in the beginning, not wanting the summer to be over just yet. Now she felt a building excitement at the idea she could be back in a classroom soon.

"Once we make the announcement, we can put out a call for them. Perhaps this building's first use will be to train capable and competent teachers to offload a portion of the responsibility," he stressed the word offload reminding her he did not want her overextending herself by adding another duty to her already full plate. She understood and would comply. Though she missed being in the classroom she knew her other duties took precedence. They spent the next half hour exploring the space while Serenity raved about all the things she could do to it to make it comfortable and fun for the kids. Kang-Dae listened, amused, as she spoke fast, hardly taking a breath. Serenity was a great queen but seeing her in this element showed him how great a teacher she also was.

When they came outside the crowd had grown. Arezoo and Gyuri kept the left side at bay with a few soldiers, while Jung-Soo and Nasreen covered the other. The crowds went to their knees as they appeared. Kang-Dae told them to stand not wanting to make a spectacle of their appearance.

"Is it true there are still enemies among us?" Someone called out. Kang-Dae stared down at Serenity whose worried face matched his. He stepped forward only for Serenity to grab his hand

and step with him. He gave her a half smile of appreciation.

"There may always be enemies among us," he began and the people mumbled. "It's easy to gain enemies when you have what so many desire. We, my people, have a lot. With blessings come enemies who will try to covet them for themselves. It is an unfortunate fact of life. However, if time has proven anything, it is that no matter who has come against us, we have always beaten them back."

"And as long as we live, we always will," Serenity added. Kang-Dae enclosed his fingers around her hand and nodded.

"Do not live in fear of possible enemies. Live in peace knowing they will never succeed."

The people cheered, voicing their approval. No one noticed the still figure in the crowd who was silent. No one saw the covered figure glaring at the couple as he released ragged breaths. No one could see the way he was clutching at his leg where the hidden dagger sat. The crowd happily accepted their king's lies and cheered foolishly for it. They had no idea that it was all about to end. He focused on the queen, holding a child he assumed to be theirs, and saw red. This life was not meant for them. He would take it all away.

Amoli gently placed a sleeping Blessing on the mat. Inside the "playroom," as her queen called it, she watched Blessing while her parents went out into the capital. Amoli stepped back waiting to see if the child stirred. When she didn't, Amoli smiled and began to pick up the scattered toys around the room. Others may whisper she had been demoted in her duties in the palace but she knew better. She had been given the most important tasks of any servant or handmaid. Other nobles thought nothing of handing their children off to be cared for and practically raised by others. Her queen was different. Not being around her child made her feel like she was lacking as a mother. It had been almost impossible to convince her otherwise so she could resume ruling by her husband's side. Putting her child in anyone's hands was hard for her and being the one she trusted to take on such a task was the highest honor as far as Amoli was concerned. She didn't miss her managing duties. It gained her respect and a name within the palace walls but that had interested her parents more than her. She would've happily served at her queen's side forever if given the choice.

Once everything was put away, Amoli pulled out her box in the corner with her sewing supplies and cloths. She'd begun making the baby some clothes for her to play in. All the gifted clothes that Blessing had were extravagant pieces people thought would earn them favor from the royal couple. She didn't have a lot of simple outfits that Serenity preferred her in as they were less trouble to get on and off and she didn't worry about letting them get dirty. Amoli took it upon herself to make a few. Once she started, she fell into a comfortable rhythm allowing the time to pass.

Someone clearing their throat from behind her caused her to spin her head around. As soon as she saw Amir standing in the doorway, with an apologetic smile on his face, she let out a small sigh of relief. "What are you doing here?" She asked quietly, mindful of the sleeping child.

Amir came inside the room. He first went to look over Blessing, with a thoughtful smile on his face and then he came to Amoli giving her a chaste kiss on her cheek. Amoli immediately looked out into the hall to make sure no one had seen anything. She could feel her cheeks becoming warm. Amir only smiled. Their relationship was not a secret even among the nobles but it still made Amoli feel embarrassed at times feeling like she was being scrutinized by many.

"I have something for you," he told her. He reached into his shirt and pulled out a gold bangle with red jewels. Amoli's eyes widened and her jaw dropped.

"Wha-," she began to ask.

"A gift from my mother. She had it sent when I sent her the news." Amoli didn't have to ask what news he was referring to. It was something constantly on her mind.

"I cannot accept such a gift," she said, shaking her head. She'd only ever handled such things if she were putting it on her queen.

Amir took her hand in his and gently slid the piece on her arm. "It's a tradition of my family. The bride-to-be wears it until the day of the wedding." Hearing the word wedding caused a tiny flutter in her belly.

"How will I explain it to others?" she asked, unable to take her eyes off of it.

"What right to an explanation do they have?" he said jokingly. Amoli gave him a look and Amir laughed.

"You could always just tell them the truth. I hear it is very easy to remember." Amoli looked away. She knew he would never voice it but he likely felt hurt at her reluctance to reveal their engagement to anyone, not even to her queen.

Amoli didn't know how to tell him her reasoning without upsetting him. She loved Amir dearly. When he had proposed she'd been elated. It was only after, when the excitement died down, that she realized what she had just said yes to. It was more than just being his wife. Marrying Amir, Lord Amir of the Dwale family would force her into a role, a position, a title she had no idea how to act in. Amoli came from a small city from a simple family. Being chosen to be a servant in the palace had been the highest honor anyone in her family had ever received. While the other female servants worked until they reached marrying age and set off to find husbands, Amoli was happy to stay, sending money to her family. When she became a maiden to the queen, she was even more prepared to stay in the palace not wanting anything else. Falling for and becoming a lady had never been an ambition of hers. She worried she would be looked down on, that she would fail in her duties, and that she would bring dishonor to two families. She worried she would have to leave the palace behind, Blessing, her queen, her life.

"I'm sorry. I don't mean to pressure you," Amir spoke after noting her silence.

"No, it's not-," she tried to tell him.

"I set off with Kahil to meet with some of the eastern lords under guard. I'll be gone a few days." Amoli felt guilt filling her. A forced smile came on his face. "When I return, I will bring you something you'll be more comfortable with."

"I love you," she said suddenly, wanting to remove the sad look in his eyes. Her tactic worked because his fake smile slipped into a true one. This time he kissed her lips and she welcomed it.

CHAPTER 6

The sound of a loud squeak followed by a child's laughter echoed in the courtyard. Jung-Soo looked on from a short distance. Kang-Dae chased Blessing around in circles as she laughed going as fast as her little legs could take her. Serenity lay on a blanket on her stomach, her head lying on her crossed arms, as she watched them both with a genuine smile on her face. It was truly an enviable sight. They were happy, truly happy, and had been since they reunited. No matter the troubles that sprouted up they overcame them together. Making decisions as one and supporting each other through everything. He had watched them from the beginning of their relationship to now. He had watched them go through trial after trial, from mistrust to separation. It all seemed to make them stronger. Whenever Jung-Soo thought about the feelings he'd had for Serenity, he knew it would never be, not just because she had never and would never feel that way about him, but because he doubted he'd ever be able to achieve the level of

trust and happiness they had for one another with
anyone. That was the kind of love you put before
anything and he could never see himself putting
anything over his duty.

The Night before the battle at Fort Chungi

*The soldiers were still up, chatting loudly,
amping themselves up for the battle to come. He
was sure Kang-Dae was "discussing" the upcoming
battle with Serenity now that he had her back. Jung-
Soo, on the other hand, chose to spend the evening
preparing. Sleeping before a battle was not
something Jung-Soo had ever been able to do. So,
he always took the time to sharpen his skills.*

*He moved his sword against invisible
enemies. Anticipating any possible move they would
make to counter it. The men he fought before had
been formidable when the numbers were in their
favor, but in an even fight, he believed they would
come out victorious. He moved to swipe at his fake
opponent's head when he noticed a shadow outside
his tent. He paused for a moment, willing to dismiss*

it as a Xian soldier moving about but the way they lingered had him thinking otherwise. He kept his sword up and moved toward the entrance. The figure moved slowly like he was trying not to get caught. Alert, Jung-Soo stood by the doorway with his hand on the flap. With a swift move of his hand, he threw back the flap and aimed his sword at his opponent's jugular. Seeing a startled Rielle rear back he quickly put it down.

"You can just say you don't want visitors!" She scolded with a whisper. Jung-Soo looked at her disapprovingly. Appearing to get annoyed at the lack of an invitation, Rielle pushed her way past him without one. Jung-Soo let the tent fall close and turned toward her.

She stared at him for a moment. "Take off your shirt."

Jung-Soo's eyes widened and he felt a kick in his gut.

"What?" He was so caught off guard he spoke in Xianian.

*"I need to check your wound, take it off,"
she said, eyeing the area where he'd been stabbed.
Understanding settled his usually calm heart.*

*"There is no need," he told her. She gave
him a hard look and Jung-Soo felt very strongly that
a 'no' would not be tolerated. He put down his
sword and did as he was commanded. Rielle pushed
him over to his cot and tried to force him to sit.
Because he didn't feel like fighting, he let her. She
undid his dressing carefully, her face the definition
of concentration. She studied his wound and he
studied her. When he first met her all he saw were
the differences between her and Serenity, how her
eyes were smaller, and her nose slightly narrower.
As he stared at her now, he didn't look for
differences, he just admired the features of her. Not
just the physical ones. He admired her ability to
keep her composure in what must be a nightmarish
situation for her. She'd been trapped in someone
else's war, held captive, and almost lost her life
multiple times. Through it all, she still found it in
her to keep going if only to help those she cared*

about. Another battle would ensue in hours, a battle if lost, that could have her once again captive to the enemy, but here she was with him. Did she care for him? The question bothered him mostly because he was unsettled by the fact that he cared about the answer. Why should he entertain such notions? What would it accomplish? He was a soldier and the only thing that mattered was fulfilling his duty to his king and friend. Anything else was just a distraction.

At the moment, a "distraction" was trailing her fingers softly over his stitches, slightly grazing his skin. He squeezed his eyes shut hoping denying his eyes would help him keep his usual stoicism. "Sorry," she apologized believing she had hurt him. He didn't correct her. Not soon enough and strangely too soon, she redressed his bandage. "It's healing good. I would recommend taking it easy the next few days but I know you won't," she told him. He felt a smile tug at his lips, but he resisted the impulse. He opened his eyes and they immediately met hers. She looked away quickly like she had been caught doing something distasteful. The two sat in an uncomfortable silence.

"How sure are you that you'll win this?" She asked suddenly, her eyes still on the ground.

"Our plan is sound. And the advantage is in our hands," he told her. While there were no guarantees in war, he believed their odds were good.

"How many of these have you been through?"

Knowing she spoke of his battles she took a moment to calculate the answer. "Over forty."

"Jesus," she whispered out loud. "Is that what life is here? Battle after battle."

"Not always," he answered truthfully. "Years of peace usually come at the cost of many battles. I imagine after this war is won; I will not have to see a battle for some time."

Rielle shook her head.

"I couldn't live like this," she said. "You never know when war is coming for you,"

"Is it so different where you are from? Is the fight shared with you before it begins?"

She gave him a look. "No, of course not, but- "

"Is your world without violence? Has peace been achieved amongst all nations?" He pressed her.

"No, it-." she started again.

"If you have no real peace, you too are unable to pick when a fight may come about." Her mouth snapped shut and her jaw clenched as she turned away from him. He had frustrated her. It wasn't his intention, but he didn't feel bad about it. He refused to believe their world was better. Serenity had chosen to come back, even if it had taken her a while to make that decision. He'd heard about their world from both her and Kang-Dae and found none of it appealing. In fact, it seemed more complicated and impossible to navigate with all

their unspoken rules and focus on material things.
He had an intense dislike of their world, and he
couldn't completely understand where it came from.

"It's not perfect, okay," she finally said.
"But it's home. Sometimes the devil you know is
better than the devil you don't."

Jung-Soo frowned, not understanding the
expression. "What is a devil?"

Rielle's eyes moved about the room as she
tried to choose her words. "He's like a really evil
entity that wants to destroy all things good," she
settled on. Jung-Soo replayed her earlier words.

"You believe it matters if you know the
evil?"

"It just means, you know what to expect
from it. There aren't any surprises when it does
something crappy."

Jung-Soo still didn't think he understood.
"How does knowing make their actions less evil?"

She hesitated before answering, "It doesn't."

"You will suffer regardless then?"

"I guess...," she trailed off.

"Does it make you feel better to choose your suffering?" He asked genuinely curious.

"No. Yes. I don't know. Maybe."

"So, it is not safety you seek, it is control. You put control of your circumstances above all?"

"No, I don't."

"Before you were ready to jump back into your captors' hands to be with Serenity despite knowing the danger. But you felt it would be a better choice than to stay put where you could be protected and trust me."

"It wasn't about trust," she argued. "I wanted to make sure she was okay,"

"At the risk of your own life. You put yourself in danger readily for others but you fear for your safety?"

"Not others, Serenity. She's my best friend, my sister. Yeah, I'm gonna risk everything for her. She's all I have," she defended.

"You know she will stay here? She won't return to your world," he reminded her.

"I know that!" She snapped. Rielle pushed herself off the cot and stormed away to the other side of the tent, crossing her arms. Jung-Soo felt he was pushing her but couldn't seem to stop himself.

"Yet you still helped her return?"

Rielle refused to face him, staring, silently, at the opposite wall. Jung-Soo waited to see if she would say something but she did not move or utter a word. Slight movement in her shoulders caught his eye. After a few more moments it happened again more heavily. At the small sound of a sniffle, he realized, in horror, that she was crying. It was not the first time he'd seen her cry, but it was the first time she was trying to hide it. Before she'd been too overwhelmed, too broken to attempt to hold back. He still had more questions, and a burning urge to get the answers from her. He needed to know her reasonings, her motives, he wanted to know...her. It was a curiosity, he was sure. How often do you meet a traveler from another world? Jung-Soo was up to two right now but it was still a rarity. He chalked his need up to a simple need for information, as a general, he didn't like not knowing about those around the ones he swore allegiance to. Jung-Soo ignored the fact that in all his years as a general, all his years on the streets, he never had such interest before. Jung-Soo tended to categorize people into three specific types. The honorable, the selfish, and the weak. Once he placed them, he never gave them another thought. Very few people moved past the categories to people worth knowing in his life and in every instance, it had been against his will. Kang-Dae had forced his way into Jung-Soo's life and not only refused to leave but refused to let him go. Jung-Soo allowed him to, of course, but it had never been his intention when the two had met all those years ago. Serenity, on the other hand, had been far less aggressive in her invasion past Jung-Soo's carefully built walls. Watching her deal with circumstances that would bring down anyone else, being around her, and having to get to know her through every trial and conflict had intrigued him. He'd been completely unprepared for it. He never expected it, so his guard had been down allowing her to traipse her way through without a fight. Amoli, was another, though he actively fought to keep her away, having no interest in her nor desire to know more. Her invasion had been the most unexpected but now she was one he considered a close friend.

With Rielle, however, it would be the first time he took the initiative. Maybe it was because Rielle couldn't be quantified. Though not as prepared for this world, he would not call her weak. Despite her ignorance, she was highly adaptable when she needed to be. Selfish, never. There was nothing selfish about her actions. She was almost stupidly selfless to her own detriment. The easiest thing would be to call her honorable and leave it at that but that word seemed not quite her or maybe too little for her. Of course, he respected her, she had earned it one hundred times over but it was something else, something behind her eyes he couldn't quite place, something familiar. Jung-Soo stood and slowly moved towards her. He thought to himself he should apologize. A word that was practically foreign to him, he almost shocked himself at the thought. He stopped within a step of her.

"Rielle....," he began, not sure what to say first. Before he could jumble out an incoherent apology, Rielle spun around and threw her arms around him, crying into his neck. Jung-Soo stood frozen, having no idea what to do. He comforted her before but he had not been the cause of her pain back then. At least then he knew what was probably going on in her head. At this moment he had no clue, and he had no idea how he should respond. He knew it probably had to do with Serenity. Stiffly, he

managed to get out a short 'Serenity," before she tensed. He wondered if he was not supposed to say anything and thought better of continuing his sentence but before he could or couldn't she pulled away. She didn't look at him, only staring off to the side. "Had he somehow made things worse?

"Your wound looks good. I'm going to get some sleep." She said softly, her voice void of any of the previous emotions she had demonstrated a few seconds ago.

"Wait," he called out before she could leave. To his surprise she did.

"Stay here." He saw her shoulders tense up once more.

"I will go stay with my men," he quickly added, fearing he had made her uncomfortable. He knew she was probably being forced to sleep in one of the smaller tents by the healers and would feel better knowing exactly where she was.

"It's your tent."

"You've slept in it more than me," he told her. She let out a sound that sounded suspiciously like a chuckle, or maybe he was imagining it. Not wanting her to fight him he quickly grabbed his sword and headed out of the tent. He fought the urge to look back at her wanting to get some kind of read on her face.

"Ap! Ap!" Blessing's cry removed Jung-Soo from his memories. On the ground Kang-Dae was kissing Serenity as Blessing hit him, trying to get his attention. Both parents seemed amused by this as they smiled at each other.

An unwanted vision crept inside Jung-Soo's head. He saw himself on the blanket smiling down at someone with the same love in his eyes he saw whenever Kang-Dae saw Serenity. A soft dark feminine hand came up to cup his cheek. He held the hand to his face and bent down toward soft welcoming lips. The pang Jung-Soo felt at the moment angered him and he forced it away along with his daydream. He had the life he wanted. He had the life he deserved. To want more was foolish, and greedy on his part. No, this was enough, it had to be.

Oblivious to the struggle happening only a few meters away from them, Kang-Dae and Serenity continued kissing, enjoying their daughter's attempts to return their attention to her. Blessing liked to be the center of both her parents' worlds and got extremely jealous if they showed affection to one another in front of her. Kang-Dae finally pulled away. "Oh, there is my Mi-Sung!" he exclaimed happily. Blessing's pouting reddening face immediately broke out into a smile and she crawled over to sit in front of them reaching out. Serenity reached for her first, giving her a kiss, making the girl laugh and returned the gesture. "Ap!" she cried out looking expectantly at him. With a chuckle, Kang-Dae leaned toward her so she could kiss his cheek as well. Serenity placed a small cup of diced strawberries in front of her and they were all but forgotten. Kang-Dae wrapped an arm around Serenity as they lay together watching her feed herself.

"Do you think we should send her to my family, just until all this rumor stuff is resolved?" Serenity asked, finally giving voice to the reservations she'd been having about everything. She hated the idea only because she had never been more than an hour's horse ride away from her child. But, given the state of things and how they had no idea what would come of it, Serenity felt she would be safer back with her parents.

Kang-Dae stared at Blessing before turning to Serenity. "Do you think you could?" he asked. Serenity gave a sad smile.

"If I had to," she said honestly. It would rip her heart in two, but she could do it if it kept her baby girl safe.

"We will make sure we will not have to," Kang-Dae assured her. Serenity gave him a hopeful look.

"Can we?" She asked, letting her confidence waver for the first time in weeks. She was used to putting up a strong front in the presence of others. It was all part of her duties as queen. The people needed to see their leaders sure so they could feel assured. With her husband, however, she allowed herself to be as vulnerable as she needed to be. Her lack of dreams as of late was adding to her worries. She had become so reliant on the dreams that making decisions without them, and facing the future without them was scary to her.

"We have, and we will again," he reminded her. Serenity leaned into him, needing his comfort and strength in place of hers. He was right, she knew it, felt it, and had to believe it. If things were to shift, if trouble came along, they would deal with it together as they had been.

CHAPTER 7

Hae-In covered his nose as he walked. The smell was so putrid it made him gag. He knew they wouldn't find anything good, he never expected something like this. The bodies scattered around had been left to rot for what must have been weeks. More than a few of them had been gnawed on by animals over time. No one had been spared, not even the children. Hae-In had to look away at that horrifying sight. Behind him, he could hear the sound of retching and vomiting. Tae-Soo must have reached his limit. The poor souls had been decimated by what looked like a combination of arrows and blades.

It didn't make sense. Bandits were never this violent and the people here had nothing of value to take. The attackers didn't appear to have taken any prisoners. This small village couldn't have been a threat to anyone, so why? Hae-In didn't understand. He walked into the first house he came across. No survivors. It didn't even look like they had the chance to put up a fight. These were simple people, not fighters. They never stood a chance against whatever or whoever attacked them.

After Tae-Soo finished expelling the contents of his stomach he forced himself deeper into the village. When they agreed to check out the scene on behalf of the King, he thought they'd just find the place abandoned. He hoped the people had just moved on, not being able to sustain the land after the fleeing Anoekan soldiers had set fires to keep the army from pursuing them months ago. The people had been adamant that they would stay and rebuild with most of the families having been there for generations. Had the soldiers come back in a cruel act of vengeance? That would have been a reckless act. He couldn't imagine them doing so when they were trying desperately to stay hidden.

The two soldiers checked every home but only found more of the same. Tae-Soo came upon another grisly sight. A woman's body lay in the street with her head lying beside her. "Barbarians," Tae-Soo spat.

Hae-In kneeled down to look closer. He noticed the drag marks and footprints by the body. "This kill was different."

Tae-Soo wanted to remark that it was obvious given she was the only victim without a head but the smell was beginning to get to him again.

"They dragged her from her home. Everyone else was killed where they found them. This one, they made sure to bring her out and they gave her a death of which there would be no doubt. She was targeted."

"If she was the target, why kill the whole village?" Tae-Soo managed to ask. Hae-In didn't have any theories on that, it made as much sense to him as it did to Tae-Soo.

He looked toward the drag marks and followed them until he reached a small home. Inside Hae-In searched around for any clues to who the woman had been. There wasn't anything out of the ordinary he could see as he scanned the room. He headed to the back. Crunch! Hae-In looked down at the broken bottle under his foot. It wasn't the only thing on the floor. Numerous vials, bottles, and small containers littered the ground along with some medical instruments. 'She was a healer,' Hae-In realized. He stepped inside avoiding the fallen items as he walked. He figured she had been found in this room and she tried to fight back. He went through her chests and any boxes he could find. Once he ran out of conventional storage areas, he started looking for more secretive ones. He checked under her bed. He tried checking for loose floorboards. But still found nothing. Frustrated, he exited the house.

Tae-Soo was examining the body, a piece of clothing covering his nose and mouth. "She may have been a healer," Hae-In told him. "Apart from that, I do not know why they came for her."

"Perhaps it has less to do with who she is and more about who she helped," Tae-Soo offered.

CHAPTER 8

One month Earlier

As soon as Jae-Hwa was brought back inside the estate, her handmaiden was ripped from her. Jae-Hwa tried to reach back for her but was pulled away as her friend cried out for her. Jae-Hwa watched them take her down the hall, helplessly fearing for her handmaid's life. While they may not have had the courage to hurt her, she knew the same could not be said for her friend. The guilt began to eat away at her for bringing her in on the failed escape. Jae-Hwa knew she should have left her behind. But the truth was she had been terrified to make such a move on her own. She had no one but her handmaiden to turn to, he had made sure of that. The gentle guard gestured for her to follow him. She didn't bother declining, knowing that it would make no difference. Instead, she lifted her chin and held her head high wanting to show she had no regrets. Despite her current fears, she would not allow herself to be intimidated.

They escorted her to the main hall. *Her* main hall that had been desecrated with the presence of her enemies. She was brought before him. Under his hateful gaze, she refused to cower, making sure she returned the glare in kind.

"You think yourself untouchable, do you?" He questioned her. She did not respond to him. As far as she was concerned, he was beneath her, no matter how his inflated sense of importance led him to treat her as though he were in charge. "I should have you struck down right now."

"Then do it, Sho. If you dare." Jae-Hwa retorted, no longer able to keep silent. The old man's eyes narrowed and his expression darkened. "You and I both know you wouldn't dare."

He held her gaze for several long seconds, fury burning off him. Jae-Hwa found a small amount of joy in his rage. "Have her cleaned up before she goes in," he grumbled. The man limped away in a huff supported by his staff.

Jae-Hwa was practically pushed into the dark room. Her skin still felt raw from how hard the servants had scrubbed her. The intricate and heavy dress she'd been forced to wear felt like it was suffocating her. Despite the warm season a chill went through her as she stood, not willing to move. "My lady," a deep voice rasped from the corner. Jae-Haw shut her eyes to silently ask the gods for strength and mercy.

"I am here," she said out into the darkness. The sound of a striker could be heard and suddenly a small light appeared from a candle. In the shadow of that light sat a figure in a chair. Shrouded in dark robes and a hood, the figure looked like a specter coming to reap her soul. Knowing the truth of the matter, Jae-Hwa didn't think it was much different. Hoping to speed things along, Jae-Hwa went over to the table where the teapot sat. She poured a healthy amount into the waiting cup and stopped to breathe, before walking it over to the figure.

She handed him the cup, feeling his eyes on her. Eventually, a scarred hand reached out to accept. "You sound much better," she told him. Unfortunately for her, it was true. Wheezing breaths no longer filled the room and he was speaking clearly without coughing. He seemed to be recovering from his illness.

"My lady, they've surrounded us!" the official reported, eyes wide with fear. It had all happened so fast that she had not been able to send word to the capital for aid. One day it was just rumors of a large force in the distance, and the next they were outside their gates. Jae-Hwa stared at the window seeing the force for herself, feeling her heart freeze at the sight.

"Who are they?" she asked, but she was afraid she already knew the answer. They wore no discernable uniform and their armor was basic as if they meant to keep their identity secret.

"Can we send word through the hidden path?" she asked her military captain.

"Even if they have not found it yet, there's no way to get to it without being seen," he

answered. Even through his calm demeanor, Jae-Hwa could tell he was worried. Their home had not been built to withstand a siege. Any additions to secure the palace made when Katsuo resided in Senoia had been destroyed at her orders. She had wanted every trace of him gone.

"They're asking to meet with you," informed the official.

Jae-Hwa pulled at the sides of her dress. What else could she do? They could tear down the gates and force their way in at any time. How many would die then? Jae-Hwa didn't want her people or the city to suffer. Maybe she could buy time until someone could learn about their predicament. She moved to leave the room when the captain, her handmaid, and the official blocked her path.

"My lady you can't!" They all said in different variations. Jae-Hwa held up her hand. "Senoia is my home and my responsibility. It has been under Gi protection for over a hundred years." I cannot hide myself away and let it fall."

She reasoned with them and herself. No one said anything, no one could think of what they could say.

"I will escort you, my lady," the captain said dejectedly. She thanked him and the two went out to meet their enemy.

From behind the gate, Jae-Hwa stood with her men at her back and her captain at her side. "Who are you?" she demanded. No one answered. "You should know this land is under the protection of the king. Anyone who attacks will be forfeiting their life!" Jae-Hwa shouted, pushing out her anger so she could overcome her fear. The men outside the gates stood silent staring past her.

Suddenly they began to part from the back onward. In the distance Jae-Hwa could see someone walking through them, using a cane. At first, Jae-Hwa could not tell who the person was. As he drew closer, the white of his beard came into focus and what she previously thought to be a cane revealed itself to be a staff. Jae-Hwa's already racing heart began to pound. Sho marched himself *in front of the gate to meet her directly. 'No!' She couldn't believe it. He hadn't been seen or heard from in months. She'd prayed he'd died or at the very least returned to his country.*

"It is good to see you, Your Majesty," the words were said with such venom Jae-Hwa stumbled back. The captain was quick to steady her.

"What do you want?" She forced out.

"Only for you to honor the agreement made. We seek shelter." Jae-Hwa shook her head. "You ask me to house known enemies of the king at the risk of my life and those I protect."

"I ask you to honor your vows to your true king! To the one who would make you his queen."

Jae-Hwa started to feel nauseous.

"He's dead," she whispered. The awful smile that rose on the soothsayer's face made her skin crawl.

"Your 'love'," he said sarcastically. "is very much alive and in need of his queen."

"Shall I bring him in without opposition, or will we need to purify this place to ensure his safety." Jae-Hwa could barely breathe. She didn't know what to do. She prayed he was lying and that it was just a tactic to scare her into surrendering. *What if it wasn't? If he were still alive, what would that mean for Xian?* Jae-Hwa fought to calm herself. Despite the awful new information, it didn't change their position. They simply could not win this fight. If they tried it would be to the detriment of all of Senoia. Maybe, if she could keep them here, she could have the opportunity to send out a message to the capital, to Serenity. Because if he truly were alive, she would be his next target.

"Open the gates," she ordered, almost choking on the words. Her men seemed reluctant to do so but chose to obey their lady.

"Have them put down their weapons," Sho told her, his harsh expression warning her not to make any missteps now.

"Do as he says," she said. As her men were forced to surrender, the enemy soldiers marched in, herding her men away in groups to an unknown fate. When one tried to force Captain Chang-Su away from her he stood his ground. "I will stay with my lady." He declared. Fearful for him, Jae-Hwa tried to convince him to stand down.

"I'm sure your king wants to make sure his lady keeps her most trusted with her," said Sho. Sho ordered the soldier away and went off to the back of the line. Chang-Su looked relieved but Jae-Hwa knew better. As her captain and one of her most trusted companions, Sho wanted him where he could keep his eyes on him and possibly use for leverage over her. Soon a carriage was being ushered through the gates. Jae-Hwa felt her hands begin to shake.

Jae-Hwa lowered her eyes as Katsuo drank his tea. Looking at him was difficult.

"You left." Jae-Hwa felt her heart skip.

"I needed to check on the people, to make sure they are being cared for," she lied.

"Do you not trust my men to do their duties?" He asked.

"With respect, given the state of things and your men, is it hard to see why I might have felt the need to see for myself?" she said, keeping her tone as noncombatant as possible.

"Sho is under the impression you sought to alert *them* of my presence." His deep voice had a darker edge to it now.

"Sho still harbors mistrust for me. I cannot fault him for thinking the worst." She heard him take another sip. When he grabbed her hand, she almost snatched it back but forced herself still.

He brought her over to stand next to him and laid his head on her stomach.

"I know my failure did not leave you without consequences. Had I been here I would have encouraged you to do what you needed to do until my return. It may take Sho longer to understand but he will. He knows what you mean to me."

Jae-Hwa felt the nausea returning.

"I am willing to do what I must to earn his trust once more." The lie came easy, like everything she said to him. Her motives for her escape attempt had mostly been for the benefit of Xian. Another part of her felt she could not stomach this act much longer without revealing herself. It wasn't just because he was an enemy of the highest type, but he represented a part of her, a part she'd destroyed some time ago. That part that was wrapped in her father's influence. That part that so desperately yearned for a throne and did not care how it obtained it. She had done terrible things to please that part of herself. Just when she thought she had overcome it, temptation came again in the form of Katsuo, offering her exactly what she desired, or thought she had. Had Serenity not entered back into her life she still did not know if she would have chosen to pledge true loyalty to Katsuo or have had the courage to give it all up without any assurance Xian would overcome him.

Jae-Hwa took his head in her hands and stroked his hair.

"When I sit on the throne none of the past will matter," he tried to assure her, only succeeding in making her more unsettled.

CHAPTER 9

Lord Goi received Fei's message about the unexpected visitors within a day. It was unfortunate but not surprising. They had prepared for this very thing just in case. They'd managed not to draw any attention for a decent amount of time. Fei knew what to do, even if he was hesitant to do it. Goi knew he would have to give him some help. If Fei fell, they would all be in danger of being next. They were too close to allow that. He sent his most trusted men over. They should arrive in time to do what needs to be done. The consequences wouldn't matter by the next half-moon. Everything was already set, and he would have a whole city for himself along with the title of Duke.

"I thank you for your hospitality. I assure you we do not mean to stay long," the old man spoke from across the table. The feast between them had barely been touched by just the two men but Goi had wanted to show his sincerity.

"I appreciate the care you are taking to keep things…discreet." Sho gave a nod.

"Of course. We do not want any harm to come to our supporters. When the time comes you will be heavily rewarded." Goi perked up at those words.

"Really?" He pressed, not able to keep his excitement to himself.

"We would not ask you to take such a risk without fair compensation." Sho leaned forward. "When everything is done you and your brethren will be called upon to help rebuild and take part in the new world, under his leadership, of course."

"Of course," Goi agreed.

"There will be a lot of places without 'proper' leadership. We can arrange a couple to be placed under your stewardship."

Goi was practically salivating over his plate. "A couple?"

"Oh yes. With such responsibility, you won't be just a lord. You'll be a Duke. A duke worthy of an even greater home, an estate." Goi smiled wide, taking hold of his wine.

"Thank you, Sir! And gods bless the true king!"

He was one of the few lords manning this city. It was one of the smallest in Xian. The other lords of Xian looked down on him because of it. The king, if he could be called that for much longer, refused to recognize his efforts in keeping it, never granting him rewards or more land. Goi had been terrified when the war ended, worrying he would be found out, but when no one came he knew he had not been. When he had been approached this time, he was tempted to refuse, to alert the king of their presence but was afraid they would reveal his previous treason. Once they revealed their plans, he felt more confident that this time things would end differently.

Amir and Kahil entered the grounds with their men. The Xian soldiers assigned to keep guard of the city were still in position. But that did not make either of them lower their guard. Lord Fei was the third stop on their list of people to question. It had been less about his actions that had put him under scrutiny and more about who he associated with. Lord Yi was a known collaborator, already put to death for his crimes. Yi was Fei's brother-in-law and best friend as many knew. There hadn't been any concrete evidence Fei had been involved with Katsuo but the leaders did not want to take any chances. So, while he was allowed to keep his land and title he had to do so under Xian's watchful eyes.

Fei met them outside his home, his young wife was standing stiffly at his side with a deep frown. Many servants were accompanying them. Fei had an awkward forced smile on his face as he welcomed them into his home. The men were led into a dining hall where there were even more servants at the ready to take on any request. The food on the table let them know they'd been forewarned of their arrival. Amir and Kahil shared a look. Neither of them would eat a thing here.

"Sit, eat," he said, taking a seat at the head of the table. The first thing Amir noticed was that his wife was no longer with him. Appearing to have noticed Amir's observation, Fei remarked, "My lady has not been very well these past few days. She has retired. Please accept her deepest apologies." An obvious lie but Amir wouldn't press them on it. She was not who they came to see. Considering they were part of the government that had her brother killed he doubted they would get much cooperation from her.

The men Amir had brought stood back, standing around the room ready for anything. Fei's eyes would shift to them every once in a while.

"May I ask the reason for this visit?"

"There have been some unbecoming rumors coming out of this province," Kahil began.

"Rumors?" Fei began piling his plate with food. Amir attributed his change in appearance to his eating habits. He had added on at least an extra thirty pounds from the looks of him. A feat not many could afford these days.

"There have been whispers, even signs claiming Katsuo has returned." Fei paused in the middle of spreading honey on his bread. He allowed it to fall onto his already stacked plate.

"My lords, I hope you are not here to continue to accuse me of something I have already maintained my innocence of," he said. His voice was worn but there was a tinge of something else in it, something that sounded a bit like fear to Amir.

"We are simply here to track the source of these rumors. To access any truth or kill them in their tracks," Kahil said, staring him in the eye.

Fei took a bite of his bread.

"Well, I can assure you, no such news has come from here. As you can see, we are under careful watch. If we had done anything sordid, you would know," he claimed, mouth full. Amir grimaced but didn't say anything.

"I hope that is the case. You should know that your city has a number of these throughout it," Kahil said, reaching into his clothes and pulling out the posters. Fei stopped midchew his face frozen.

"I know nothing about that," he sputtered.

"Are you sure? It seems a big thing to go unnoticed by you in your city."

"I do admit I may have been a bit lax in my duties following the king's ruling. It is not an easy thing to be accused of," he tried to sound offended but was coming off more and more anxious.

"You and Yi were very close," Amir reminded him. "Close as brothers many would say." Fei tensed at the mention of Yi.

"Yi was a traitor and he was justly …punished. He did a most egregious act," he looked like it hurt him to say the words.

"An act you were completely unaware of?" questioned Kahil.

"I have already said that I was not," gritted Fei.

"And now, you are still maintaining ignorance of all the rumors pouring out of your province?"

"I am."

"And where are your men?"

"You know that I have been unable to keep my own men at this time. They have all been dismissed save the few hundred you-, our king allows me to keep."

"And where are they?" Amir asked again, choosing to ignore his slip of the tongue. "I haven't seen any, not in the city nor on the grounds."

"Well, who would want to work with someone under the king's suspicion?" He deflected. Amir scanned the room once more, eyeing the many servants. He couldn't help but notice that he'd yet to see one female among them. His eyes met Kahil who had yet to pick up on it but he could tell Amir was concerned and became more alert.

"We thank you for your time and your hospitality," Amir announced, suddenly standing to his feet as Kahil did the same. The Lord looked surprised by the abrupt ending of his interrogation but became relieved.

"You're welcome to stay," he offered with no sincerity.

"We have other places to visit," Amir said.

"Of course. I do hope you find who you are looking for so this nasty business can be put to rest for good."

"We will."

They exited the house alone, Fei not even bothering to escort them out. The servants were still around attending to various tasks, various unnecessary tasks in Amir's opinion. He felt when Kahil finally caught on, as his body slightly tensed. They walked down the steps without urgency. Their men followed behind and at their sides. They mounted their horses and made their way to the gate. Half a dozen men, also servants, were manning the gate. It was still closed even as they approached. Kahil cleared his throat loudly, an innocuous sound for anyone else but he and his men knew it was a warning to be on guard. The "servant" stared at them without making any attempt to open the gate. Amir could feel his heartbeat increase and his body was feeling an awful sense of dread. Kahil's hand slowly made its way to his sword.

"Open!" the man finally shouted. From the outside, the gates were pulled open, revealing another five servants. A few of Amir's men went ahead. Amir and Kahil trailed behind, keeping their eyes open to any movement. The men closed ranks around them little by little. The gate had yet to close behind them. Amir didn't have to look back to know there were eyes on them. He was beginning to suspect there would be even more away from there.

CHAPTER 10

The funeral was packed. There were hundreds, if not thousands, of people filing into the room. Serenity could hear soft music playing. No one was wearing black. Everyone was dressed in white. She walked through the crowd. Everyone who saw her looked at her with big smiles like they were celebrating. Something caught the corner of her eye. Just as she was going to look, Kang-Dae grabbed her arm and kissed her. Though she couldn't see it she knew everyone was watching. She clung to him as he kissed her, over and over. The people were laughing and clapping now. The clapping was so loud it sounded like thunder. As she pulled away, she couldn't see beyond his loving smile. She reached up to touch his hair. That was when she saw it again, the movement. But once again her attention was stolen by Amoli who was also dressed in white, holding Blessing in her arms as she led her through the room. They passed by Jung-Soo who was talking with Rielle, wearing street clothes with white robes thrown over them.

*Her mother-in-law was sitting at a table. Satori
walked up to her offering a cup which she accepted.
Queen Prija was also at a table, trying to engage in
conversation with the Xians around her while
handing out goody bags with large swords sticking
out. Within the crowd, for just a split second she
thought she could see Ami. There was a large
shadow behind him. She tried to call out to him but
he disappeared. Amoli brought her to a large table.
It was so long she couldn't see where it ended. The
table was empty, only having empty plates and cups
on it, as far as she could see. When she turned to
ask Amoli about it, she was gone. Not just her, the
whole room, which had just been lively with
thousands, was completely empty. She turned back
to the table which now had a great feast spread out.
Beyond the table, she could see two figures,
wearing all black. They were seated but didn't touch
anything, though it appeared they wanted to. The
plates in front of them were still empty. Serenity took
a step closer only to bump into something. She
looked down and gasped at the casket in front of*

her. When she looked around, she saw there was a long row of caskets between her and the table. Whatever she'd been seeing made an appearance again. This time there was no one to stop her from looking. She turned and saw a blazing blue fire climbing the walls and eating at the tables and furniture in the room. The room slowly turned black and the charred walls began to crumble. Panic filled her but she couldn't run. Her feet only moved so fast. It was like trying to run in tar. She could only make it to the next coffin. In the distance, she saw each casket begin to pop open, one after the other. She tried moving but she was now stuck. The caskets popped open faster. Suddenly, the one next to her opened. Curiosity began to override her instinct to run and she slowly looked into it. A charred hand reached out and grabbed hold of her causing a fire to run up her arm. Serenity let out a wild scream trying to pat the fire out but it continued to spread.

Serenity came awake with a gasp. She'd had this dream before. Serenity panted, holding her chest as she struggled to slow her breathing. She remembered it now. The last time, it had left her as soon as she woke up but the fear remained as Kang-Dae did everything in his power to calm her. Now, she was still frightened but there was some clarity. Her dream was more than a warning, it was a promise, in more ways than one. She looked at Kang-Dae who was sound asleep. She leaned down and whispered his name while gently tapping him. He awoke a couple of seconds later. It took a moment for him to realize what was going on but as soon as he looked at her, he sat up quickly.

"Are you alright?" He asked checking her over. Serenity nodded even though she was still shaken.

"I had the dream again," she told him. He tensed and wrapped her up in his arms. With effort, she slowly recounted her dream to him. He listened while she spoke, never interrupting or showing signs of concern. He only continued to hold her. When she was done, she fought back tears. She had snuggled into him as much as she could.

"Whatever's coming, I don't think we can stop it," she cried.

Kang-Dae shook his head. "We will." Serenity sniffled, and he stroked her cheek. "We'll gather the lords and the others, and start putting measures in place."

CHAPTER 11

Traveling on the back road, the last thing Tae-Soo or Hae-In expected was to run into the very officials they were meant to be visiting. Located in the nearest town by the village, it was their next obvious destination to get a clue as to what had happened. From the looks of their reactions, they too had not expected to run into their party.

"Hang, Guan," Hai-In greeted evenly. "Where are you heading?"

The officials would never be great spies. Their faces instantly gave away their guilt and fear. Tae-Soo kept his eyes on the men escorting them. They were dressed for battle it seemed. In armor much more expensive than anything their town could afford. The men, having more composure than their leaders stood calmly betraying no thoughts or actions. Tae-Soo, Hae-In, and the men with them were outnumbered, but only by a few.

"We were called to meet with the king and queen," Hang lied without convincing anyone.

"Even though they ordered you to stay in Isheng?" Tae-Soo rebutted. The sad excuse for a man didn't even try to come up with an explanation and immediately called for the soldiers to attack. Just as the men approached Hae-In, Tae-Soo ducked along with the others in front and the men behind fired off their already-loaded arrows. The running men were forced to stop and take cover behind shields as the other unlucky ones fell. The frontline ran out to attack while they cowered. Hae-In beat mercilessly at the shield of the first man he approached until he had hacked into the wood surrounding the small patch of metal splintering it. The soldier tried reaching for his sword but Hae-In had already stabbed him in the gut.

Tae-Soo used his shield to bat away the arrow that came barreling toward his chest. Before the archer could get off another shot Tae-Soo slammed the edge of his shield into his face, caving the man's nose in. As he screamed Tae-Soo hit him again pushing the rest of his face in. Tae-Soo removed his blades and went after the other two archers hurriedly trying to reload. The blade in his right hand sliced the man on his left's face into his eye. While the man on the right took Tae-Soo's other dagger in the gut. After the man on the right fell, he used the left dagger to finish the now one-eyed soldier. Another soldier came at him with his sword raised. Tae-Soo ran at him at the same speed only to quickly shift to his right as the sword swung down. The soldier stumbled forward and Tae-Soo daggered him in the spine before back kicking him in the leg and sending him face down.

Hae-In and a comrade, Gang, took on two soldiers wielding staffs. The one across from Hae-In tried jabbing him with the point but he jumped back in time. He went for Hae-In's legs. Hae-In jumped again, landing on the weapon. The man tried to pull back. Hae-In kicked him in the face and ran him through. Gang had caught the staff of his opponent on his first swing and had wrestled it from the man's hands without much effort as Gang was two times his size. With his strength, he broke the spear across his knee and jammed both jagged ends into the man's chest and stomach.

Hae-in could see two of their men shot down with arrows from the men on the back of the wagon. He whistled, getting Tae-Soo's attention. Tae-Soo looked toward him and Hae-In gestured his head to the wagon. Understanding without words he ran toward the front horses and gave a hard smack to the rear of one. The horses took off causing the unprepared men to tumble off. Before they could get up Hae-In and Tae-Soo were standing above them. Hae-In stomped on one's neck and gave a hard twist breaking it while Tae-Soo picked up one of the archer's fallen arrows and stabbed his opponent in the heart.

In the midst of all this Hang and Guan watched uselessly and helplessly from their horses. Any attempt to try and run off was blocked by men fighting. When more of his men were dead on the ground, Guan attempted to dismount and run for the trees. Unfortunately, in his panic, his foot caught on the saddle and he fell, barely able to break his fall with his hands as he dangled helplessly. Hang took his chances on his horse going back up the road, possibly trying to get back to the safety of his town. An arrow to the back ended that plan before his horse could even fully turn around.

Tae-Soo and Hae-In approached the still-living and incapacitated Guan. Tae-Soo kneeled down with his head tilted. He would have laughed if he weren't so angry. "Where were you going?" he demanded. Guan was crying, desperately trying to shake himself free. Hae-In stepped up and pushed his foot loose. Guan fell to the ground with a hard thud. Guan pushed himself up. Tae-Soo only allowed him to get to his knees before pressing one of his daggers to the man's throat.

"I will not ask again."

Guan had to swallow several times before he could speak.

"We were told to bring our men and supplies to the capital."

"Why?"

He shook his head. "I don't know." Tae-Soo applied pressure and a drop of blood slid down his neck.

"I don't! We were just meant to be a small supply party, one of several."

"By whose orders?" Hae-In asked. Guan hesitated before Tae-Soo pushed again.

"The soothsayer. He claims to speak on behalf of Katsuo. He said we had to be there before the new moon."

"Captains!"

Tae-Soo and Hae-In left Guan in one of the men's care and went to the wagon where they were being called. They had gotten several of the barrels open. Tae-Soo jumped on and looked inside. He put his hand into the black powder. He took some out and sniffed, confirming his worst suspicions. Hae-In was checking out another barrel with presumably the same cargo.

"How long?" Tae-Soo asked Hae-In.

"Two days," he spoke with horrified realization.

"Collect everything you can, we leave for the capital at once!" Tae-Soo shouted.

***

Kahil had not relaxed since they left Fei's grounds. He was too unsettled by the strange behavior within his estate. He knew his lord had been suspicious as well. Even though they were several miles away they still felt the need to keep up the illusion that they did not suspect anything. The forest seemed to have ears. No birds sang, no bugs chirped. But there was breathing amongst the trees. The men had already been signaled to keep their wits about them, and they too were staying alert to their surroundings. Their next destination was Lord Chamas in the city a couple of hours' ride away.

A snap within the trees had all eyes and weapons pointed in the same direction. Unnerving silence filled the area. Seconds passed. Minute reached. Nothing. The men continued on but no weapons were re-sheathed. "Is our lady prepared for her journey?" Kahil asked. This was not a casual conversation. It was a disguise. A way to put anyone who may have been out there at ease. Amir's eyes stayed ahead while subtly checking the trees every few seconds.

"I can't be sure," he admitted honestly. "I do not know if she truly wishes to go."

"You don't know if she truly wishes to marry you?" Kahil clarified, making things plain as he always did with his lord. Amir and Kahil had grown up together. Kahil's mother worked in the house and his father was one of the soldiers pledged to Amir's father. When Amir began training under his father to become the next Lord, Kahil was training to be a soldier. They saw each other very little for years until Ami's father became ill and Amir had been forced to step up sooner than planned. It was only by chance or perhaps fate that Kahil worked his way up the ranks and was randomly chosen to be a part of Amir's protection. It was Amir who granted him the title of Captain after they survived the Anoekan ambush a few years ago. That ambush had almost taken Amir's life but he survived.

"There are days I know she does," Amir said. "The others…," he trailed off.

"It is a big change for her. Naturally, it would take some getting used to," Kahil told him. He could see him nod from the corner of his eye but there was a weight to it. Kahil didn't know if it was due to the conversation or their current situation. Given the way he tensed as the wind blew causing the leaves to shift, he guessed it was the latter. It was that slight shift in the weather that caused the arrow going by to hit the tree and not his lord. "Cover!" Kahil screamed. He jumped from his horse and Amir did the same. The men took formation with shields covering Amir and themselves as well. The arrows rained within seconds. Many bounced off the shields while a few were embedded in them. Kahil peeked out through a small sliver of space between his shield and another. While the arrows continued pouring, he could see a hint of movement in the distance. Ten, no twenty, no at least thirty men heading toward him, and that was only who he could currently see.

"Archers!" he called. The men enclosed within the shields already had their bows out and loaded.

"Front defense!" As soon as he spoke, the front of the soldiers moved their shields and the archers stepped forward sending a score of arrows into the crowd of men heading their way. Most went down.

"Cover!" Kahil said again. He noticed as the shields were moving back in place there were more men heading their way.

"They're coming from the rear!" A soldier shouted from the back line.

"From the sides!" Another yelled.

'So, they were surrounded,' Kahil realized, dismayed. Amir and he looked at one another, both most likely thinking the same thing. Amir took hold of his sword, keeping it at the ready, a determined and ferocious look in his eyes. "Get me back to her," he ordered Kahil. Kahil knew he wasn't just giving that order to him but to himself as well. They would not accept defeat.

"Side Defense!" he shouted. As the shield went down and the arrows flew, Kahil, Amir and the others ran out to meet their enemies and their fates.

CHAPTER 12

Katsuo watched the flames from a distance. He found himself unable to get close to any fire bigger than a candlelight flame since his "defeat." He raised a scarred arm to drink the medicine the healer had given him to fight the infection that kept rising in him. He no longer winced at the bitterness, having gotten used to the taste. The healer had been kind, something Katsuo had not appreciated at the time. Back in those first few weeks, all he could think about was the pain. His burns had overtaken his body and his mind.

He couldn't stop screaming. The flames licking at his leg only compounded the pain he felt on his face and arm. He tried to move away. Drag himself out of the flames but his leg was broken as was his arm. He could only stare as his other arm turned from pink to red, and then black. His screams never died down as he watched his body slowly become increasingly engulfed in flames.

What should have been salvation, two arms lifting and dragging him away only brought more pain as his mutilated limbs were roughly dragged on stone and rock. He was finally able to stop screaming, only because he'd passed out from the pain.

His reprieve ended when he awoke in a darkened room. The burning was gone but the pain remained. He didn't dare move though he doubted he could. He could hear quiet mumblings around him and soft movement as well, but he couldn't even manage to turn his head to look. Stone ceilings in dim light was all he could see along with stone walls in his peripheral. The narrowness of the walls led him to believe he was lying in a hallway.

"Quiet, do you want them to hear us?!" A hushed voice whispered.

"Does it matter? Whether they kill us today or tomorrow, all we are doing is putting off the inevitable."

"Coward!" Someone spat.

"They defeated us! We lost! There's no bravery in denying it," the second voice continued.

"They haven't found us yet. If we wait it out a little longer, we can escape, find our brothers still out there, regroup and-," another started speaking.

"And what? Confront the Xians once more? For what? This war was all his doing! Look what it's gotten us, look what it's gotten him. Is that what you want for yourself?"

The words would have enraged him any other time, but the pain he was in took precedence. They also may have been true. He'd bet everything on this war and it all had been ripped away.

"The best we can hope for is to get home and hope we are accepted back."

'Home,' the word was foreign to him now. He tried so hard to make Xian his new home, wanting to carve out a greater legacy than his land could provide. Now he may never see his true home again. He didn't realize how much he'd come to regret that until this moment. From the corner of his

eye, he could see a figure standing right beside him.
He shifted his eyes to it and felt his heart pound.
'Ami.' Standing next to him with a sad and pitying
look on his face. He wanted to reach out to him but
he lost consciousness again. He drifted in and out
for days barely able to register what was going on
around him. For a few of those days his
surroundings never changed, trapped underground
under the broken remains of the fort. Until one day
he opened his eyes to see the night sky moving. He
could hear the sounds of the night and the soft pants
of those around them as they carried him on a cot.
He vaguely wondered how they'd gotten out and
when but couldn't voice his questions.

The next time he awoke he thought he was
on fire again. The pain had returned with a
vengeance. He opened his eyes to see a woman
hovering over him dousing his burns with
something. He didn't know what it was but it felt
like she was burning him all over again. He moved
his good arm to push her away but was stopped by

someone. He looked up to see Sho standing next to him holding his arm down.

"You must let her treat you," he told him, in a grave voice. He didn't care what kind of treatment this was; he couldn't endure it another minute.

'Don't fight sweet boy,' This voice was different, softer, it sounded far but close. Katsuo looked up to see a woman in the corner of the room, tears in her eyes as she held her hands in front of her like she was pleading. 'Get better and come home,' the woman said. 'Mother.' The pain intensified and his mother screamed out as if she were feeling it.

"Stop!" he screamed out hoarsely, struggling against Sho's hold to no avail. Sho placed something over his mouth, a cloth with a strong scent.

"Don't!" the woman scolded. Before long he felt himself slowly fading back into the darkness.

"-ind won't be able to handle such a high dose," the voices came to his addled mind slowly. He could barely comprehend them.

"If it takes his pain it doesn't matter," a voice he recognized spoke. Sho.

'Pain away,' sounded nice. He wanted that.

"The infection is strong. Mixing the Mugana with the Giseng could have long-term effects."

"Just cure him. Whatever effects there are will be my problem to solve."

"He's leading you back to the abyss." Katsuo looked down to see another figure at the foot of his bed. Unlike his mother or Ami, she held no look of sadness or worry. Her brown skin darkened significantly in the shadows of the room. She smiled gleefully while he lay broken. "Right back to me."

Katsuo wanted to speak out and tried to but only a hard and harsh cough came out. Once it did, he couldn't stop. He felt something thick and nasty filling his throat. He began choking on it. Suddenly hands were on him and a cup was being forced onto his lips. He didn't want to swallow, he only wanted to spit out whatever was making its way up his throat. Despite his wishes, he was forced to take in whatever was inside the cup. Almost immediately, the thickness went back down. 'Dreamwalker' was his last thought before he closed his eyes once more.

He was awake again. He hated it when he was. The pain was unbearable. In his waking moments, the woman would give him medicine but it only took away the worst of it. The rest was still agonizing. He still could not sit up or move. He wore more bandages than clothes on his body. He would do his best to focus on something, anything, else hoping his mind could wander from the pain even just for a few minutes, long enough for him to drift into blissful darkness. There was a hanging talisman above him. He recognized it as one of the older gods of Xian. Tai-Lusa, the goddess of health and vitality. The woman must be a follower of her teachings. This was what he had been reduced to. A disfigured broken man at the mercy of low-born peasants and their gods. He hated this. He hated her. Didn't he? It was hard to keep his thoughts together sometimes. He hated that she was seeing him in this way. Hated that she was their only option when he used to have a dozen healers at his call. He hated the one who'd put him in this position. In his dreams, he could see him, with his arrogant expression. He would laugh at Katsuo in all his nightmares. Sometimes he was chopping off his limbs one at a time. Other times he was having him burned at the stake, howling with laughter as Katsuo screamed and begged. It was his fault. He had stolen his destiny from him. Hadn't he? He was meant to be the one on the throne. That's what Sho said, everyone around him told him so. It must have been true. Then why was he like this? Why had he failed? Maybe his mother would know. She would welcome him back home no matter what. She'd stood by him after Akimitsu's death, she would stand by him now. Akimitsu, Akimitsu wasn't dead, he remembered. He'd seen him, right before his life ended. Was it his fault? Because Katsuo had failed to kill him. When he was told the deed was done, he never checked the body himself. He couldn't. He didn't want to see his brother in such a way. He wanted to hold on to the last time he saw him playing happily with his nanny not knowing what was to befall him. Katsuo never wanted to, but Sho was adamant. He made it clear he would one day take the crown he worked so hard for. But where was he now? Had Sho's premonition come true? Did he now sit on his throne wearing his crown? The anger built up once more and with it a fresh wave of pain. He whimpered, unable to do anything else. He wished he were home.

***

Katsuo was propped on a pillow as the healer woman fed him broth. He couldn't open his mouth very wide. He dribbled more than he swallowed. It was embarrassing. He wanted her to leave him. He'd rather starve than continue to suffer this humiliation. When he would try to turn his head, she'd gently but firmly pull it back. He would try to yell at her for her impertinence but could barely get out one word. "You need to eat to get stronger," was all she would say.

This continued for weeks. Slowly, he was able to sit up, with help. As his burns slowly healed the pain became more manageable. He was able to eat soft foods, porridge, and mushed fruits, like a child he'd lament. But he could at least feed himself. In those weeks Sho only saw him a few times. When he asked him where he had been he'd always say he was making arrangements for his return. He had wanted to ask to return home but had been unable to voice it aloud. Returning home would be admitting he had failed. It would mean everything Sho had spoken over him had been a lie. Since he was a child Sho had been at his side. Teaching him, guiding him, informing him of his great destiny. Even when his father had been busy with his whore, it was Sho who taught him to be a king. It was Sho who brought him here. It was Sho that had him risk his crown back home to pursue his prophecy. It was Sho who did not see the outcome that would befall him.

Katsuo thought on the past as he did all day every day ever since he'd come back to his senses. He constantly wondered what decisions led him to his defeat. One day he'd put the blame on his men's ineptitude; another it was all because of the Xian king. Sometimes he wondered if he'd sealed his fate when he took on this quest of his. Sho constantly told him who was to blame but he didn't want to hear it. He refused to entertain the idea that it was his own naivety that brought them here. He'd asked for her, one of the many times he'd awaken in his delirium. Sho had always ranted that she was to blame and how she'd deceived him. Some days he outright refused to believe it. Others he imagined wrapping his hands around her throat. As the days brought him closer and closer to his throne, he thought hard about what he would do once he saw her again. He would soon find out.

CHAPTER 13

Serenity placed another book back on the shelf. She could hear Blessing babbling in her own language to Amoli. Arezoo stood on guard by the door. She'd come to the library in search of a specific book. She wanted to read about the voyages of the historian Myung-Dae once more to see if there was something she missed last time. He was the only historian to interact with the Assani people. She wondered if there may be some clues to the Anoekan people in his tales that could help them establish a dialog. She had not given up the hope that they could be of help to them in case things went south.

"Will you address the lords with the king?" Arezoo asked. Serenity nodded but quickly said yes, remembering she was behind the shelf.

"I'm about to head over there as soon as I find it," she told her. Kang-Dae was most likely already in the throne room awaiting the lords' arrival. Though they still had not heard back from

Kahil and the others, with the reappearance of the dream, the need to come together and strategize was urgent.

"Should I take the princess to the Dowager? She wanted to visit with her," Amoli mentioned.

"That's fine. She hasn't seen her in a while. You can probably leave Blessing with her. Take some time to yourself." She responded, still scanning the shelf.

"It is no trouble, my queen, I do not mind staying with them. My schedule is very clear," asserted Amoli.

"You could take some time to prepare for your journey."

"Journey, my queen?" questioned Amoli.

"To your future in-laws," Serenity hinted, revealing her knowledge of the situation. Amoli was silent and even Blessing had gone quiet as if sensing her surprise. Serenity came from around the corner to see her staring at the floor, a pink blush on her tanned cheeks.

"As bad as you are at keeping secrets, Amir is worse," Serenity joked. "Jung-Soo got it out of him that same day."

"Are you sure you wish to tie yourself to such a man?" asked Arezoo. "If he is unable to withstand such small pressure, he could never withstand torture."

Serenity held back her laughter. "Well, we all have different standards for men," Serenity joked.

"I-I, just do not think it is the right time," Amoli finally said. "There is so much going on."

"There's always something going on," Serenity countered. "You don't let life stop because of it or you'll always be postponing your happiness."

"Is it my happiness?" Amoli spoke softly, hesitantly. "How can I know that it will be? It's completely-."

"Unknown." Serenity finished for her. Serenity walked over to her and knelt beside her. Blessing, seeing her mom so close, reached out to touch her face. Serenity smiled at the girl before turning her attention back to Amoli. "There's always a little bit of fear in things we don't know." Amoli looked at her friend, her face full of worry and uncertainty. "And you won't know. The only thing you can know is what you feel."

"Do not make the error of mistaking familiarity for happiness. Just because it is different does not mean it will be a mistake," Arezoo spoke up once more, in a surprisingly thoughtful tone. Both women looked over to her surprised at the wisdom that came from her.

A loud crack, almost like thunder, sounded outside in the distance.

***

As the Lords began to file in, Kang-Dae ended his conversation with Jung-Soo who went to take his position at the side. He wouldn't start until Serenity arrived, knowing she was most likely on her way. Satori stood in Amir's place in his absence. With all his years of experience, Kang-Dae felt his input would be valuable. The men took their seats and Kang-Dae couldn't help feeling a tug of disappointment at the empty spots where the traitorous lords once occupied. Despite suspecting the truth, it still burned him to know they still were dealing with such matters. It brought many unwanted feelings back to when he'd felt his greatest betrayal with Kyril. Though these weren't quite as personable, it still left an ache in his heart and a sense of paranoia about those in the room with him. Could he be sure of their loyalties, and even if he could trust them now, who was to say if they wouldn't betray him later? Kang-Dae had spent much of his early years as king not trusting those around him, seeing how they could so easily bend the rules for their own wants and ideas. It was why, back then, he'd jumped at the chance to seize his true power through marriage with Serenity, a plan he would be thankful for until the day he died. A small smile reached his face at the memory of his decision and all the joy that had come with it.

"Will my mother be joining us?" Kang-Dae asked Satori knowing he would know. The man shook his head.

"I believe she had plans to spend the day with the princess, my king," he answered. Kang-Dae wasn't surprised. Ever since Serenity had stepped fully into the role his mother had slowly pulled back to give her the chance to flourish in the role without her influence. There were times when Serenity would feel unsure of herself and she would go seek his mother's council, without him knowing, or so she thought. His mother would not step in no matter how she pleaded, encouraging her to trust herself and forgo trying to do things the way others had. Her mother had told him once that her and his father's way of ruling was for their time and that he and Serenity would have to discover their own way.

She had since thrown herself into the role of grandmother, spending as much time as she could with their daughter.

As the last of the lords came in, Kang-Dae turned to head to his throne seated by Serenity's. A thunderous boom echoed from outside. Just as the lords looked at one another trying to determine where a storm had come from so suddenly, the ceiling crashed down on them.

***

The sound had Serenity going toward the window to see if the blue skies that had been present when they arrived had shifted into stormy ones. It wasn't until the thunder sounded once more and she saw no clouds but a large object hurtling towards the main hall she felt pure terror. Eyes wide, she watched in horror as the roof caved in knowing her husband was inside. She was about to warn the women when that sound happened again only it sounded like it was coming right for them.

"GET OUT!" she screamed out, turning to get to her daughter. She only made it two steps before the ground collapsed from under them.

CHAPTER 14

Kang-Dae slowly sat up from where he had ducked to save himself from debris. Dust and smoke burned his eyes and obscured his vision as he attempted to look around. Some of the lords were attempting to pick themselves up. An unfortunate few weren't moving at all, trapped beneath large pieces of wood and stone. A small fire was burning in the middle of the floor and a couple of lords burned in it. Kang-Dae couldn't tell who it was. He looked at the large opening in the ceiling revealing the skies. His ears were ringing and he felt a bit dizzy. His head was throbbing in the back. He went to touch the spot and was bewildered when he felt wetness. He brought his hand back to his face and saw the blood. For some reason, he had a hard time comprehending what he was seeing.

"My king!" a voice shouted. Kang-Dae slowly turned toward it. Satori was in front of him, his face dirty. Satori struggled to help him on his feet, or maybe it was him who was struggling,

Kang-Dae wondered as his legs started buckling from under him. Before he hit the ground Jung-Soo was next to him, helping him stand. Together the two men helped to usher him out of the throne room as the other lords rushed out with them, some pushing past in desperation. Kang-Dae could see Yu, lying unmoving, beneath a large piece of rubble. He only lingered for a second before he was led out. They all stepped outside into even more chaos. People ran about screaming and crying. Nobles and servants. The screams increased and some of the noblewomen looked up screaming. Kang-Dae wasn't sure why at first until he looked up to see a large round burning object crash into the temple. 'A hundred-year structure gone in an instant,' he thought to himself. The men tried to keep him moving but it was getting harder and harder for him to get his legs to cooperate. Not even a minute later, another hit the ground only a few meters from where they stood.

"We have to evacuate everyone!" Screamed Satori, trying to be heard over all the noise.

"Get to the Dowager," Jung-Soo told him. The man nodded and gently gave Kang-Dae over to Jung-Soo and took off towards his mother's hall. Kang-Dae, feeling slightly more oriented, stood straight.

"Serenity," was all he said before forcing his now working feet to move toward the hall of knowledge. Jung-Soo was at his side as they forced their way through panicking people and out-of-place debris. As they turned the corner past the courtyard they came to a stop. Kang-Dae felt his heart seize and his breath got stuck in his throat. The hall was in shambles. The entire second floor library was gone and the first floor looked to have caved in on itself. Kang-Dae flew toward the building.

CRASH!

Another boulder had launched itself into the ground in front of them, exploding on impact, sending both men flying back.

***

Blessing was crying. Serenity struggled to open her eyes so she could get her baby. 'She must be hungry,' she thought to herself. The more she tried to move, the more difficult it was, the more Serenity slowly began to realize something was wrong. Blessing's cries were shrieks, pain-filled screams that tore at Serenity's heart. She managed to open her eyes and gasped. No longer in the library, or even the hall of knowledge, they had fallen beneath the building into the tunnels below. There was nothing but the remains of the hall and the books of the library to break their fall. Suddenly, aware of everything, the pain in her abdomen flared, making her cry out.

"My queen," she heard Amoli call out.

"Amoli! Blessing, is she okay?" She couldn't see anything over the shelf that had fallen and was now hovering above her. The silence between her question and Amoli's response was more frightening than anything she had just experienced.

"I think she's fine," Amoli called. There was a slight uncertainty in her tone that told Serenity she was probably injured. Given the state of everything she would accept that over dead. Serenity attempted to push at the beam pinning her to the ground, ignoring the pain she felt but it didn't budge. She could hear shuffling and Blessing's cries getting louder. Soon Amoli was above her, with Blessing wailing in her arms. Even though she hated to see her baby so distraught she was so grateful that she was moving. Amoli dropped to her knees and attempted to move the beam with Blessing clinging to her. Serenity tried as well hoping their combined strength would be enough. They pushed and pulled as the sounds of chaos rang out from above them. Serenity feared what was happening out there but she mostly worried for Kang-Dae and prayed he was okay. The beam shifted a few centimeters but that was it.

A clattering had both women jumping. Arezoo was making her way to them at a low crawl. Her left leg, she let drag, using her hands to pull herself over to them. "Arezoo, don't move," Serenity told her, seeing she was hurt. Arezoo ignored her. She slowly but determinedly made her way to them. Upon closer inspection, Serenity realized her leg was badly injured. Arezoo seemed to be completely ignoring this fact as she took hold of the beam as well and began trying to pull it off. Serenity wanted to tell her to stop but knew she wouldn't listen. All three women put everything they had into moving the beam.

***

Satori was running as fast as he could toward the back of the palace. He could see the Dowager's hall had not been hit yet and moved faster. From the corner of his eyes, he could see movement in the distance. He turned and blanched as scores of men in armor began pouring in through a hole in the wall. Not having time to waste he sprinted to the hall. Dozens of women and men were making their way out the front. They appeared unharmed but were notably terrified. Satori pushed past and went inside. He was making his way to the

Dowager's room but stopped when he spotted her in the middle of her courtyard directing people out. Relief filled Satori and he made his way over to her.

"Your majesty, we must go," he told her. She continued guiding a young woman toward the exit.

"We have to get them out, send them to the fortress," she told him.

"The men will do that. You need to get out of here now. We're being invaded."

"I am aware," she said snippily.

"No, right now, They've already infiltrated the walls," he told her, trying to get her to understand. She paused and he saw a flicker of disbelief in her eyes.

"Where's my family?"

"They're being escorted out," he told her. He had no idea if it were true or not but he knew if she thought otherwise, he'd never get her to leave.

"You need to get to safety," he reiterated. She paused, taking in his words. With a short nod, she reached out for him. Satori took her arm and led her out of the yard.

CHAPTER 15

Jung-Soo pulled out another large splinter from his side. Whatever the enemy was using as fodder was created to burst upon impact to cause even greater damage to anyone who may be around. He held his hand over the wound trying to staunch the bleeding before checking on Kang-Dae. He had taken a bigger brunt of the blast as he had been in front. Jung-Soo crawled over to him but he was not moving. "Kang-Dae!" Jung-Soo called to him. He didn't stir. Jung-Soo checked over him, finding more than a few splinters sticking out from his body but none long enough to cause major damage. Jung-Soo called out to him again, gently shaking him trying not to cause more damage.

Kang-Dae's head shifted from side to side. "Serenity," he mumbled. He barely opened his eyes and they looked past Jung-Soo. "I have-, Serenity," he continued having trouble forming his words.

"I'll find her," Jung-Soo told him to put him at ease. Without warning Kang-Dae fell unconscious once more.

"General, we have enemies entering through the rear gate!" A soldier came running up to him. He was accompanied by a small troop. Jung-Soo imagined the bulk of their palace forces were busy engaging the enemy at the front gates.

"Take him!" Jung-Soo ordered getting to his feet. "Take the hidden path to the fortress. Stop for no one." The men took up Kang-Dae.

"What about you, General?" The soldier asked.

"Just go! If he awakens, he'll want to come back, don't let him." The soldier nodded and the men carried Kang-Dae off. Still clutching his side Jung-Soo stumbled toward the hall.

***

Clashing swords and painful cries could be heard above. Serenity, Amoli, and Arezoo desperately pushed knowing they needed to escape before those sounds made their way towards them. Amoli attempted to quiet Blessing who had stopped screaming but was still crying. The women knew the sounds would alert anyone nearby to their position and since they had no way of knowing if they would be heard by friend or foe, they did their best to minimize the sounds. Long minutes passed and they had yet to get Serenity free, only managing to get one of her legs out.

"I should go get help," Amoli said after another failed attempt. Serenity shook her head.

"You could run into trouble," she told her. She didn't have to elaborate on what kind of trouble. "You need to get Blessing away from here."

Amoli shook her head. "I will not leave you," she stated. She took hold once more and pulled. A scream from just above them sounded.

"We don't have time," Serenity cried. "Get my baby out of here!"

Amoli once again shook her head, tears springing to her eyes.

"Amoli, please!" the sounds were getting closer. They were above them now. To her horror, she heard someone shout to check inside.

"Take Arezoo and get out of here," she pleaded.

"No," Arezoo said defiantly.

"Arezoo-," Serenity began.

"My place is by your side, protecting you. I will not leave. I will not," she declared. Serenity didn't know when she had begun to cry but she could suddenly feel the tears flowing from her eyes. She looked back toward Amoli.

"Go, please. Save my Blessing," she pleaded again. She could tell when Amoli accepted her request because her shoulders slumped and a sob escaped her. With a slow nod, she took Serenity's hand and squeezed it. Serenity kissed it and looked at her daughter for what she feared would be the last time. She reached for her and Amoli handed her over. Blessing immediately wrapped herself around her mother's neck.

"I love you," she whispered into her hair. Serenity's heart broke as thoughts of never seeing her daughter grow up overtook her mind. "Stay safe." It took every ounce of willpower to pull her off. Blessing cried and fought to remain with her mother. Serenity cried as she forced Blessing back into Amoli's hands. "Go," she told her friend. With a sad look, Amoli headed down the tunnels.

Above them, Serenity could hear someone attempting to climb down. Arezoo took out her sword with much effort. She pulled out another dagger and handed it to Serenity who gratefully took it. They stared at the opening waiting, as it was all they could do.

***

Satori took the lead as the Dowager and he made it to the gate. This lesser-known gate was painted and built to look like a piece of the wall and

only a few knew how to open it. He found the latch
hidden in the ridge of the wall and undid it. With
great effort, he pushed the gate open. A whistle
above his head made him turn to look behind him. A
number of soldiers were heading their way, some
with bows drawn. There were many, too many and
it was only the two of them. Satori looked to the
Dowager who had a trace amount of fear on her
face but greater than that was determination. She
clutched her sword in front of her, steeling herself
for a fight. But it was a fight Satori knew they
would not win.

Satori grabbed hold of the Dowager's arm
and pushed her through the gate so hard she fell.
"Satori!" she shouted but he ignored her.

"Get to the fortress," he told her. He
watched as understanding filled her brown eyes and
she started shaking her head.

"No, no!"

Satori reached for the gate latch. "It has
been my honor, Your Majesty," he told her before

slamming the gate shut with all his might. He could hear her shouting for him as he locked it. The first arrow hit him through the arm making him grunt. Without hesitation he broke it off and jammed it into the lock before breaking it off, making it impossible to open. The first soldier to make it to him suffered a slice to his face, taking out his eye. Satori's mind was suddenly filled with memories, things he cherished and things he'd long forgotten.

He recalled the last dinner he shared with the entire royal family and how the Dowager had laughed most of the night. It had been a beautiful sound.

The second soldier managed to nick his hand, but Satori recovered swiftly, swung, and cut into the man's underarm, burrowing his sword all the way through into his chest. He had to use his foot to force the soldier off.

The image of the king as a young child sitting in his mother's lap on the throne while his

king and friend appointed him as his most trusted
advisor. He had been so happy that day, proud.

The arrow hit him in the shoulder this time.
Satori ignored it as another two soldiers came
charging at him.

The young queen-to-be took him down
again. The future king stood on the sides laughing
as Satori lay on the ground embarrassed at how fast
she had defeated him but secretly impressed. She
stood above him with a confident smile, her hair
swinging in the breeze.

He blocked the first soldier's blow but was
unable to stop the second who had jabbed him in the
gut. Satori pushed at both with a shout. He stumbled
back. 'I loved you since I saw you,' he thought. He
didn't tell her, he never wanted to as it would have
made no difference and would only hinder him from
doing what he wanted, which was serving her with
his whole heart. Satori moved back to the gate,
positioning himself in front of the latch. The two
came at him again. He dodged the first swing,

grabbed the attacker's arm, and elbowed him in the face before stabbing him through the heart. As the soldier fell the second came forward. Satori took the first's sword and swung upward, catching the soldier in the chin. A pain in his chest gave him pause. He looked down to see an arrow. He coughed and a spurt of blood came out.

The queen Dowager had come to visit him after his duel with Sun. She had stayed with him for hours, and they reminisced about the past. For a moment, a small moment he let himself pretend she cared for him the same way he cared for her.

Satori fell back onto the gate. The men drew their bows once more. Satori smiled. He could see her, standing in front of the men, until they faded away and she was all he could see. She smiled at him the way she smiled at the king; the way he had only dreamed she would smile at him. He never felt the arrow that hit his heart.

CHAPTER 16

Jung-Soo was moving as fast as he could, given his condition. From the distance, he could see a large group of men attempting to make their way into the remains of the hall. Someone had to be alive in there for them to make the effort, Jung-Soo told himself. He went toward the back hoping to get in before them.

Only one made it down at first. Serenity held the dagger in front of her. The soldier wore black armor, with no discernable colors but it was clear who had sent them. The man held a crossbow in front of him as he got closer but upon seeing Serenity and her state, he visibly relaxed and even laughed at her. So unbothered by her he walked toward her without noticing the unmoving but very much alive Arezoo by his feet. Before he could take another step. Arezoo swiped at his leg, sending him to the ground. A clean cut, admired Serenity while also being slightly disturbed by the sight of the lone foot standing on its own. The man cried out for help from his comrades. Arezoo crawled over to him and silenced him with her sword. Arezoo relieved the corpse of its weapon and handed it to Serenity along with the spare arrows. With the help of her sword, she managed to get to her feet. She leaned against the debris near her but held her position, ready for anyone who may approach her.

Serenity took the bow in hand and aimed it toward the opening. She wasn't the greatest shot, having little experience with the weapon beyond what little teachings Arezoo had shown her, but today she prayed God guided her hands. This time two men made it down, stumbling as some of the debris moved under their feet. Before one could regain his footing, Serenity released an arrow, hitting him in the thigh. The man tumbled down the rest of the way landing on his back before Arezoo who made quick work of him by Stabbing him in the heart. The second man came down with more ease, sword raised. Arezoo, using the debris for support leaned back as he swiped at her head.

Arezoo swung her sword hard into the soldiers, and it fell from his hands. Faster than Serenity could comprehend, Arezoo swung again, this time at the soldier's throat. Gurgling and clutching at the wound the man fell back. He was dead in seconds.

Jung-Soo had just made it to the back of the hall, which was still intact. "Jung-Soo," someone called. Jung-Soo turned to see Amoli limping toward him with something in her arms. Jung-Soo rushed over to her and she threw herself into him with a cry. Jung-Soo hugged her quickly and pulled back. Noticing Blessing in her arms he quickly scanned behind her.

"Where?" he huffed out. Eyes red, Amoli pointed behind her.

"The tunnels. You have to save her!" Jung-Soo took off before she could finish, not noticing her collapse to the ground.

Serenity shot off another arrow at the soldier engaged with Arezoo. He was bigger than the other two that had come down with him. They lay dead on the ground, thanks to Arezoo's efforts. The arrow sailed past his head. Serenity was scared to aim lower, fearing she would hit Arezoo. As another soldier made his way down Serenity turned her focus on him. This time she hit her target right in the collarbone. His eyes went wide and he fell off to the side. Whether or not he was dead Serenity didn't know but she didn't care. She turned her attention back to Arezoo who was trying to keep her own blade from touching her throat. The soldier was pushing at the blade and Arezoo was slowly losing ground. Serenity aimed once more. 'Please God' she prayed as she fired. The arrow only grazed the side of the soldier's face but it was enough to throw him off. Arezoo, using the strength of her good leg, pushed him back. She slammed her sword into his foot. The man howled. Taking out her other dagger she slammed it into his temple. Serenity released a relieved sigh. Arezoo slumped back panting.

"You are hesitating too much," Arezoo said. "And you are too tense."

Serenity let out a dry laugh.

"How do you know?"

"I know," was all she said. Serenity smiled sadly.

"You were the one who wanted to work on swordsmanship more than anything else. Bet you wish you'd let me use your bow more huh?" she joked. To her utter shock, Arezoo let out a small but clear chuckle. It was a sound she had never heard come from the woman in all the time she knew her.

"A sword is always more reliable," she countered with words she had said to Serenity dozens of times before. Serenity could hear the smile in her voice.

"Says you."

"Says me," Arezoo said looking back at Serenity. Her face showed all the fatigue and pain she was in but with a genuine smile that made her look more beautiful than Serenity had ever seen her look. Serenity felt the tears returning but she forced them back. She returned her smile. The sound of more men descending drew both of their attention back to the opening. This time Serenity didn't wait as soon as she saw legs she let loose. The soldier fell forward, an arrow sticking out his leg. Arezoo killed him quickly but as she did another two came down. Serenity shot, hitting one in the shoulder but due to his armor, he barely flinched. The men went after Arezoo. Serenity aimed again but found the weapon to be empty. Panicked, Serenity felt around for another arrow as she watched, fearfully, as Arezoo tried to fight off the men. The soldier Serenity shot, was making his way over to her. Serenity took hold of Arezoo's dagger. The red-faced soldier limped until he was standing above her. He drew out his sword, a hateful look on his face. There was murder in his eyes and Serenity could feel a spirit of death creeping around her. Heart racing, she couldn't take her eyes off the sword. The man reared back, Serenity leaned forward and grabbed hold of the arrow sticking through his leg. He screamed. Serenity pulled hard causing the back end to snap. Taking a page out of

Arezoo's book, Serenity jammed the broken end into his foot. He fell onto his back.

A cry from Arezoo made Serenity look over. 'Arezoo!" she shouted. One of the men was holding her against the debris while the other was slowly piercing her with his sword. The area around them began to shake as more debris began to fall.

"Arezoo!" Jung-Soo heard Serenity's cry and forced his body to move faster. He turned the corner and saw Arezoo locked in a hold with two men slowly being stabbed. Serenity was on the ground, looking to be trapped beneath some of the wreckage. He could only see the top half of her. As Serenity looked over to Arezoo, she didn't see the man in front of her removing what looked to be a broken piece of wood from his body.

"Serenity!" Jung-Soo screamed in warning but it didn't stop the man from jamming the piece into her neck.

Serenity felt the blood fill her mouth. She touched the piece of arrow sticking out of her throat. A loud groan sounded from something, no someone, Serenity could barely keep her eyes open in shock but she could see Arezoo take the force of the blade that had been slowly making its way into her body. Once she had been run through, she took her dagger and stabbed her killer in the eye. The other man reared back in shock. She tossed the screaming man into him making them both fall. Serenity could see the other man coming toward her with his sword once again, but before it could connect Arezoo threw herself in its path. Serenity couldn't scream or even speak. Blood began to trickle from her mouth as the tears fell as she cradled Arezoo's head in her lap.

Jung-Soo went to get to her when the rest of the roof collapsed. The last thing he saw was Serenity slumping over as debris fell around her until he couldn't see anything. Jung-Soo ran into the wreckage and began pulling up different pieces of wood trying to get to her. His vision was obscured, but he wouldn't stop. He could hear someone behind him but he couldn't turn around, he couldn't stop.

"Jung-Soo," Amoli cried out to him. Jung-Soo ignored her frantically tossing more and more pieces out of the way, but making no real headway. A hand on his shoulder made him falter for half a second before he kept going.

"We have to go," pleaded Amoli. Jung-Soo shook his head, still focused on his task. It was only when he heard a small cry that he stopped. He turned to see Blessing reaching for him. Jung-Soo's shoulders slumped and he let out a scream. Blessing managed to stretch her body over to him and grab onto his shoulder before pulling herself into him. Jung-Soo clutched the child to him. He looked up to Amoli to tell her they needed to go but froze at the reddening of her dress around her stomach. He looked closer and saw a tear in her dress that covered what looked like a gaping wound. Wide eyed he looked up to a weary looking Amoli. "I am alright," she claimed. No sooner did she say it that she began to sway. Jung-Soo moved quickly to catch her. She fell into him. He helped steady her.

Jung-Soo, not having many options, removed the outer layer of his robe and constructed a makeshift carrier for Blessing to carry her on his back. Once she was secured, he took Amoli into his arms and carried her out toward the west gates in hopes of making it to the path to the fortress without running into any more enemies.

CHAPTER 17

Someone kept calling his name. Kang-Dae couldn't recognize the voice, it sounded so far away. Was it his father? He tried to open his eyes but it felt impossible. He tried to move but he couldn't. He felt nothing, only numbness. Where was he? Had he fallen asleep? He would be in so much trouble if he had fallen asleep in the woods again. His father had already warned him about sneaking out alone. Wait, no, this wasn't right. Kang-Dae tried to open his eyes again and failed. This time a few sounds begin to pierce the emptiness. They were soft, barely discernable but they were there. Feet. They were footsteps. Was his Mi-Sung awake? Mi-Sung, the memory of his child slowly poured memories back to him. Where was she? Where was Serenity? Something had happened, but he couldn't recall what. He tried to open his mouth to call out for them but he was paralyzed.

***

Eun-Jung, the former queen of Xian, had been walking the hidden path for what felt like hours. There wasn't anyone behind her, which was good in the sense that the enemy had not followed her but was disheartening as it meant few of their people had been able to make it. There were some prints in the dirt that gave her some hope but she would not let it take root. During the entire journey, her thoughts were composed of worry and fear for her family. Wondering if they were safe, fearing the worst had happened. The more screams she heard in the night the more she feared. She needed to be prepared for anything. She clutched the hilt of her sword.

Up ahead she spotted several Xian soldiers standing at the entrance to the path up the mountain. She quickened her pace. The men recognized her though she couldn't recall their faces. "Your majesty," they greeted in unison.

"Has my son made it?" she asked. The men looked at one another, neither wanting to speak first.

"He has, your majesty," one finally spoke slowly. Eun-Jung felt a lump in her throat.

"I'll escort you up, Your Majesty," The one closer to the entrance spoke up.

The trek up the mountain was not an easy one. The path was one of the only practical and safe ways up but it was still arduous. When they finally reached the doorway, she felt like she was ready to collapse. They entered the open area; the darkening sky was visible to them. Inside, Eun-Jung was happy to see some of the palace workers moving about around the yard. Some of the soldiers were already prepping the place in case of siege, lining the walls with arrows, rocks and what she assumed were vats of oil. Looking up to the second level she could catch a glimpse of more movement above. She needed to get a count of how many had made it. "Your Majesty!" She saw one of the female workers running toward her.

"Ji-An. Where's my family?" she asked as soon as she stopped.

The woman looked down. "I will take you to him," she said softly.

Ji-An led her inside the fortress stronghold. They climbed the stairs all the way to the third floor. Deep inside the mountain, they walked until they came to an open room. Eun-Jung went inside and gasped. Kang-Dae lay on an old cot, a remnant from the last great siege. Kang-Dae was pale, so pale she feared he was dead until she saw his chest rise. Other than that small movement he was still. His head was wrapped heavily. She ran over to him.

"My son!" She cried as she touched his arm. He didn't stir. "Where's the healer?" She asked.

Ji-An refused to look at her. "None have arrived yet," she told her. Eun-Jung looked down at Kang-Dae. She stroked his cheek, alarmed by the coldness. She shifted the blanket on him.

"The queen, my granddaughter? Where are they?" she asked, realizing she hadn't heard a word about them.

"They have not arrived, Your Majesty." Eun-Jung shut her eyes in despair. No, she couldn't stay here while Serenity and Blessing were out there. She kissed Kang-Dae's cloth-covered head and stood up.

"I want men with me to go back out," she said, turning to leave the room.

"Your majesty, you cannot," Ji-An protested.

"The queen cannot be left on her own amongst the enemy!" she told her.

"The soldiers said no one should be going out. It risks the enemy finding us."

Eun-Jung shook her head but her words gave her some hesitation.

"So few of the people made it here. The soldiers that venture out to bring more," she paused. "Not all of them return."

It was hard to hear. Eun-Jung knew their situation was dire but hearing this reminded her this could still get worse if they were not careful.

"You should take a rest, Your Majesty. Sit with the king. There is nothing more you can do tonight." Eun-Jung felt tears of frustration well up and she stubbornly wiped them away.

"I need a change of clothes," she told the woman. Eun-Jung went back to Kang-Dae and sat down beside him.

CHAPTER 18

Jung-Soo was tired. His arms and legs were burning. The injury in his side was throbbing and his chest was burning from all the heavy breathing he was doing. Still, he kept moving, Amoli in his arms and Blessing crying at his back. The poor thing had been terrified the entire time, screaming for her parents. Jung-Soo's determination to get them both to safety was all that was keeping him going. The last image of Serenity was burned into his brain allowing him not a second of peace but driving him to save her child at all costs. He didn't know how he was going to tell Kang-Dae. He didn't even know if he would be able to tell him. There was no guarantee he had made it. The thought dismayed him even more.

Cries in the distance behind him made him pick up his pace. He had been hearing it for a while now. As more and more people escape into the woods more soldiers would run them down. From the sounds of things, they had exterminated more than four groups of people. The fighter in him wanted to go and help, give the people a chance, but he couldn't. The child was his priority. He could not jeopardize her safety for anyone. If he could just make it to the hidden path, he may be able to slow them down. If the enemy failed to find it would be a much-needed reprieve for not just him, but all survivors. As Blessing's cries increased Jung-Soo feared she would lead the enemy to them. Knowing he couldn't lead the enemy to the path he reluctantly stopped behind a tree. He gently laid Amoli down. She had lost consciousness a while ago, something that had alarmed him greatly, but once again he could do nothing about it. He swung Blessing around to face him. The poor girl's face was red from all the screaming. Fluid leaked from her eyes and nose. Jung-Soo tried shushing her and holding her to him. Once she was on his shoulder he noticed the small stain of blood in her ear. He also saw she had a bad burn on her collarbone, most likely from the remains of the projectile that had been used. Knowing she had been in such pain hurt his heart even more and he hugged her tighter as he whispered soothing words to her.

At his feet, Amoli began to stir. He slid down next to her and took her hand in his. "Amoli," he whispered. Her eyes fluttered open. She looked out blankly as if she were trying to process where she was. Once she scanned the trees her eyes landed on him. As if seeing him was all her mind needed to remember, tears immediately filled her eyes. Jung-Soo had to look away unable to handle her grief along with his own.

"We're close to the path. We're almost there," he said because it was all he could say.

"Is she okay?" For a second, he had to remember that she could not be talking about Serenity and he had to choke back his emotions. He nodded and cleared his throat.

"I think the blast may have injured her ear." Amoli nodded as if she already knew.

"It was bleeding," she told him. "That thing, it landed right next to us. I tried to cover her as much as I could," her voice broke.

"You kept her safe," he assured her. He had no doubt it was due to Amoli that the child only sustained a couple of injuries.

Sounds of screams filled the sky. Amoli looked around with wide eyes. Jung-Soo held a finger to his lips to keep her quiet. Luckily, Blessing's cries had died down some. He continued rubbing her back to keep her calm. The snapping of twigs drew their attention. Jung-Soo and Amoli shared matching looks of concern. He carefully placed Blessing in Amoli's waiting arms. As quietly as he could, he stood to his feet and drew out his sword. The sound came from in front of them. Jung-Soo debated whether he should lead them away, and keep them from finding Blessing, but given the state of Amoli, he had serious doubts she would be able to get them to the fortress on her own. The steps were coming closer. He wished he had grabbed a

crossbow on his way out, despite knowing he had
no room to carry it.

He went to a tree opposite the girls and hid
behind them in wait. If he were lucky, they may
pass them by. They moved almost silently, which
was contrary to the others. Jung-Soo wondered why
this group cared about stealth. The shadows of them
hit his eyeline before he could hear another sound
from them. Jung-Soo held up his sword preparing
himself. He wasn't at his best, but he could not
afford to falter. The first thing he noticed was the
armor. It was Xian. But Jung-Soo knew better. That
didn't mean anything when dealing with the
Anoekans. He was prepared to let them continue on.
If they happened to notice Amoli, he may be able to
catch them off guard from behind. The chances of
him taking them all out was nonexistent. He just
needed to keep them from finding Blessing. Maybe
someone else would come along and find them. He
was sure more Xian soldiers would be coming soon
if someone had been able to get the word out, he
realized. It was possible they had no idea what was

transpiring here. The thought deflated him. Too focused on the ones in front of him Jung-Soo had not noticed the one creeping behind him until he felt his presence at his back. Without thinking, Jung-Soo swung, hitting the blade of Tae-Soo whose wide eyes met his. Jung-Soo almost collapsed from relief.

"General," Tae-Soo breathed out, relieved. "It's the general!" he called out to the others who all stopped in their tracks. Peeking around from the front of the line, he could see Kahil and Hae-In. Hae-In immediately came running.

"General, are you okay?" Asked Hae-In as soon as he took in the state of him. Jung-Soo sagged against the tree.

"We need to get to the fortress," he told them. By now Kahil and Amir had made their way over.

"We were too late," Kahil said grimly. Jung-Soo led the men over to where Amoli and Blessing were. Seeing Amoli, Amir sprinted to her.

Amoli felt a burst of happiness when Amir appeared before her. She reached her hand out to him. He knelt beside her, taking her hand in his.

"Your back," she said.

"Are you okay?" he asked, fear and concern etched over his face. She nodded, squeezing his hand, needing his comfort more than anything in that moment. Jung-Soo came up and took the, now sleeping, Blessing in his arms ignoring the words and pleas of his men to allow them to carry the child. As gently as he could, Amir lifted her into his arms and she wrapped her arms around his neck. Despite the pain she was in, she wanted to cry tears of joy, having been so afraid she would die without seeing him again.

"We have people in the area that need help," Jung-Soo told them.

Tae-Soo and Hae-In nodded. "We'll go out and collect them," said Hae-In. Captain Kahil gave orders to his men to find and help any survivors. A small number of men stayed with them to escort them to the fortress. Feeling a tinge of hope for the first time that day, Amoli prayed they would make it.

CHAPTER 19

The screams of his enemies were good.
Their attack had been successful. He should relish
in them, Katsuo told himself, and a part of him did.

For the first time in what must've been
weeks, Katsuo regained full consciousness. He was
able to turn his head to see the numerous bandages
engulfing most of his body. He no longer felt the
horrible pain he had before, as it had been reduced
to a strong but dull ache all over his body. He could
hear movement from a short distance away. He
checked his surroundings, finding himself in a small
room in what must be someone's home. From the
furniture and design, he figured he was still in Xian.
Judging from the condition of everything, a very
impoverished part of Xian. Most likely a village on
the outskirts of a larger city or population. He
couldn't figure out what he was doing here.

"Sho?" He called out hoping the soothsayer
was nearby and able to give him answers. Instead,
an older woman came into the room. Her long

graying hair was pushed to the back of her head and tied with a white ribbon. She dressed simply in beige pants beneath an open skirt with a beige shirt to match. She had a serious but calm expression on her face.

"Your father, will be back soon. He's gone to scavenge more herbs for your treatment," she explained. 'Father' Katsuo thought. That wasn't possible. He was back in Anoeka. and he was in no condition to travel anywhere.

"He left some of his men here to look after you if you are worried," she told him. 'His men?' He wondered. 'Sho,' Katsuo realized. He was hiding their identity. A smart and necessary move. That Xian king most likely thought him dead. It was best to keep it that way while he recovered. Looking down at himself, he wondered if he ever would. Remembering the damage and how he'd felt that day, it seemed unlikely.

"Who are you?" he asked, wondering why he'd been left in her care.

"I am Yun-Sing. I am a healer in the village. I work on many with afflictions such as yours." An affliction, such a word seemed insignificant to describe what he went through. Recalling the pain, the humiliation of it all, started filling him with a new burning. Kang-Dae. It was all that Xian king's fault. That final fight between the two of them had only gone in the Xian king's favor because he'd distracted him. Though at the moment it was hard to remember what he had told him. Whatever it was he was sure it had been lies. He'd never trust the words of such a deceitful snake.

"Would you like some water?" the woman asked, barely turning him from his anger. He nodded slowly and watched her leave the room. He had to be careful. If she knew his identity his life would be over. He was in no position to protect himself. He didn't know how many men Sho had brought with them. If he were smart it would be few so as not to draw suspicion. They had to find somewhere they could be safe until they could figure out their next move.

***

Yun-Sing had finished helping him dress after she washed him. He was a bit more mobile and able to move his arm into the shirt. Yun-Sung was patient with him, allowing him the dignity of doing what he could on his own. Sho pushed his way inside. "Leave!" he barked at Yun-Sing. Katsuo didn't like that he spoke to her like that. She was the one who had been helping him recover all these weeks. She had been there for him in his most painful and horrible moments of agony. Katsuo didn't voice this. Yun-Sing did as she was ordered, a slight defiant expression on her face. Katsuo admired her control. He would never have been so submissive in the face of such disrespect. Sho came to sit in front of him. Katsuo continued putting on his shirt with much difficulty. Sho reached out to help but he pulled away, ignoring the pain the action caused him. Sho looked a bit surprised at his refusal and Katsuo thought he looked a bit guilty. Katsuo almost felt bad for making him feel that way.

"We will need to be moving on soon. It's no longer safe to stay here," he said. Katsuo tied his shirt close. "I've already made arrangements. We'll be accepted in Undi. Lord Goi has graciously offered us a place on his land."

'Another greedy Xian lord,' he thought to himself. Were these the people he fought to align himself with?

"And you trust him?" Katsuo asked.

"I trust what he desires. He can only get it through our triumph."

Katsuo chuckled mirthlessly. "Triumph," he scoffed.

"What a great triumph it was," he said sarcastically, leaning back against the wall. Sho frowned.

"He knows, like all of us, that we will fulfill what we set out to do. This setback is not our end," he said.

*"Setback!" Katsuo yelled. Sho blinked.
Katsuo gestured to his mangled side. "Is this what
you call a setback?!"*

*"Greatness has consequences," Sho said.
Katsuo rolled his eyes. "Destiny is not an easy thing
to carry. With one as important as yours there has
to be...pushback." Katsuo shook his head. "You
want to be the ruler of this world; you are going to
have to deal with unpleasant things. Make hard
decisions." Katsuo had heard all this before. He
was not in the mood to hear it again.*

*"I want to return home," he said, shocking
both Sho and himself. He hadn't voiced such a thing
since they landed on the Xian shores.*

*"This is your home," Sho insisted. Katsuo
shook his head.*

*"They reject me, this land, the people, they
all reject me. Why should I stay?" The room was
filled with silence. Katsuo felt warm, his forehead
started to sweat.*

"I did not think you would give up so easily."

Katsuo's shoulders fell and he shut his eyes. "The day of your birth I was there. I saw the truth of your destiny. You weren't meant to rule one little piece of the world." Katsuo wanted to cover his ears. "This world needs you to take your place atop it. I saw you on the seat of the world. I was by your side. There were no wars, no infighting. We all had peace because you were our king."

Katsuo didn't think he could believe that any longer. How could he? Sho moved closer, getting in his face. "What hope with those you fought for have if you give up now?" Katsuo shifted uncomfortably. "You remember that day. You remember what we lost at their hands and the ones who refused to help."

Katsuo didn't want or need the reminder. He would dream of it repeatedly. He was awoken by his father as people screamed and ran trying to escape. He remembered begging his father to find his mother and the cold reply he'd received. The race to the ships as their homes and city was ransacked and burnt was etched into his memory. He also recalled the fit his father had when he received the response from the Xian king when he'd pleaded for their aid.

"You cannot have forgotten why we did this, why we still need to do this." The memories reached deep inside him pulling out the rage that was always just at the surface. The broken and sad eyes of his mother, the first time he saw her in years, still haunted him. The guilt he felt for being unable to protect her, for abandoning her, he had vowed to do everything in his power to keep what happened from ever happening again. Katsuo stared into Sho's desperate face. Could he just return home and tell her he'd failed? Was he to be known as the king who lost everything? Katsuo's thoughts started becoming too much. Too jumbled with past and present.

"I do-, I can," he tried to say but he couldn't figure out what it was he wanted to say. Sho took him in his arms.

"It's alright my king. I know. We will get through this, and return stronger than before. I'll see to it," he promised. Katsuo could barely hear him over his racing thoughts. He wanted to tell him no, he wanted to tell him yes. There was still a war going on. But it was inside his head.

The smell of smoke reminded him where he was, bringing him out of his memories. This was a culmination of everything he did, all his triumphs and failures. He could see some of the palace still aflame even from where he was. Once they were sure they had wiped away all traces of the old, he would have his men put it out. They would build their palace right where this one stood. Once he settled in the heart of Xian the people would have no choice but to accept him as their king. After he took the head of the former king, of course. He had given orders to leave King Kang-Dae alive for him if he wasn't dead already. Katsuo hoped not. He wanted that pleasure for himself. He wanted to enter himself and face the man once more, but Sho had advised against it, believing this was the best option. He should cripple him as he had been crippled, Sho had said. Looking at his disfigured face Katsuo had to agree. The men he had stationed in the surrounding area had strict orders to execute everyone they came across. They couldn't let anyone escape. They could not take the chance. They needed to secure their position before word got out and the lords of Xian, whichever ones were left, tried to come for him.

Sho sat on his horse beside him, a stern look on his face. Katsuo wondered if this was what he saw. When he had first been told about the prophecy, he never imagined what it would end up costing him in the end. Now with everything at hand, Katsuo had a fleeting thought, a thought he immediately dismissed as it came. 'If he'd known, would he still have done it?'

CHAPTER 20

Pain and darkness. That's all there was. Yet somehow there was also a feeling of nothingness. This wasn't right. No one was meant to be here. Eyes tried to open but they were not connected at the moment. The body was far away. Light in the distance. A pinprick of it but enough to give hope. Get to it. Fight. It's right there.

A hand twitch, that was all that happened. No one would notice it though. They were too busy trying to stop the bleeding.

***

He could see Serenity out in the water. She was floating. There was no pain, and he felt so peaceful. Looking towards the sky he almost gasped at the beauty of the night. Above him thousands of twinkling stars shined. "You're going to drift away," he called out to her, amused. Serenity looked down at herself and saw she was floating. She wore a red two-piece bathing suit, as she would call it, sprinkled with gold. She flipped over to swim back toward the shore.

On the grass Kang-Dae sat with his leg up, his head resting on his knee as he watched her. He was wearing only his white pants. Once she could, she stood and walked over. Kang-Dae's head raised as she moved toward him, a warm smile coming on his face. He reached for her and she took his hand allowing him to pull her down into him.

"It's pretty here," she told him, staring out at the water. It looked so much like the lake, only grander somehow. The grass was soft as feathers and the breeze was the perfect temperature.

"Hmm," Kang-Dae hummed as his thumb stroked her arm in a comfortable rhythm. They sat quietly, content, neither moving, not feeling the need to. It could have been minutes or hours but it didn't matter there. There was only peace. Serenity looked up at the ledge, the same ledge she'd fallen from only a couple of years ago. It looked impossibly high in that moment, stretching to the clouds.

"Blessing would love it here," Serenity spoke without thinking and suddenly it was like a switch in her mind.

"I'm not here. We're not really here," she realized.

'I do not think we are," Kang-Dae responded.

"Are you real?" She asked, looking up at him. He pulled her up to look at him.

"Are you?" he challenged back. She looked around at her surroundings once more. She looked as if she were trying to remember what had happened before she arrived here. He had tried as well, but it was like trying to remember a dream that had faded.

"Are you dead?" She asked, her voice wavering. He shook his head even though he was starting to doubt himself.

"I think I am," she whispered.

"No," he said authoritatively. "You aren't. Neither am I."

"It feels wrong to be here already," she said.

"We're not here," he reminded her.

She looked back at him before lying on his chest.

"We can fix this," she told him. "We have to." He was quiet. The moon felt like it started shining just a little bit brighter. As she looked back towards the water it looked so peaceful, so inviting. "Maybe I should go for a swim," she said suddenly, forgetting everything else.

CHAPTER 21

Once inside the Rocky Fortress, Jung-Soo immediately went searching for Kang-Dae. Amir took Amoli inside in search of a healer. He had been directed to the third floor. Blessing was asleep once again having woken up only once on the climb up. She needed to be changed and fed but Jung-Soo's singular focus was getting her to her father.

When he stepped into the room the queen Dowager looked up at him. He watched as her face scrunched up with emotion.

"Mi-Sung!" she said hoarsely. She struggled to get on her feet after sitting in such an awkward position for so long but she didn't seem to notice as she charged toward him and snatched the sleeping child from him. Jung-Soo let her, knowing she needed it. Jung-Soo looked past her to Kang-Dae who looked worse than when he left him. It worried him greatly but a small selfish part was glad he didn't have to give him the news of Serenity yet.

Jung-Soo turned to leave, to finally see to his own wounds now that Blessing was safe.

"Serenity? Is she with you?" Jung-Soo's heart dropped. He didn't have the energy, or the nerve, he realized at that moment. He had nothing left to give. He shook his head and kept walking. He found a vacant room with a lone cot and box in the corner. He looked through it and was pleased to see some shirts and clothes inside. He slowly changed out of his bloody and dirty uniform. He slowly cleaned himself as much as he could. He wrapped his stomach with a sash as tight as he could not caring about the pain. He would go in search of a needle and thread later. Once he was done, he just sat on the floor staring at the wall. It hit his hand first. That was when he finally noticed. He ignored it at first. When another few drops hit his legs, he couldn't pretend any longer. He felt his shoulders shake. His breaths came out in harsh pants. The noise escaped before he could stop it. A cry. Before long Jung-Soo, the stern-faced general, was sobbing in the dark room.

***

The nervous man shook as he checked Kang-Dae's bandage. The only healer who'd been rescued in the night, he was no Medhi and clearly lacked the vast experience of Hui but he was all they had. He checked Kang-Dae's eyes and pulse. Jung-Soo watched him getting less and less impressed with his abilities. The Queen Dowager watched with Blessing in her arms. She had not put the child down since they arrived. Jung-Soo wondered if she slept in her arms.

"There's no response, Your Majesty," the man stammered.

"We know that, tell us why," Jung-Soo snapped, having lost any and all patience. The Dowager gave him a stern look but it did not intimidate him.

"W-W-Well, the king seems to have suffered a very serious head injury." Jung-Soo rolled his eyes in the manner he'd seen Serenity do many times.

"Is there anything you can do?" the Dowager asked. The man's face reddened and he began to sputter.

"I do not have very much experience with this kind of injury," he admitted sheepishly.

"Leave!" Jung-Soo shouted.

The jittery man was quick to grab what little supplies he brought and rushed out of the room. The Dowager shut her eyes in frustration.

"There's no one else," she reminded Jung-Soo. Unfortunately, neither Hui nor Medhi had appeared. From the few accounts he was given, Hui had been last seen in the lower level of the hall of vitality. No one had seen him beyond that. The hall had been one of the buildings that had been decimated so his survival was unlikely. Medhi, on the other hand, was seen helping some survivors escape out of one of the western gates. But after that, no one had come across him. There was the possibility he was in hiding, having not been able to reach the fortress. Jung-Soo had been tempted to go out in search of him but the Dowager had deterred him from it. It was dangerous enough. Going out, having to wonder about, not knowing where to look. It would be irresponsible.

"It does him no good to have the inept treat him," Jung-Soo defended his actions.

"He needs a healer."

"I know," Jung-Soo told her. He stared down at Kang-Dae whose breathing was steady. He had not awoken for more than a few moments in the last few days. He didn't speak, and when he did Jung-Soo was unsure if he was even aware of his surroundings. Those moments were becoming fewer and fewer. Jung-Soo knew they needed help but sending out men they could not afford to lose on an impossible search was not the way. Going into the city was likely to be just as dangerous given the blockade the Anoekans created to keep them from seeking help. If they could make it to the stream maybe he could bypass the soldiers but it would take him far out of the way. A day trip could easily become a week with all the detours he'd have to take to avoid detection. Even then, finding someone capable would be an even greater challenge. He trusted no healer outside of the palace to have the ability to treat Kang-Dae. Except there was one. The thought came out of nowhere. He couldn't possibly, it was a ridiculous notion. But the more he thought on it, the more sense it began to make.

"I may know of where we can find him real help," he spoke carefully, still unsure himself if this was the right choice.

"Where?" asked the Dowager.

He reached for the necklace around Kang-Dae's neck. The one gifted to him, by Serenity, which held the key to traveling safely between worlds. The Dowager looked up at him, face shifting from confusion to utter disbelief.

"You can't mean-," she started.

"She has knowledge beyond any other healer in Xian. Who knows what medicines that world holds. We know exactly where she is. I can bring her here."

"You cannot go. It's too dangerous. And it is wrong to bring her into our fight especially after-," her voice caught in her throat and she hugged Blessing to her. "She would never agree to such a thing," she told him.

"To save him, I believe she would."

"She would not risk her friend's life," she doubled down. "Rielle was as close to her as her family, she would never want her put in harm's way."

"She's not here!" He snapped. Blessing whimpered in her sleep and the Dowager flinched instantly filling him with guilt.

"This is our best option," he said softly. "I can be back in a week's time."

The Dowager patted the child's back lulling her back to sleep while staring at him with sad eyes.

"The people need their king. We need him. I'm going," he said because he would and to take the burden of guilt off of her. This was his decision. He would bear the consequences.

CHAPTER 22

Three Days later

Rielle had been scrolling through posts absentmindedly for over an hour. She'd gotten home from work and immediately took a nap. She had still been exhausted from the night before waking up with the consequences of her overindulgence in cheap shots. Now she was surrounding herself with people who were more likely to cheer her on as she drank and throw her into the arms of a cute man on the dance floor. Without Serenity, she'd leaned more into her other friendships, women from work, or those that she'd met on her nights out. It was nice to have someone to do things with but the next morning she'd always be reminded why she preferred hanging out with Serenity. Serenity was good at being the angel on her shoulder. Rielle knew she had a penchant for going with a flow even to her own detriment. Being around Serenity helped her set limits for herself and boundaries with others. Without her, she seemed to become her own worst enemy. She had to stop herself from reaching out to her ex, Marcus, several times with only the thought of how disappointed Serenity would be if she knew she'd gotten back with him after trying to break up with him for so long. Sometimes it wasn't just Serenity's ire she imagined but the disappointed harsh stare of a stoic general.

It wasn't just her mornings being affected. She felt like her job was draining her soul. It was the second job she'd gotten in the past year after being let go from the other when she'd shown up late too many times, after oversleeping once again. She had started with what she now believed was a foolish endeavor to try and become a doctor once more. She hoped she might be able to get back into the residency program she'd dropped before but they required her to go back to med school and take several courses before they'd consider it. She tried but it had all felt like too much. Things that had been easier for her the last time felt much harder. She didn't have any free time to study and she found herself having to drop two of the three courses to save herself from failing. After that, she hung up the dream of ever becoming a doctor, accepting she had just missed her opportunity. The knowledge of that had sent her into a depressed state. She hovered between hardly leaving the house to staying out almost all night. She only slowed down when Serenity's mom had come over to check on her and she had been dressed in her same club outfit from the night before, still slightly drunk. Her shame in that moment was enough for her to make some changes but not many. Rielle just didn't feel she had much to look forward to anymore.

Rielle continued looking at posts, trying to work up the energy to fix her some food. She considered just ordering something and calling it a day. The text notification only drew her eyes for a split second before she decided to ignore it and continue her scrolling. It was only after she realized who the sender was that she sat up.

She was in her car in minutes. According to the schedule they managed to come up with,

Serenity wasn't due for a visit for another two months. From the one-word summons she figured maybe it was Kang-Dae, but if Kang-Dae was coming alone that meant something had happened. Her mind was abuzz with all types of scenarios and possibilities, many, not great but she pushed them aside. Most likely he wanted to bring her parents over to give them some big news. She had told herself that as she grabbed her bag of medical supplies. She told herself that as she grabbed her designated Xian pack. Yeah, that had to be it. Even as she thought it, Rielle could feel a tightening in her gut.

Her bad feeling only got worse when she saw who was sitting at the tree where they'd buried the emergency contact pack. His hair had grown out a little. And he was sporting a small shadow of a beard but it was him, dressed in all black. He held the phone in his hand awkwardly, not used to the machine. He'd only used it one other time. He'd been sent to bring her when Serenity's due date approached. Rielle knew at that moment, looking at his grim expression, that this was not happy news.

He wouldn't look at her. That was the first hint something bad had happened. Before he gave her blank expressions of indifference but now, he couldn't even meet her eyes.

"What happened?" she asked, fighting to keep her voice steady.

"We need your help. Kang-Dae needs your help." He said, finally raising his eyes to meet hers.

"Is he hurt?"

He gave a short nod. "None of the healers you have-," she started.

"We cannot count on them," he interrupted. "He needs help beyond their capabilities."

Rielle started feeling nauseous. Her abilities were questionable in her mind. Her failed attempt at returning to complete her residency had shaken her confidence.

"How'd it happen?" She asked. Once again, he hesitated.

"We were attacked. The Anoekans have resurfaced." Rielle felt lightheaded.

"So, you guys are at war again?"

"As of now, we do not know how numerous the enemy is. It may just be a small faction." He didn't sound too confident in his assessment, and given the fact that he was the one in front of her, she doubted it as well. "They attacked the palace. As far as we know it is the only place they've attacked. The child is safe in our fortress. It's our best stronghold. You will be safe there. I will keep you safe." That was the only thing he said that she believed wholeheartedly.

But she also noticed and she knew he knew she noticed how careful he'd been with his words.

He continued avoiding her eyes and despite his assurances of safety, he looked as if he'd been through his worst defeat.

"Tell me," she demanded. He kept his eyes downcast but she could see him flinch. His head gave a small twitch, like he couldn't outright deny her but his body refused to cooperate.

"Tell me," she said more firmly.

"We need to go," he said, turning his back on her. Rielle ran up on him and hit him on the back with both of her fists.

"Tell me!" She shouted, her voice breaking. He refused to turn around, staring out into the water. She grabbed onto his shirt and shook him. "TELL ME!!!"

Jung-Soo released himself from her grip and took a few steps toward the water before stopping. "I di-, I could no-," he started and stopped. Rielle let out a cry. She could stop him. Not allow him to have to suffer the burden of saying it but she needed to hear it. She had to. She deserved it. She deserved that pain for how she had treated her these past months. She deserved it for every time she declined to see her. For every time she had to choke down her inner feelings of envy for her friend who seemed to have everything.

"I could not get to her," Jung-Soo said so softly she could barely hear him. "I- I could not, I tried," his voice cracked and Rielle rushed him again, only this time she hugged him from behind. She could feel his body shaking as he fought against his emotions. Rielle sobbed into him seeking her comfort as she attempted to comfort him.

CHAPTER 23

He was by the lake again. Serenity was no longer in his arms. Kang-Dae jumped up in a panic. "Neeco!" He shouted for her. "Neeco!" He could see no one in the water. His memory went to the last time he saw her drifting out there. Had she drifted away? Had she left this place? Had she gone…on?

"Neeco!" His voice came out more pleading this time.

"Hey!" Serenity's voice called out. He looked up to see her on the edge of the ridge. He was about to shout for her once more, fearful of what she planned to do but when he blinked, she was gone.

A hand on his shoulder had him spinning around ungracefully. Seeing Serenity in front of him smiling so radiantly calmed all his fears. He pulled her into his arms.

"I was afraid you'd left me," he admitted. She rubbed his back.

"I wouldn't. Ever. We promised, remember?" He did. After being reunited before the final battle with Katsuo they swore to one another they would never part again. "Where'd you go?" she asked as they pulled back. She took his hand and began leading him along the shore.

Kang-Dae was about to answer but closed his mouth. He couldn't recall. He was with her one moment, than he wasn't. That was all he knew.

"I do not know."

It didn't seem to concern her as much as it did him. She just nodded and grabbed onto his arm. The water kissed at their bare feet as they continued to walk. It felt warm.

"There's so much to do," she said suddenly. Kang-Dae looked down at the top of her curiously. He didn't know what she meant by that. What could they need to do here?

"He thinks he's going to keep me. He won't," she said. She spoke so casually about it like she wasn't worried. He stopped walking, pulling her to a stop as well.

"Who?" he asked, genuinely confused.

She looked up at him with the same smile.

She reached up and tucked his hair behind his ear. "You can't rush it. Healing always takes time. Especially here." She laid her palm over his heart and used her other hand to touch his head. Her words bothered him for some reason. Even if he couldn't quite grasp what she was talking about he didn't like hearing it. He felt a need to argue with her.

"I have to find you," he said unsure why he felt the need to say it while also feeling a sense of déjà vu.

She took him by his hands and shook her head.

"You won't have to worry about me," she assured him. "You have to get stronger for what's coming. While you do, others will get the help we need."

"From where?"

"Where all the trouble began."

CHAPTER 24

One Week After the attack…

"Hello Rielle," Kang-Dae's mother greeted her kindly. Rielle remembered to bow before returning the greeting.

"How is he?" Rielle asked. She looked over to the unconscious Kang-Dae laying in the bed. He didn't look good at first glance. He was pale. His breathing looked uneven and the bandage around his head told her he was dealing with a serious head injury.

"Better than a few nights ago," The Dowager spoke with what Rielle could tell was forced hope. Rielle went over to him and listened to his chest. His heart was still beating strongly, so that was something. She didn't want to move him any more than he already had been to check on his injury but she didn't have many options. As gently as she could she turned his head. She opened her bag and took out her scissors to cut the bandage off.

The wound was hard to see, still covered with hair that was matted with blood. She took out some alcohol and cotton swabs and started cleaning. She could already feel the area was raised. The knot was probably the size of a golf ball. As she cleaned, she noticed it wasn't just blood that she was removing. Rielle let out a soft curse.

"What is it?" The Dowager asked, her voice rising.

Rielle did not want to give this news. "The blow to his head caused his body to overproduce," she paused trying to think of a simple way to explain it. "The fluid in his head needed to protect his brain."

"If it protects, isn't that good?" she asked.

Rielle shook her head.

"Too much of it puts pressure on the brain. It can cause some serious problems."

"Will he die?"

Rielle could lie, she wanted to, but what would that do?

"He could."

"What can you do?' Jung-Soo spoke from the doorway.

Rielle sputtered, "Me?"

"You can help him. You know what's wrong."

"Knowing and being able to fix it are not the same thing," she said as patiently as she could.

"You could try," he challenged in a way that really irked her spirit.

"This isn't a cut I can just wrap a bandage around. What he needs is surgery. I'm not even a doctor!"

"You're his best chance."

"Hell no!"

"Would you say that if she were here?" It was a low blow, and they both knew it but only

Rielle could be mad about it. Jung-Soo stared back without showing an ounce of guilt.

"Even if I was going to try, I don't have what I'd need," she said half-heartedly.

"Tell me what you need and I will get it to you."

"And if you don't have anything like it in this world?"

"I'll build it," he said with a straight face. She almost laughed. She pulled one of the several medical books she'd brought with her. After checking the index, she found the page she needed.

"First, I need a really big needle."

CHAPTER 25

Opening her eyes was not something she wanted to do, so she didn't try. She already knew nothing she saw would give her any reassurance. She wasn't among allies. She knew that already. She kept focusing on just breathing but every pull of air hurt so much. Eventually, she had to cough which only made the pain that much greater. Something came up her throat and came bubbling out her mouth. 'Blood' she was coughing up blood. The notion scared her, but still, she kept her eyes closed. Someone turned her head on its side to keep her from choking.

"You should let her die," she heard an angry male voice speak. "Sho would reward us."

"But *he* will have us killed," another voice responded. "You heard him. She dies, we die."

"Sho wouldn't allow it."

"Why do you think he's in charge?"

"Isn't he? Katsuo-,"

"Our king," the other corrected.

"He hasn't been the same since his return. He probably never will be. He could end up just like his father,"

"Do you want us flogged? Keep your voice down."

Another cough came out of her along with more blood. She felt something wiping at her throat, it felt so tender. She fought not to flinch. Something soft was being pressed against the area and secured.

"She should be dead," the first man spoke up again.

"She's strong," the other remarked with a hint of admiration.

"She's a dog. Almost cost us everything."

"I don't need your help anymore. You can leave," the exasperated man said to his companion. There was some silence then the sound of retreating feet.

"My queen, don't worry," the voice whispered in her ear. "You'll be okay."

'Medhi,' she thought. Inwardly she smiled. No, she didn't have to worry at all. They, however, did, she thought as she began to drift off once more.

"He won't be here for much longer, will he?" Serenity asked her grandma, as she bent over to pick up a smooth stone from the water. Her grandma stood just a few feet from her. She looked almost how she remembered her but younger somehow too. She appeared right after Kang-Dae had disappeared the first time.

"No baby," she told Serenity with a warm smile. Serenity smiled as well. While she'd miss seeing him when he left for good, she knew it was good that he would be gone from where they were. This wasn't a place meant to stay. He had things to do. So did she.

Serenity stood up. "I feel like I may have messed up. Like I didn't do things right," she confessed. Her grandmother came up to her.

"A life without trials is a life without miracles. A world without sickness is a world without healing. People without needs are people without blessings," she told Serenity.

"Can I fix this?"

"Can you? Is it in your power to fix it?"

"Will He fix it?" Serenity rephrased her question.

"What do you think?"

"I know he can, but-," she began.

"Yes, he can," was all her grandmother responded.

"I saw that he can. I saw that he did," she corrected herself.

"So, then you already know how this ends."

Serenity glanced out at the water.

"I never thought it would look like this."

"I know. No one does."

She went over and hugged her grandma tight and she did the same.

"I miss you."

"I miss you too. We'll see each other again. Just not now."

Though she did miss her grandmother, that information was good to know.

"Remember, everything you need, he already gave it to you." Serenity nodded, still holding on to her as tight as she could.

CHAPTER 26

The Night of the Attack…

Medhi had just helped another two servants escape the palace while directing them to the path. He was finding fewer and fewer of his people and the enemy had come in in great numbers. He did his best to stay out of sight. The instinct to get himself out was pressing on him but he still felt there were more people he could help. The enemy looked to be settling in. He saw a couple of them dressed in civilian clothing. There even looked to be a couple of healers. He watched, helplessly, as several Xian soldiers were surrounded and mercilessly killed. They had managed to injure a couple before they were taken down.

"Find a healer!" One of the enemies shouted. Medhi heard footsteps coming up behind him. He could not stay put without being caught, he realized. Making a choice he quickly shed his green head scarf and vest leaving him in plain white clothes.

He ran out to the injured men. "I am a healer!" He announced his heart beating furiously in his chest. The men who called inspected him while the dying man at his feet begged him for help. Medhi got to work staunching his wounds. He ordered the others to find a place to take their wounded until he could get to them and properly treat them. The men hesitated, making Medhi feel sick with anxiousness. After a few seconds, the soldier helped the man up and took him away. Medhi helped the other injured man, having to reset the bone in his arm. He sent him after the other two. More soldiers ran by, but seeing him work on their brethren had them completely disregarding him. It only eased his nerves a bit. Medhi planned to escape as soon as he could. He was about to head toward the nearest gate when he caught sight of a group of soldiers walking. There were two in front and two behind. In the middle, there were two more carrying something. No, someone, he realized seeing a glimpse of a red dress. He got just a little closer. His eyes widened when he saw who it was *the men were carrying. Any notion of escaping left him and he quickly followed behind them. He was about to call out to them when someone pulled his arm causing him to stop. Medhi looked up into the green eyes of an enemy soldier wearing a helmet. Medhi feared he'd been caught but as the soldier continued to stare without speaking, he started to get the feeling he knew this person. Before he could figure it out, he was being pulled inside one of the still intact buildings. When the soldier removed the helmet letting loose brown wavy hair. Medhi let out a sigh of relief. It was Nasreen.*

"What are you still doing here?" She asked.

Medhi looked around to be sure no one was near or listening in.

"They have the queen," he whispered. Nasreen's eyes widened. "She's hurt. Badly, I think."

"They won't let you near her," she told him.

"They will if they think I'm one of them," he countered. Nasreen looked back out making sure no one was around.

"It's dangerous," she warned. He just stared at her pointedly, eyes lingering on her enemy armor. Nasreen scoffed and rolled her eyes.

"Engaging in this act may require you to step out of your role as a healer. Are you willing to do that?"

Medhi knew what she meant. It may come down to killing if it meant protecting their identity and helping the queen. As a healer, it went against his core principles. He thought back to how the queen had looked and how there was no one else who could and would help her the way she needed.

"I will do what needs to be done," he vowed. Nasreen seemed unsure but took him at his word. The two exited the building and went in search of the queen. They passed a small group of sitting soldiers seemingly taking a break from their invasion. One of their healers was with them *wrapping the wrist of one of the soldiers as they laughed about their victory. Nasreen stopped Medhi from continuing on. The men were facing away from them, too involved in their own conversation to notice their presence. Nasreen looked around the area, checking if there were any more soldiers or enemies around. Medhi was unsure why they had stopped until he saw her reaching for the sword at her side. Medhi felt his anxious nausea return. She handed him a dagger. He hesitated, before reaching out with a shaky hand and grasping the hilt. He tightened his hold trying to steel himself for what he was going to have to do. He took several deep breaths. Nasreen was staring at him, a flash of sympathy going across her face. She put her finger to her lips, signaling him to keep quiet, and gestured for him to stay put. Medhi was about to protest, but in a way that showed her great skill, Nasreen had already made it over to the men. The first never saw her coming or felt it when her dagger pierced his heart from the back. The men were frozen in shock for a moment giving her the chance to toss her dagger into the throat of another one. As the two jumped up to face her she had already removed her sword and went to her knees. With a graceful spin, she swung at the legs of the one on her right. He howled before falling right into her waiting sword. The other moved his sword down at her but she had already removed her blade and blocked him. She kicked at his knee forcing the appendage inward making Medhi wince. The man fell to his side and was permanently silenced with a sword to the mouth. The healer, still frozen in fear, finally found the ability to move and started to run. Nasreen was up and on him before he could make it ten steps. She jumped on his back, grabbed his head, and twisted with a quick jerk.*

When she was done, she signaled for Medhi to come over. Medhi quickly did as he was told. Together they switched the healer's clothes for Medhi's. During this time, he realized why she'd chosen such a brutal way of killing the healer when he noticed how clean his outfit was, compared to his comrades. The fact that she could consider such a minute thing during her actions both frightened and impressed Medhi. Dressed in the right attire Nasreen walked him to where the prisoners of war were taken and where their queen may be.

CHAPTER 27

Rielle's heart was pounding. In her time as a
resident, she hadn't observed anything like this. She
felt like she was flying blind. The books could give
only so much information but not the confidence to
feel like she was equipped to do this. While
preparing, she did something she very rarely did.
She prayed. She prayed harder and longer than she
ever had before. Her relationship with God was not
as strong as Serenity's so she hoped maybe he'd
taken their relationship and the fact that this was her
husband into consideration. If Serenity were in
heaven maybe she could even put in a good word
for Rielle. She prayed for guidance and she prayed
for Kang-Dae. She prayed she did not kill this man.

What Jung-Soo had been able to scrape
together wasn't ideal but she could work with it.
The biggest thing was keeping the place as sterile as
possible which, in this space, seemed impossible
but she had the people do what they could. Clean
sheets hung up around the area. The many burning

lamps provided enough light. Hot water was sitting on a small table in a metal bowl. She pulled the needle from the bowl. She had Jung-Soo and a couple of men prop Kang-Dae up in a chair. She sat behind him with a lamp so close to her face she could feel the heat. With the book open right next to her, she stared at where she was meant to place the needle for longer than she should have, trying to delay things as long as she could. Her hand started shaking so bad she had to stop and put the needle down to collect herself. She paced back and forth arguing with herself that this was crazy, impossible, she couldn't do this she couldn't save him. She felt the tears coming and the pressing need to start crying. She stopped pacing and fell to her knees. "Please God, please help me. I know I haven't done things right. I know I gave up on a lot, med school, me, even you. But if you get us both through this, if you help me save him, I promise to start doing things your way from now on." She sat on the rocky ground until her knees became sore. She didn't move until that urge to cry started to fade and her heart took on a regular beat. It was subtle at first, slow, a calm that started from her chest and radiated throughout. A peace, unlike any peace she felt before. She went back to her chair and took hold of the needle once more. With a deep breath, she positioned her needle at the base of his head and began to push.

Jung-Soo was waiting outside the room where Rielle worked on Kang-Dae. The Dowager wanted to be there as well but he sent her off with Blessing. If things were to go wrong, he didn't want the child near. It felt like hours, and it might have been. As time crept by all he could think about was losing his best friend, but there was also another scenario, one that filled him with greater trepidation…having to be the one to tell him about Serenity. If he did survive this, would he want to, would he still be the man he knew without her, would Jung-Soo? The depressing thoughts came in waves he tried to refocus each time. The enemy still did not know if Kang-Dae was dead or alive.

The door opening had Jung-Soo rushing to meet Rielle. He couldn't even let her walk out before he was in her face. She had a type of mask over her mouth and nose that she removed. Jung-Soo couldn't help but notice she looked a lot calmer than she did when she first went inside. He knew this was an unfair thing to ask of her, to put on her shoulders. If Kang-Dae didn't make it, he would never blame her or want her to take on that blame. She looked up at him with watery eyes and his heart seized.

"He's doing good," she said. The relief felt too much like good news and Jung-Soo didn't think he could believe it.

"Really?' She nodded. "He's still unconscious and I can't tell you when he'll wake up, but for now he's out of the danger zone."

Jung-Soo swallowed the lump in his throat and looked past her to see him still propped on the chair unmoving, but alive.

"Can I go wash up?" She asked, reminding him that he was blocking her.

"Oh, yes," he said, moving out of her way. "Thank you, Rielle. I can never repay you for this," he told her. She gave him a small smile and continued down the hall.

CHAPTER 28

The throbbing in his head was like nothing he'd ever felt before. He wanted to open his eyes but it was difficult and the effort he put forth to try just made his head feel worse. He felt like his whole body was numb except his head. Was that all he was, a head? The thought scared him enough he forced his eyes open just so he could look and see for himself that he was still all there. It took several tries before his lids moved at all. At one point he feared he was blind. He pushed through and felt the flutter of his lids. Blurriness. That was the only way to describe what he could see. He could barely make out the fuzzy ceiling of rock above him. "Kang-Dae," he heard a voice speak.

Someone was squeezing his hand, which relieved him to know it was still there. He tried moving his eyes to look down but it was like his eyes wouldn't cooperate. It took great effort. His eye finally shifted just a bit to his left. There was a blurry figure next to him. "Serenity?" he questioned, trying to squeeze the hand in his but failing to even move his fingers.

The figure was quiet and released his hand. "He's waking up," the voice said. It sounded garbled, muffled. He couldn't distinguish anything about who it was. He hoped it was Serenity, he needed her. Another blurred person came to stand by the other one. This one he could almost tell they were male but that was all. The smaller figure came closer, bending over him. He could feel their fingers opening his eyes wider. He wanted to stop them but he couldn't. He could barely muster out a 'stop." After doing the same thing to his other eye, the figure pulled back. "Can you hear me?" The figure spoke, or he thought they did. It sounded far away.

"If you can, blink one time for me."

Kang-Dae wanted to speak to move to get up. A blink to communicate was infuriating to him. Was that all he would be capable of? Despite his anger, he forced himself to do as he was told.

"That's good."

"You're still recovering. It will take some time but take it slowly. Things will start coming back slowly."

He didn't want to take it slowly. He needed to get up, he needed to see his daughter. He needed his wife. 'Where was Serenity?' he thought.

"Rest is the best thing you can do for yourself" the figure spoke again. No rest. His family. He needed his family. Even as he thought it and tried to keep his eyes open, he could feel himself drifting once more.

CHAPTER 29

Medhi jumped away from her as soon as the door opened. She still couldn't turn her head but she knew someone had come in. Judging from Medhi's pale face it was someone she should have been worried about. She didn't have to wonder long when the person spoke.

"Is she awake?" That voice. It was a voice she had truly believed she would never hear again. She couldn't believe this was actually happening. She was once again back at his mercy. They had hoped and prayed that the rumors had been false when they should've been preparing for him. She felt him come near her. She wasn't able to move, she couldn't even scream at him. Katsuo stood above her. She took him in, his scarred face, his cold eyes, and his menacing expression only made worse by his burns.

She never heard Medhi's response to his question, too focused on not dead man in front of her but it didn't matter as their eyes locked. There was genuine hatred in his stare. Serenity began to doubt she would survive this. It looked like a rage was building in him and he was set to go off at any moment. When she was sure he would strike, he stepped back out of her sight.

"Will she be able to speak?"

"It's too soon to tell," Medhi answered. He'd told her it was very likely her throat and voice would heal. "She's still very weak. It's better to keep her resting. Give her body a chance to heal." It was quiet again.

"Just do what you have to do to keep her alive," he ordered. "No matter what it does to her," he added with no trace of warmth, not that she expected any. Once he was gone Medhi let out a heavy sigh of relief. He came over to her.

"My queen," he whispered sympathetically. She wasn't sure why until he took a cloth and dabbed at her eyes. She hadn't even realized she'd been crying.

***

Sho looked down at the palace workers who'd surrendered during the raid. There were not many, less than a dozen, mostly women. Once the palace had been secured, he and Katsuo made their way inside. He ordered the men to help Katsuo get settled. He had protested at first, wanting to hunt around the grounds for the Xian king but Sho managed to convince him to rest and began their reign in the morning.

"If you wish to live you must do these three things. If you refuse you have forfeited your life and will be strung up at the gates for all to see."

The peasants trembled and cried. "If you will renounce your former king, swear your unwavering obedience to me and accept the great Katsuo as the true king. You will not be harmed. That is my word to you."

"Is there any among you not willing to do this?" He didn't expect any refusals and he didn't receive any. There was one though, a young woman covered from head to toe who seemed not to have heard him. She stared at him but showed no reaction. "Bring her to me!" he ordered.

As soon as the guard grabbed her, she looked frightened, looking around frantically.

"Do you wish to die?" he asked. The girl had tears in her eyes but she didn't answer. Not a sound, a whimper, or a shake of her head. He had the guard hit her and though she keeled over in pain she still did not cry out.

"Will you renounce your king?" he demanded. She just stared at him, more tears falling into her facial covering.

"She's deaf and mute," announced the soldier who'd brought the prisoners to him.

Sho looked down in disgust. What use could she be? It might be better to just have her killed anyway. He almost gave the order but stopped himself. A worker who could not share secrets could be beneficial. Especially now. He had the perfect person in mind.

Sho raced over to the room after receiving the news. He couldn't believe it at first. Then he took it as a sign that they were on the right path. But when he'd been blocked from entering and seeing the treacherous woman himself, he became angry. "How dare you!?" He demanded. The two soldiers looked nervous but did not back down.

"The king has ordered that no one is to enter but the healers."

"Healers?" he spat. He couldn't be. He was actually trying to save her? Sho wanted to force his way in and put an end to this once and for all. It was for his own good, the good of them all. Sho had to stop himself. He didn't know how Katsuo would react if he did what needed to be done. Katsuo had been more withdrawn from him lately. Though he seemed to go along with his plans and take his advice it was more because of resignation, than belief in him. He didn't want to do anything that may jeopardize the fragile bond they currently had. No matter how much he wanted to. Sho looked over the shoulders of the guards staring at the healers *working frantically to keep that woman alive. For now, he would just pray for her death, until the opportunity arose for him to make his move.*

"Take her back," he told the guard who placed the mute woman back in line with the others.

"Well? Have you come to a decision?" he asked. One by one the workers went to their knees in submission.

This was just the beginning, he thought. More people would begin to turn their backs on what was and pledge their full allegiance to Katsuo.

CHAPTER 30

This time, when he opened his eyes, things were much clearer. The pain in his head was still present but it was a dull ache, not quite as sharp as it had been before. He looked around without moving his head. Someone with dark hair was standing away from him. He could hear the babble of his daughter. "Serenity," he tried to call out but it was too weak for anyone to hear. He swallowed with difficulty and tried once more. The figure spun around. Though she had his daughter in his arms, it was not Serenity. Seeing Rielle with his child had him thinking he was dreaming for a moment.

"You're awake," she breathed out. Already Blessing began reaching out for him. He wanted to hold her. He managed to raise his arm a little.

"You can't hold her yet. It's going to take some time to build your strength backup," Rielle told him. He wanted to argue but the way his arm felt heavy he knew she was right. The more Blessing reached out to him and the longer she couldn't get to him, the more she began to whine. It tore at his heart. Rielle rushed her out of the room even though Kang-Dae tried to get her to stay. She came back without Blessing, but Jung-Soo was now with her. She had something in her hand as she bent over him. She pointed the thing at his eye. The burst of light made him hiss.

"Sorry, sorry," she said but still proceeded to do the same thing to the other eye. After that, she started asking him questions, simple ones like his name, where he was, and the last thing he remembered. He didn't understand why but obliged. His voice got a bit stronger the more he spoke. His answers must have appeased her because she told Jung-Soo he was doing well before turning to leave them alone. Jung-Soo stopped her. They talked quietly among themselves. Kang-Dae couldn't understand what they were saying. Jung-Soo's face gave nothing away as usual and Rielle was facing away from him. But the way her hands would move and how she never broke eye contact with Jung-Soo led him to believe it was an intense conversation.

Before he could inquire about it, she turned to him, face crestfallen, and walked out of the room. Left with Jung-Soo he hoped to be able to get some answers of his own.

"The fortress is well protected. I've assigned men to always be on guard at the entrance. No unnecessary travel if we can help it. We don't want to draw any attention. We haven't had any sightings. No one has been seen. It's possible they have not realized how many of us made it here. Most likely they are searching within the city."

The more he talked the more impatient Kang-Dae became. Important as this information was, it was not what he wanted to know at the moment. "Serenity-," he began.

"We've been unable to send word to General Wen. He still has no idea what's happened," Jung-Soo continued on as though he'd never spoken. "The fortress supplies will last another few months if we're careful. Once we can establish a safe path in and out, we can send out for more."

"Serenity!" Kang-Dae managed to shout. "Where is Serenity?"

Jung-Soo finally quieted. "I'll let you rest," he said without emotion. He even turned to leave. Kang-Dae, fed up and desperate, unwisely tried to get up. He only succeeded in falling off the bed landing in a painful heap. Jung-Soo was instantly at his side trying to help him up. Kang-Dae grabbed onto his shirt.

"Where?"

Jung-Soo's face remained stony. "She did not make it out of the palace." Unbelievable words in such a cold voice. Kang-Dae took a second to comprehend it. Once he did, he shook his head. He started trying to stand on his own, but Jung-Soo stopped him. Weak as he was, it barely took a push.

"We need to send out a party to bring her back. We can't leave her out there." Jung-Soo held him to keep him from flailing and ending up on his side once more.

"You have to calm yourself. You still need to recover."

'Healing takes time' The words came into his mind out of nowhere. He could hear it in her voice, but couldn't recall when he'd heard her say it. Kang-Dae stopped struggling against Jung-Soo.

"It's my fault," he heard Jung-Soo whisper. Kang-Dae sat unmoving, not saying a word. Jung-Soo truly believed she was gone but he felt no such indication. In fact, his heart was desperate to find her because he knew she was not safe wherever she was. He didn't know how, he would never be able to explain it, but he knew she was not dead. No matter what Jung-Soo saw. Kang-Dae reached up and grabbed Jung-Soo's head, leaning his forehead against his. Jung-Soo continued babbling his apologies but Kang-Dae held him until he calmed.

"Help me up," he said after a minute of silence. Once he was safely back in bed, he finally addressed Jung-Soo.

"I will heal. Regain my strength. Keep the people safe for me. Keep the men sharp. We need to be prepared for when they find us. Once I am able, I will find her and bring her back."

Jung-Soo began to speak, most likely to reiterate what he believed to be true.

"Have Rielle brought to me, I need her to tell me how I can expedite this process," he cut him off, not willing to argue when he knew it would not change his mind or his heart. Unfortunately, Jung-Soo was not privy to his feelings. He could only believe what he saw. Kang-Dae on the other hand would trust in his heart.

CHAPTER 31

One Month After the Attack

Serenity stared at the food being offered to her. She hesitated to eat, not because she feared what might be in it but because eating was difficult for her. Swallowing was getting easier but the pain was still there. Only taking the tiniest of bites helped. Judging by what she had been given this time she figured this must be a good day for her captor. Trying to guess his mood was a not-so-fun game she had been forced to play these past weeks ever since she woke up in her room/cell. She had been sure she was dead. When she first realized her situation, she wanted to be. She had been unable to move but was in so much pain. Whatever they had given her to keep her from moving did nothing to numb the pain which she imagined was intentional. Mehdi did what he could but with eyes lurking over him he had to do what he was told. Those days when he would come to see her had been like being trapped in her nightmares.

"Until I can be sure you will not run from me again, I am afraid this is a necessary precaution," Katsuo spoke from above her. Serenity could only follow him with her eyes. He placed his hand gently on her cheek. "This is for your own good. You need to be protected even from yourself." Serenity struggled so hard to move, to slap his hand away. She felt herself tearing up in frustration. Katsuo wiped at the tear affectionately making Serenity even more incensed.

"When you've recovered, I will show you the truth of your vision. I know you feared the consequences of my victory. It was why you chose to align yourself with," he paused, unable to finish saying his name. "I can forgive you for that. After all, you led me to my greatest victory."

Not only was he disfigured, but he was also absolutely deranged. The sad part was Serenity was having a hard time deciding if this was a new development or if he had always been this out of touch.

"The hard part is over. Now the work can begin and I will finally bring about peace everywhere."

He'd spoken of such things before, Serenity recalled back when she'd first met him. In his demented way of thinking he believed the peace he dreamed of could only come from war and an imagined crown where he ruled all. Sho's influence, she figured.

"If only you had believed in me. You would not be in such a state now." His voice dropped an octave and his eyes darkened and Serenity shivered as his demeanor shifted. His hand went toward her bandaged throat as he stroked lightly at the material.

"If only you had not abandoned me," he gritted. His hold on her throat tightened. The pain was sharp but Serenity couldn't even cry out. "and sought out our enemy, perhaps we both would not be what we are today." As he continued his grip began to shake and his voice was almost trembling *from rage. Serenity shut her eyes, trying not to become overcome by the pain and unable to stare into his hateful eyes any longer. Finally, he let go. Serenity's neck throbbed and she could taste blood. She slowly opened her eyes and was relieved to see he was gone. A shuddering breath escaped her lips as she silently cried.*

She never knew when he would make his little visits. When he did, she could never predict how he would act. At times he'd come seeking support, or maybe validation from her for his actions. Other times he came down to blame her for his failures and threaten her with a public execution. She couldn't speak regardless but she never gave him any reaction. She refused to show fear on his violent days and would never acknowledge his "kindness" on his good days. Crazy as he may be, he wasn't foolish enough to give her any information. She still had no idea if her family was alive or dead. A part of her felt like they had to be alive. She tried to confirm this feeling by telling herself Katsuo would have used their deaths to torment her and get her to lean on him as the only one she had left. She wouldn't put it past him to think that way.

The servant they said was mute was feeding her today. She was still too weak to do it herself. The girl's green eyes avoided her gaze. The guard inside the room hovered uncomfortably close. Serenity didn't know why he bothered. She couldn't pick up a spoon let alone try to escape. Not yet anyway. "the king approaches!" Serenity tensed and the girl quickly went to her knees. Katsuo entered dressed mostly in black. He wore no sleeves so his arms and burns were visible. He scanned the room. Seeing the bowl on the table his eyes flared for some unknown reason. "Out! All of you!" he ordered. Everyone moved quickly. When they were gone, he sent the men in the hall away as well. Serenity did her best to press herself as far into the wall as she could. She didn't like being alone with him. Witnesses would not stop him from doing what he wanted, she knew that logically. But being alone with him felt worse, more dangerous.

He walked in silently. He snatched the bowl from the table and stared down at it like he hated it and was a second away from tossing it. She fully expected him to. What she did not expect was for him to sit where the girl had been and offer her a spoonful of porridge. She'd already been eating it, so if it were poison, she'd already be screwed but it felt wrong taking it from him. She could see him becoming impatient. Not wanting to provoke him in her still weakened state she opened and allowed him to feed her.

"Sho has disappeared again," he started speaking out of nowhere. "He will not inform me of his plans." He scooped up more porridge. Serenity watched perplexed. Still confused as to why he was here, feeding her, talking to her. "Even my men will not inform me of what he does." He shook his head. "He looks down on me. They all do. They think I'm a failure."

Serenity had no idea what was happening. Did he want her to disagree? Reassure him? Comfort him? It was a no on all fronts for her.

"He blames me for the loss that day. He thinks if I'd listened to him, it would have gone differently. I have been listening to him my whole life!" He tossed the bowl down.

'Well, it took a little longer than she expected but there he went.' He stared down at the mess he made. Serenity couldn't get a read on what he was thinking. His mind was unfocused, switching on a dime.

"None of it happened the way it should have," he whispered more to himself than her. He looked lost in these moments. If Serenity could muster a speck of sympathy for him, she probably would have when he got this way. What was left of her compassion for him was destroyed with her home. His gaze suddenly turned to her so fast she almost jumped. She waited, trying to steel herself for anything. But he just stood and left. She heard him ordering someone to clean up as he left the hall.

She released the breath she'd been holding once she was sure he was gone. One thing she took from his ranting was that although they had failed to kill him, they'd managed to cause a break in his relationship with Sho. Something Katsuo was absolutely right about. The soothsayer no longer trusted him. It probably didn't help that he insisted on keeping her alive. She was sure Sho was advocating for her execution repeatedly. Still, he hadn't budged, a choice she was grateful for even if it confused her. He didn't realize how right Sho was. Leaving her alive was going to be very dangerous for him.

CHAPTER 32

Rielle held onto his hands as they walked the hall. His mother and Jung-Soo stood at the end. "Good, very good. You're doing great," she encouraged as they moved. He appreciated her words of encouragement but didn't need them. Although he was recovering it was taking longer than he liked.

"Let's head back," she said. Kang-Dae shook his head.

"Not yet." He wanted to keep going. The further he got, the stronger he got.

"You've done enough. You've gotten way farther than yesterday. Don't overdo it," she warned, trying to steer him back to the room. He tried pulling away from her to continue on his own only to stumble and fall. Jung-Soo came over in an instant to help him up. He tried to push him away to do it himself.

"Stop it," Rielle fussed at him almost as if he were a misbehaving child.

"She bent down to meet him at eye level.

"Stubbornness doesn't heal. As hard as it is to hear. The best thing you can do for your body is take it easy. Rest does more for the body than anything. If you push yourself too far too fast, you won't get better. You'll just give up what you have left." It was hard to hear, she was right about that. He just wanted to be useful again. He couldn't help his people lying in bed most of the day. He couldn't find Serenity if he couldn't make it outside. With a sigh, he lifted his arm to Jung-Soo who helped him up. Together the two walked him back to his room and sat him on the bed.

"Have any of the other lords reached out?" he asked.

Jung-Soo shook his head.

"Perhaps they are still unaware."

"Or they've made their choice."

"Don't say that," his mother said.

"It would not be the first time," he grumbled.

"Even if they did come, we would not have the manpower to drive the enemy out. They could fortify themselves for years if they wish. Longer, if the Anoekans who retreated return."

Jung-Soo raised a very true and disturbing point. These were not all of Katsuo's forces. Many had been sent back to their home country in accordance with the deal he'd made with the new king.

"We need to make sure that doesn't happen," Kang-Dae said. "Bring me paper and ink."

Kang-Dae finished his letter and sealed it with his mark. Jung-Soo had watched him without asking a single question although Kang-Dae knew he had several. He handed it to Jung-Soo. "Go to Anoeka."

Jung-Soo stopped mid-reach when he heard him.

He looked at Kang-Dae like he was sure he had heard him wrong and wanted him to repeat himself. "The new king doesn't want Katsuo to succeed any more than us. He may find it in his best interest to join with us and remove a dangerous threat to his rule."

"Or he could side with him and send all the men at his disposal to wipe us all out," countered Jung-Soo.

Kang-Dae shook his head. "If their country wanted to war with us, they would have done so already. They had their chance to support him and chose to stay out of it. Perhaps if they had reason to fear his retaliation, they would be more inclined to step in."

Jung-Soo wasn't so sure. In his opinion, their lack of interference either way made them opportunistic cowards who would rather sit and wait to see who came out on top than choose a side.

This new king may not want to lose his throne but would he fight for it, or would he just hope Katsuo never came back for it?

"Can you get there?" Kang-Dae asked. Jung-Soo pushed back his reservations and thoughts.

"If we can get to the docks, I can sail. Though I wouldn't put it past them to have men waiting in case."

Speaking of help, Kang-Dae remembered another part of Serenity's dream.

"Take Amir with you as well,"

"Why?" Jung-Soo was unable to hold back the questions this time. Amir had barely left Amoli's side the whole time they had been there. It might be a test in itself trying to talk him into traveling so far from her in her unstable condition.

"He needs to sail to Kah Mah, seek Queen Prija. She may be willing to help." Relations between the countries had improved over time, thanks to Serenity's influence. Regular trade and their unprovoked aid in their rebuilding months had sealed an unspoken alliance between the two. It would not be a foolish act to appeal to her.

Jung-Soo was tempted to say maybe that would be enough as he really did not relish leaving Kang-Dae on his own to hold out against Katsuo while he traveled to seek help from their enemy's homeland. He took the letter from KangDae's hand. "Outside of the king, do not allow word of Katsuo's survival to spread." Jung-Soo understood.

"The blessed moon will be approaching soon. Return Rielle to the lake so she can return home. She has done more than enough."

Jung-Soo ignored the tightening in his heart. He nodded again.

CHAPTER 33

Rielle packed up the last of her things and tossed them in the bag. When she tried to close it, it wouldn't as it was too overstuffed due to her lazy packing. Getting frustrated with the thing she pushed the bag to the floor in a huff. She plopped down on the cot and hung her head in her hands. She couldn't figure out why she was so annoyed. Jung-Soo had told her Kang-Dae wanted her to go back home to keep her safe. She should have been glad, and appreciative of the gesture and she was. She thought she was. Everything that was going on was exactly the reason she'd avoided coming to this world. She felt like she never had peace whenever she was here. Yes, there had been moments when she came to be with Serenity during her labor that she had been pampered. She had been too frightened to set foot outside the room let alone the palace. Memories of fear and death were all she felt she'd find there. Maybe this annoying feeling was her concern over Kang-Dae. He could suffer complications and she wouldn't be able to help. It felt like more than that though. Maybe she was dreading coming in contact with Serenity's family and having to be the one to tell them the awful news but even that didn't feel right. Something was bothering her and it was more than just the obvious. She reached down to pick up the fallen bag and poured everything out to repack. 'You shall return where you belong,' the words and the annoyingly monotone voice of the person who said it penetrated her thoughts. It was what he'd told her when he broke the news. 'Where she belonged,' she thought bitterly. Like he would know anything about where she should be. She barely knew where she should be. He was probably thrilled to be getting rid of her now that she served her purpose. The way his eyes had stayed downcast as he told her said otherwise. She knew it wasn't true, she knew that even as she thought it but it gave her something to rage at other than the million other horrible things that had happened. She would go home and have to pretend that her best friend wasn't gone, missing, or otherwise but gone all the same. She'd have to pretend that there wasn't a whole group of people living under constant threat of death, people she'd come to care for. She was to pretend there wasn't a possibility that her niece could fall into the same type of hands that had haunted her nightmares for months after her ordeal. She had to completely forget about the one who had saved her from evil men and her own stupidity. The one who was so good he'd put aside all his feelings for those he loved. The one who carried the weight of unbelievable guilt over something that couldn't possibly be his fault. The one who would go off and risk his life for the hundredth time for his friend and his country with no one there to remind him that his life mattered as well. What if she got back and never heard from him again, from any of them? The thoughts were starting to make her feel nauseous. She got the stupid urge to ask Kang-Dae to let her stay. Give him the excuse she still needed to monitor him. He would never go for it, she decided. He was even more stubborn than Serenity. The thought of her friend had her swallowing back a lump trying to form in her throat. If she were truly gone, she didn't know if she could stomach any more loss in her life. She could appeal to the Dowager but she doubted she would speak against her son, especially in the state he was in. If she were honest with herself, she didn't want to stay just to be stuck inside the fortress worrying. But maybe it wasn't a matter of getting someone to say she could stay. Maybe she just had to stay close to the right person. An annoying general came to mind. He would never agree of course. But she didn't necessarily have to let him know.

CHAPTER 34

She was watching her eat again. The servant with mean eyes. Unlike the others, she was a Xian citizen happy to give her allegiance to the would-be conqueror. She also seemed to delight in seeing Serenity in this position. Serenity supposed she was one of the not-so-uncommon people who never took to the idea of having a foreigner as a queen. A lot of them had fled during her pregnancy when the rumors of her aiding Katsuo had been making rounds across the city. Only a handful returned once the truth was brought forth.

Serenity ignored her as she often did, taking several handfuls of rice and shoving it in her mouth. Manners were not her priority. She'd eat whenever she could, needing to keep up her strength. Her throat wasn't as sore lately which Serenity took as a good sign. She still couldn't talk very well but she didn't need to. Not yet.

As she reached for the cup of water the woman's foot shot out kicking the cup, sending it scattering on the floor what was left of her water a useless puddle. Serenity glared up at the woman who had a smug and nasty grin on her face. The woman didn't speak, only snatching the plate from in front of Serenity. She turned on her heels and sauntered out of the room obviously pleased with herself. Serenity waited until the door closed and locked. Hearing the heavy footsteps get further and further away, Serenity slowly moved to the corner of her pallet and lifted the sheet. The small cup of water she'd hidden away a couple of days ago was thankfully still there. She took a couple of tiny sips before placing it back in its spot. She'd wait for the next meal without that servant. The guards who brought her food during their shift didn't care about watching her so it was easier to square things away for later. She had several things hidden away, just waiting for her moment.

***

Rielle had done pretty well staying out of sight, she thought. It had almost been two full days and they still had no idea she was following them.

She stayed back far enough, mostly following whatever footprints they'd managed to make. When he had taken her to the lake she had played her role well, swimming out, going under, even staying down long enough to fool them into thinking she'd returned. Once they turned to leave, she surfaced without making much noise watching which direction they were traveling. After she got a good idea of where they were going, she swam back to shore and changed into some dry clothes. Toting her large bag, she started after them. It wasn't easy. They barely made noise, she supposed that was the point but she doubted General Silent would have much to say anyway. She hoped they would stop to camp soon. With all the walking while carrying the heavy bag, it was very tiring. The sun had set over two hours earlier. It had gotten colder. Not caring how it would look she set the bag down and pulled out her leather coat. She knew she probably shouldn't have brought it but she brought a couple of things with her for her comfort. Hiding her origins just was not a priority for her when she came here. Staying alive was. Once she had it on, she went back to following but had to pause. They were no longer in her sight. 'Oh man, how'd they disappear so fast?' she thought. With the sun no longer shining trying to search for prints would be nearly impossible. She would've taken out her flashlight but she didn't want to draw attention. She kept walking in the direction they were going, hoping they had done the same. She walked another half hour still without seeing any trace of them. Now she was starting to get worried. If she lost them, what would she do? She may have been able to go back to the lake but the moon was long gone. She would be waiting weeks for the next one. Would she have to make it back to the fortress? She staggered up an incline still unsure whether she should continue on or not. Huffing and panting she made it up the hill.

"How long did you expect to keep this up?" Jung-Soo asked, coming from around a tree. Rielle froze. She noticed Hae-In a few feet away from him, a sympathetic look on his face. She stamped down any embarrassment and held her head high.

"How long did it take you to notice?" she fired back. Hae-In looked back and forth between them. Jung-Soo didn't say anything, just turned and headed into the woods. Hae-In came up to her and took the bag from her. She thanked him.

She was about to follow him into the woods but pulled him to a stop. "How long did it take you all to notice I was following?" she asked curiously. It took him a minute to comprehend what she was asking, with his limited English skills but when he did, he smiled. He held up one finger.

One day, he was telling her. That may have hurt her ego just a bit but the fact that he knew and continued without forcing her back made her just a little bit happy.

When they made it to an opening with some of the other men everyone got quiet. She recognized some of them as part of Jung-Soo's personal group having traveled with them before. Hae-In sat her bag down on the side of him and motioned for her to join him, which she did. Jung-Soo sat on the other side as far from her as he could get while staying close to the fire. He never met her eyes, only staring into the flames, but Rielle felt like she was definitely on his mind.

CHAPTER 35

Kang-Dae ignored the light throbbing of his head as he took the lead in front of the small group of men. They moved in the dead of night only being guided by the small light of the moon and their own knowledge of the land and layout of the trees. Kang-Dae knew they were outnumbered but this was their home no one knew it better. Every hidden way in was etched into his memory. His goal was simple. Kill Katsuo. If he took him out the rest would scatter like before. He ignored the pleading of his mother to wait until he had fully recovered or at least for Jung-Soo to return but he refused. He couldn't stand having the enemy in his home, on his throne. There was the other part of him that needed to know if Serenity was inside. If she was, he had to get her out. Once he made up his mind he moved forward with his plan. Many of the men who came with him were eager to join him, feeling the same need for retribution he did.

He led the men toward the back, in search of the drainpipe. It was small but big enough to get through if one tried. If they could get inside, they would come out inside the washhouse within the servants' wing. Once inside they could sneak into the armory and grab what they could and take them all out. He stepped over what looked like a giant ant pile ready to make the sprint to the next blind spot in the trees. They could see the walls in the distance. 'Almost there,' Kang-Dae encouraged himself. His throbbing head matched the beat of his racing heart. The rush of adrenaline kept him upright as he pushed on, determined to destroy Katsuo that very night.

They stuck close to the trees. If anyone was looking out, he hoped the dark armor they sported and the night sky would keep them from being spotted. It was silent, there was not even the chirp of insects. It unnerved him but he kept pressing. He passed another pile after almost tripping on it. It was irritating the back of his mind as he'd never seen so many before. A dark knot started to form in his belly. He pressed on, ignoring it.

A whistling sound filled the air and a source of light gave them clearer sight for just a second before Kang-Dae noticed the flaming arrow sticking out a tree bathing the few soldiers sneaking by in light. Kang-Dae was about to order them to get out of sight when another whistle filled the air, this time the arrow lodged itself into another nearby "ant pile" a short distance away from him. The sight barely registered in his mind before ....Boom!

A burst of fire and the shout of one of his men filled the sky. Kang-Dae looked up in horror to see the bright burning fire and one of his soldiers desperately patting his burning side. Some men went to help him and Kang-Dae heard the whistling again.

"Get away!" He shouted but it was too late. Boom! Another burst of light and flames. This time five men were left burning on the ground, but two were unmoving. Suddenly Kang-Dae was back in the palace hearing the loud blasts and the screams of the men in the room with him. The whistling became faster and more numerous. A tree caught fire, not five feet from Kang-Dae. His men were beginning to lose their nerve staring at the flames and their fallen brethren. Kang-Dae got behind a tree and some men followed suit. He could see the men on the walls arrows aflame taking aim. They had no element of surprise and trying to get past this field of fire would cost them more than they could afford to lose. He cast a longing look toward the walls, towards his home. With a loud curse, he turned toward his men.

"Fall back!"

They didn't hesitate, wanting to get out of there as fast as they could. They ran back the way they came, hearing and feeling even more explosions at their backs. Luckily there was no one following, it was too dangerous to have his own men on the ground after such a maneuver, Kang-Dae thought. He wondered if he was watching. His head was now pounding and he felt slight dizziness but he kept moving. At the very least he would get his men back to safety. He didn't want to lose any more on his foolish mission.

CHAPTER 36

Serenity sat in her little room at the table. The room was a bit bigger than it was in real life. It looked more like a cottage. She looked up to see Snow White walking around cleaning. Serenity watched in anticipation because she knew what was coming. The knock on the door came and Serenity watched from her seat as the princess went to open the door. Just like the fairy tale, the witch was at the door, only this witch was a man in a cloak. Sho. He spoke in an obviously threatening manner but the princess was oblivious, stuck in her role. Serenity just watched as she stupidly accepted the apple and took a bite. Only instead of simply falling asleep she began to choke and gag. Her face turned green and she fell dead to the floor. Sho watched with no emotion before turning his cold eyes to her. He looked startled to have been caught. His appearance changed to the harmless old woman he was meant to be in the story. Acting as though she had not witnessed what he'd done he gave her the same spiel while offering another red apple for her to "enjoy." Serenity stood and took the apple in her hand. She could feel Sho's eyes on her, eagerly waiting for her to take a bite. Instead, Serenity gripped the fruit and threw it as hard as she could into his face. "Witch Sho" flew back. Serenity stepped over him into the outside where the sun was shining brightly.

The sound of the door opening jerked Serenity out of her sleep and her dream. She slowly sat up. When Sho walked through holding his staff with the same air of importance he always carried, Serenity didn't bother moving from her spot on her bed. He had the same guard with him and the mute servant. The girl immediately went to work taking up her empty plates and cups.

"Your false king's failure tonight will only push the people to our side," he began. Serenity didn't let his words affect her. She heard the explosions in the distance. She had not known what was going on but she made a guess. She had hoped it would bring an end to all of this but when the sounds stopped after such a short time and she vaguely heard the men in the halls gloating over their victory her hope for a rescue had diminished. But then she felt a burst of happiness because she realized only one person would be that brave and crazy enough to attack in the night for a half-destroyed palace. He was alive and that realization gave her even greater hope than before.

"You may think yourself to be safe but do not be fooled. Soon his clarity will return and I will have your body strung up outside the gates for all to see." Sho's confident words were meant to fill her with fear but Serenity only stared blankly at the man, refusing to give him any kind of response. Her tactic made him bristle and his grip on his staff tightened.

"Already the people are flocking to the true ruler of this kingdom. Once the lords bow before him the people will follow and they will beg for the heads of the false rulers," he continued to taunt. Again, she gave no reaction, only looking him up and down. The action brought a scowl to his already pinched face.

"Rest well. Tomorrow you may rest eternally," he threatened again. Serenity let out a snort. Unable to hold back his anger, he stepped forward and swung his staff into the side of her face. The blow made her numb at first, only able to feel a whooshing dizziness before the pain came. Serenity placed her hand on the side of her face attempting to soothe the growing ache. She wasn't bleeding but she could guess there would be an impressive bruise forming soon. The soothsayer must have realized as well, as a hint of fear entered his cold eyes. With a 'humph' he turned and walked out of the room. Serenity smiled to herself despite the pain.

CHAPTER 37

Rielle stared at the horizon with her hands resting on the railing of the ship. Trying to stay below deck in hopes that not seeing the ocean would quell her sea sickness had not worked at all. As a last-ditch effort, she made her way to the front of the ship for some air. She locked her eyes on the horizon and felt some of her discomfort diminish. This was probably not one of her smartest moves but she'd never admit it out loud. He would love to shove an "I told you so" in her face. Except he wouldn't say it. He'd just give her one of his blank stares that somehow said everything he was thinking.

A cool breeze licked at her skin and she closed her eyes to enjoy it. The seas were calm despite her earlier nausea and it was quiet save for the sound of the waves beneath her. No hum of engines or planes above. If she had been exposed to this side of this parallel world perhaps, she wouldn't have been so reluctant to come visit. No war or threat of death, just nature and peace. She supposed that was something she could get used to.

They'd been on the sea for two days now and according to their captain had another three to go. They were going the long way around to avoid any ships manned by Katsuo men who he may have left around just in case.

"Feeling sick again?" the question startled Rielle, making her grab at her chest.

"We talked about you making some kind of noise before you speak right?" she reminded him. He gave the barest form of a smile and for some reason, her heart skipped.

"I'm okay," she answered his previous question, turning back to the water. She felt him come up behind her and then he was standing beside her. "Never really been on a boat before."

"My first time on one wasn't as pleasant as this. The seas weren't as calm and neither were my captors."

So shocked by hearing him voluntarily speak about his past she almost didn't register what he'd said.

"Captors?"

"I was born in a small village near the sea, far from places with many rules or regulations. Bandits used this to their advantage and would come through to take us as slave labor. I was one of the unlucky few."

He talked about it so nonchalantly, but Rielle doubted the effects of such a life didn't linger.

"How long were you-?" she started to ask, not sure if he would answer.

"Eight years. Until I escaped."

"What about your family? Did you ever go back to try and find them?"

"Not until after I met Kang-Dae. He was kind enough to help me find my way back. But there was nothing left to go back to." Rielle didn't inquire anymore. It was clear that whether they were alive or dead he had accepted he'd never see them again. Rielle's heart hurt for him.

"I lost my parents when I was 11," she found herself blurting out. She could feel him staring at her but she kept her eyes on the horizon. "It was an accident, a car accident. I don't even remember it. Sleep in the backseat one minute, waking up in the hospital the next."

She woke up to a nurse hovering above her. Strangers had to give her the worst news of her life. Her godmother hadn't arrived till days later as she lived in another state. But even when she did arrive, she had only stayed for a few days before leaving her in the care of her grandmother, something her parents had never wanted, a fact even Rielle knew.

The sound of waves was all that was heard. Neither offered up any more information nor shared any more of their past.

CHAPTER 38

Dinner that night came courtesy of the mean servant. A change from the normal rotation, Serenity noted. It was also more than she would ever give her. Serenity's eyes narrowed as she placed the plate on the floor. On the side, next to the rice was a small portion of glazed apples. Serenity was immediately transported back to her dream. The smell of the rotten apples came to her memory so strongly she wanted to gag. Serenity looked up at the woman who was staring at her with her usual disdain but there was something else, something more subtle. She stood stiffly, anxiously. She was staring at her but her eyes would wander away for only a second or two. Maybe out of nervousness, Serenity wasn't sure. Serenity looked back at the food before turning to face the wall. After only a minute, she heard the woman huff and step toward her. A hard stare from Serenity made her falter.

"Eat!" she demanded. Serenity turned away from her once again. The larger woman reached down to pick up the plate and stormed over to her, intending to shove the plate in her face. As soon as she was in reach Serenity wrapped her chained arms around hers trapping the woman in her hold. The woman let out a painful shout. Serenity took one hand and grabbed a piece of apple and quickly shoved it in the woman's mouth. Serenity kept both her hands over her mouth and nose effectively closing it and keeping her from spitting anything out. As she struggled to escape her hold and breathe, Serenity held her tight. Once she was sure she couldn't hold out much longer she let her go. On instinct, the woman took a breath with it taking in the fruit. The woman gasped and coughed on her hands and knees as Serenity looked on unremorseful. Once she had her breath the realization of what had happened and what she just swallowed hit her and her eyes became wide with panic. She scrambled to her feet with a sob and threw herself out of the room, falling on her hands and knees. The guards outside tried to help her, but she was busy sticking her fingers in her throat trying to vomit. As she gagged and choked, she incoherently kept stammering out how Serenity had tried to kill her and begged for help. Eventually, the guard called for help as the panicked woman began throwing up. One of the guards came inside the cell to check on Serenity to make sure she had no weapons. When he saw none, he ordered her to stand and pulled on her chains forcing her to follow after him. As she gazed down at the still sobbing and vomiting woman, she couldn't stop the smirk from coming on her face.

The guard took her outside. The fresh air felt like heaven. She soaked in every second of it as they walked her toward the northern part of the palace. They walked her through familiar halls she felt like she hadn't seen in years. They made it to what used to be the formal dining hall but had been reorganized into what she assumed was a throne room as they had destroyed the real one. Inside, she was met with the scowling face of Sho and the curious but annoyed expression of Katsuo as they appeared to have been in mid-conversation. Behind them, the guards were helping the woman into the room. She looked terrible. Her face was red, covered in tears and snot. Vomit stained her robes and she looked like she could barely stand.

"What is this?" Sho demanded.

"There seems to have been an incident," the guard responded. Before the guard could explain, Katsuo stormed up to them with a reprimand ready on his lips when he stopped short. His eyes fixed on the bruise on Serenity's face. Serenity fought to keep from smiling. Katsuo's eyes darkened and his nostrils flared.

"Did you hit her?" He demanded. The guard quickly dropped her chain and went to his knee.

"No, my king. I would never disobey your command." Katsuo gently took hold of her chin and lifted her face to the light, inspecting it.

"Who did this?" he asked, his face taking on a much gentler expression. Serenity stared past him to see Sho frozen. If she were closer to him, she would see the sweat pouring from his temple. Sho stared back with hatred and fear. To his surprise and utter confusion, she turned toward the still-shaking woman and pointed a chained hand at her.

The woman, taking a second to realize what was happening earnestly shook her head.

"No, my King, I-I would never," she stammered. She pointed back at Serenity. "She tried to kill me."

"The woman speaks the truth. I believe she tried to poison her," the guard corroborated.

"With what?" Asked Katsuo. The woman froze as she realized her error.

"She only has what I allow her to have and what I order given. Where and how could she have gotten poison?" He gritted out.

The guard faltered, unable to answer the question. "I do not know."

Katsuo turned to the woman.

"Well? How did she poison you?" The woman swallowed fearfully multiple times, opening her mouth only to stutter and shut it.

"Answer!" The woman fell to her knees.

"I-I do not, I believe she-," she sputtered.

"Lock her up until she can remember," Katsuo ordered. The woman let out a cry.

"No, please my King, I am loyal to you!" she claimed as two guards picked her up and dragged her away.

"Take the chains off and return her to her room."

"My King" Sho began to object.

"Not now Sho," he cut the soothsayer off.

"From now on I want her food prepared in front of me."

Sho's eyes met Serenity's as Katsuo turned back toward him. This time she allowed him to see her smile before she was led away.

CHAPTER 39

A storm was raging above. Gone were the calm seas from the previous day. Many of the men stayed packed below deck. Rielle was in her cabin probably fighting to keep from being sick. Jung-Soo had tried to check on her but every knock was met with a forceful "Go away!" He didn't take it personally. She was probably not doing great and had no intention of allowing others to see her in such a state.

"Ship!" a crewman from above called out.

Jung-Soo raced to the deck. He looked up at the man positioned at the top of the mast.

"Civilian!?" He asked, hopeful.

"Their flying Anoekan colors," the captain said, voice grim.

"How far away are we?" Jung-Soo asked.

"At least a day," the captain breathed out in frustration.

"Can we outrun them?" Jung-Soo questioned, already dreading the answer.

"They're fast and with these winds, they're quickly gaining on us."

"Do what you can to keep us ahead," Jung-Soo told the man.

Rielle had stumbled up from below deck and made her way to him with a deep frown. "What's going on?'

He almost wanted to lie but knew it wouldn't help the situation.

"We're being followed."

She raced to the back to see for herself.

The sails shifted in an effort to catch the wind.

"Can they catch us?" Rielle asked with a twinge of panic.

"I do not know," he answered honestly. "Stay below deck out of sight." Rielle turned her frightened eyes back to the ship. Jung-Soo grabbed her by the arm and pulled her away from the railing. "Rielle, you need to go below deck," he repeated slowly and strongly. The rain was beating down on both of them. It took her a second to understand his words before she gave a short nod and went to do as she was told. Jung-Soo stared out at the still approaching ship. If it had firing capabilities, they would only need to get a bit closer to use it on them. The civilian ship they were on had no defensive weapons. If they were attacked, they would just be a sitting target. He looked at the small boats on the sides of the ship. Not ideal but good to have if the worst should happen. There was land in the distance. If they had to abandon the ship, they had an opportunity to make it somewhere they could actually stand a chance to fight.

"Pack up some of these boats!" He ordered going down to get what was important and do the same. They needed to be ready just in case the worst happened.

CHAPTER 40

"It is time for another show of strength," Sho said as he approached Katsuo. He looked preoccupied in his mind. Sho was sure it was with thoughts of that witch. He needed to remove her now before she could cause any more damage. He thought by staying in the background of the plan to poison her he would keep his involvement out. He was sure that even if the plan failed there'd be no way to tie it to him. He was still confident this was true, as there was no actual proof. But judging from that witch's smile there may not need to be. She knew and as long as she did, he was in danger of falling out of favor with Katsuo. He was already giving him more pushback than he had in months. It was all her influence. It was why he could not allow her one more day alive.

"What kind of show of strength?" Katsuo asked in a bored tone. He didn't even look at him. Sho choked down his annoyance at the disrespect.

"It's time for the people of Xian to know who their king is. Take the men into the city. Make yourself known to them. Reveal the defeat of their king from your own lips. Once you do, those willing will submit to you."

"If they don't?"

"Many will. For those that refuse, there is only one way." Katsuo showed no reaction, nor did he agree or disagree. Sho moved to stand directly in front of him. "Once you do this, we will have the backing of all the lords of Xian. That is all we need to strengthen our hold."

Katsuo lazily sat up straighter. He looked up at Sho.

"You said they would come to me if I had the throne," Katsuo reminded him. Sho was taken back.

"And they will. Once they know you have it," he reiterated, trying to get him to understand. Katsuo had not been the same since his injuries. Sho had taken charge of things because of it. It was why he had left him out of the more extreme but necessary decisions, like destroying the village that they had sought refuge in. He knew Katsuo would not have agreed even though it had been the safest option for them.

It never used to take much effort for him to move when he said so unless it was something he truly did not want to do. It reminded him of all those years ago when he'd ordered him to remove his brother to secure his future. He'd argued with him for weeks until Sho had to display his power and ensure it was for the best. Now he was questioning things he never would have before. If he didn't do this now, it may be he who Katsuo chose to remove.

"I've seen them all bowing to you." And he had, a short but clear vision of the Xian lords submitting at his feet offering gifts of black flowers. Sho knew it would come to pass. Whether this was the move to bring it about he was not as sure. But that was not his true purpose at the moment.

"Tomorrow, take them into the heart of the city. Make your announcement to all the people. Once you've staked your claim, everything will fall into place. Katsuo stared into his eyes. Sho tried not to falter under his gaze. He could not determine what he was thinking. When Katsuo gave a short nod, he felt his tension ease.

"Give word to the men, we move out in the early morning."

"I will, of course, maintain your will here in your absence with a few men," he told him offhandedly, hoping Katsuo would not disagree. Katsuo only nodded, which Sho was grateful for. Perhaps he had just needed a reminder as to what would be gained.

Sho backed away with a bow and went to inform their men. By tomorrow his problem will be wiped from this world and he'd have Katsuo's full trust once more.

***

Serenity was tightening her mini twits. She didn't have a window so she could not tell what time of day it was but it felt early. With nothing to do she split her time between prayer, plotting, and hair care. She paused mid-twist hearing the keys jingling from the hall. No one announced anything so she assumed it was another servant or Sho trying to make his threats. When Katsuo came in, she was surprised and immediately put on alert. He came alone as far as she could see. He was in full armor, holding a plate of food in his hand. 'Who was he off to fight?' The question put a knot in her stomach.

"I will be going soon. My fate is being set and I will see it through."

She eyed him carefully, not saying a word. He stepped forward and she stood, not comfortable being in any type of vulnerable position around him, at least not any more vulnerable than she already was. He didn't appear offended by her actions. He only came closer and sat on the bed himself.

"It seems a lot," he began staring at the wall. "to secure a fate that is supposed to be inevitable." There was bitterness in his words.

"I won't be long," he said matter-of-factly. The shift in his demeanor was jarring even if she'd seen it numerous times now. "Until I can secure a more obedient server, no one will be bringing you anything today."

No one should be coming down here, is what he was saying. He put the plate on her bed. Immediately, she noticed the large amount of food. It was way more than what she was normally given. But what caught her eye was that there was no spoon, but chopsticks. Gold and pointed chopsticks. No matter what she was given, she'd only ever been allowed a wooden spoon. She tried not to react; afraid he'd remove them but he didn't seem focused on her at all. He was still staring at the wall.

"It's not just the disobedient we must be weary of," he said. It was so quiet she didn't know if he was even talking to her anymore.

"Even the most loyal, will try and seize their moments." She was struggling trying to keep up with what he was saying. His words, though they could easily apply to her, did not feel directed towards her. He stared down at her food. She became worried he would take the chopsticks but he just stood and walked out the door. 'Okaaay' she thought to herself. There was clearly more going on than she knew about but she would not let herself be thrown. If she needed to be prepared, she would be.

CHAPTER 41

"Incoming!" The crewman shouted just before the floor next to Jung-Soo splintered into nothing. Their time and luck had run out. After managing to stay ahead for only a couple more hours the ship finally was able to get them in range. They wasted no time, firing on them immediately.

"Get into the boats!" shouted Jung-Soo as he went below in search of Rielle. They had packed them with as much as they could without trying to overload them, bringing only what was absolutely necessary. The men scrambled to lower the boats as another cannon hit the side. Struggling to stay on their feet, they continued to work. Jung-Soo made it two steps before another shake had him tumbling the rest of the way. Unfortunately, it seemed like the sea had joined with the enemy becoming rough and turbulent. The storm they'd managed to sail through without issue had become more fearsome, making it almost impossible for the captain to keep control. Unable to dwell on the aches and pains Jung-Soo forced himself up. He rushed to his cabin first. He pulled out the small letter box and shoved it inside his robes for safe keeping. He grabbed his sword and went out to find Rielle.

"Rielle!"

Rielle was huddled between the bed and the wall. She squeezed in there when the first hit sent a cannon through the hall. Taking a page from Serenity, she had been praying nonstop.

"Rielle!"

With the ringing in her ears, she thought she might be hearing things and continued her frantic prayers. "Please God, protect us, keep us safe. Don't let us die here," she pleaded again and again.

"Rielle! Where are you!" Finally realizing she wasn't imagining it she shakily pulled herself out of her safe place. The jerking ship made it difficult to walk straight, forcing her to hold onto the walls. She tumbled out the doorway but was quickly caught.

Jung-Soo held onto Rielle keeping them both upright.

"We have to go," he told her. The fear in her eyes told him she'd been afraid he would say that but there was also a grim understanding. She gave a nod and Jung-Soo held her closely as they made their way back to the steps. They were halfway up when a loud groan sounded and the ship lurched once more, this time throwing them into the wall as the entire ship felt like it was falling over. Rielle let out a scream. Jung-Soo threw his body over hers as they were taken on and off their feet several times.

The ship finally righted itself but the damage had been done. The cabin was filling with water fast. Jung-Soo kept sight of Rielle, slightly pushing her toward what had been the stairs and the only way out but was now filled with rushing water. They needed to get out before the ship brought them down with it. Luckily, Rielle appeared to be a strong swimmer. She pushed ahead, only looking back to make sure he was still with her. She hesitated at the exit that now only led to an almost nonexistent deck and the sea but took a deep breath and continued on. Jung-Soo followed suit. Once in the open water, he had hoped there would be some reprieve, but the currents among the storm were strong, pushing at them, making it difficult to keep afloat. Muffled sounds of more canon fire sounded above. Jung-Soo tried to keep Rielle in his sights but the harsh waters raged and it made it hard to see. A strong push of the current hit him and he felt himself being tossed to the left. He rolled as the water mercilessly pummeled him over and over. He struggled to keep what breath he had left. Not wanting to waste his strength fighting nature he allowed it to take him hoping it would calm soon. Seconds rolled by. The last of his breath was leaving him. Eventually, he was pushed out far enough from the currents, just as he felt himself go lightheaded. As soon as he was free, he used all his might to swim toward the surface. He breached the water with a heavy gasp. Ahead of him, at a good distance, sat the sinking ship now completely overturned. The enemy ship was still further out but getting closer.

Jung-Soo looked around hoping to see signs of other survivors, but was quickly disappointed. He prayed they had gotten to the boats and made it to the shore. "Rielle!" he shouted, not seeing any sign of her.

"General!"

Jung-Soo's head spun and he saw Hae-In swimming toward him clumsily. "None of the boats made it. The waves were too strong," he informed him. Jung-Soo's heart dropped.

"Have you seen Rielle?" he asked. Hai-In shook his head.

"We need to get to land." Jung-Soo would agree but he refused to go without her. He continued looking out hoping to catch a glimpse of her. His vision was heavily obscured by the heavy rain. "General," Hai-In pleaded before he let out a short cry. Jung-Soo turned toward him. Seeing his paling face scrunched up in pain he moved toward him, taking hold of him before he could sink. He was obviously injured but Jung-Soo couldn't see where. With the waves moving them closer to shore he gave one more desperate look for Rielle. As Hai-In began to go under once more he held him up and swam toward the shore. She was a better swimmer than he was. She would make it, she would, he assured himself even as his heart got heavier with every stroke.

CHAPTER 42

The city reminded him so much of home.
Katsuo and his men rode out in the afternoon.
People saw them and quickly began to flee. Katsuo
ordered his men to round up anyone they could find
and corral them into the center of the city. The cries
and screams were not as pleasant as the ones before.
These weren't his enemies. They were to be his
people. He knew firsthand what it was like to feel as
though your home was being invaded. He hadn't set
out to be looked at in that way originally. Sho told
him fear was the quickest way to get people to
respect your authority. When you were sure you had
it, only then could you begin to show them the good
you would do for them.

He guided his horse to the city's center
where crowds of hundreds huddled together in
mass. What few Xian soldiers were in the area tried
to protect them but they knew they were
outnumbered. "Today is a day you will all
remember. Today is the day you welcome the one

and only true king!" He announced. The people were silent, some too afraid to make a sound.

"What have you done to our King?" one soldier demanded, face angry, defiant.

"Your king is dead, as is your queen" he lied. The people began to cry out in mass. They denied it and called him a liar. Fear was quickly becoming replaced with anger. Katsuo steadied his horse who began shuffling nervously as the crowd grew louder.

"The undying prince will never perish!" someone shouted. "Our queen lives!" He searched the crowd for the culprit but everyone's face had the same hard look. It could've come from anyone. He hated the fact that so many in the crowd would rather believe Kang-Dae was still alive and speak so reverently about him rather than accept him. Was he really to believe they would ever speak of him in such a way?

"The man you once called king is no more. I've taken his life, his home, and his throne." he tried again. "I am your new ruler."

The women and children cried out their despair while the men angrily denied his claim feverishly. The screams were becoming too much. He felt like he was back on the streets of his home that night. He could hear the people cry out for help as their homes were burnt. The woman and men seemed to be getting impossibly loud until all he could hear were the screams. A rock flew past his head. Katsuo's eyes widened in shock at the boldness. Soon other random things were thrown at him and his men. In his head, he could hear Sho's voice. 'A show of strength.' A piece of fruit hit him in the temple. The Xian soldiers started advancing on his surrounding men. Unable to take anymore he screamed out. "SILENCE!" All his men drew their weapons. The screams and throws finally stopped. Katsuo needed to stop them for good. Sho was right, fear was the best way.

"Destroy it all, burn it down," he ordered his men. The people began to beg and curse him. Good, he thought to himself. Now they knew he was the one they had to rely on for the rest of their days.

CHAPTER 43

It didn't take as long as she thought it would for Sho to make his appearance. She figured he'd want to make sure Katsuo was a good distance away before he enacted his plan. He entered with one guard and the mute servant at his side. Serenity met him on her feet, the chopstick poking at her back from beneath her pants and skirt.

She gave him a look that basically asked him 'are you sure you want to do this?' The man had the audacity to smile.

"You still overestimate your importance. You have plagued me with your presence for long enough. Thinking you were greater than me, than my power. He will mourn you, be angered by your death but it will only push him into his destiny. The destiny I foresaw that will come to pass because of my sacrifices, my guidance." Serenity rolled her eyes.

The guard shut the door behind them to prevent her from escaping. Sho pushed the girl toward her. She looked confused as to what he wanted of her. When the guard stepped forward with only a jagged broken spoon in his hand it was clear to Serenity how they meant to frame her for the girl's murder. It was most likely to sell their story that she'd tried to escape and they had no choice but to put her down. As the soldier went to strike, the girl, moving faster than anyone in the room could have anticipated, caught his arm just as the sharp edge was an inch from embedding in her throat. Caught off guard, he wasn't prepared for her to use his weight against him and throw him over her shoulder onto the ground. Before he could comprehend what happened, the spoon was taken from him and the girl quickly punctured both eyes, causing the man to shriek. She swiftly put an end to that by grabbing his dagger and slitting his throat. Too stunned to move, all Sho could do was stare in shock. Removing her head scarf, allowing her wavy hair to spill free, Nasreen handed the head piece to

Serenity before removing the guard's weapons to claim as her own along with his armor. Finally coming out of his stupor, Sho began to shuffle over to the door frantically trying to get it open and get help. Before he could open the door fully, Serenity slammed into him so hard it shut. Sho grunted as his face hit the door. Serenity backed up enough for him to turn and face her, his eyes brimming with hatred. Serenity lifted her bloody hand to take his staff and tossed it to the floor. Upon seeing it he gave a confused look before reaching behind him. His eyes widened and a look of pain came on him as he pulled out the chopstick in his back. By now Nasreen had removed her outer clothes and already had on the fallen guard's breastplate. She handed Serenity the dagger.

Nasreen quickly ducked into the next room she came across. The soldiers and intruders had begun moving into the different areas of the palace. They had started by rooting out or straight up killing anyone they found hiding away. Nasreen had unfortunately been privy to the horrid sounds of the poor people being caught and pleading for their lives before being dragged away or worse. She had wanted to help but knew she was outnumbered. She knew she had to keep herself alive long enough to get their queen out. Medhi had successfully made it in with the enemy. He would be able to safely keep an eye on her and help her recover while she worked on how to get them all out.

She knew trying to continue her ruse as a soldier would not be practical. They had no women soldiers as far as she knew and trying to maintain two disguises was a quick way to get caught. She knew she needed a different approach. A harmless one. She looked around and realized she was in a servant's quarters. She looked through the wardrobe and found a uniform. She quickly changed and snuck around until she found a group of men gathering survivors for capture. Thinking this was her best chance she made her presence known and was promptly captured with the rest. When the soothsayer demanded their allegiance, she fought to keep quiet. It was an out of nowhere idea for her to pretend to be mute. Once she made the decision, she stuck with it realizing it made her seem like even less of a threat. She never expected the fool to make her his personal servant. Day after day she thought of new ways to kill him and then to go off and take out Katsuo. But she waited.

When she had been sent to finally serve the queen she'd been overjoyed. Her queen hadn't recognized her at first which was probably a good thing, as the soothsayer had kept close watch on her in the early days. When he became sure she couldn't do anything he began leaving them on their own, or at least with his one guard. She had to carefully reveal her identity to her queen not wanting to startle her too much. One day, in the middle of feeding her she let her face scarf slip just enough. The queen's eyes widened and she almost laughed but stopped herself. The two couldn't speak, not wanting to alert the guard but they exchanged a meaningful touch of hands. When she saw the queen fighting back tears unwilling to release her hand she knew at that moment, her sister was dead and she was trying to apologize. Nasreen felt her own eyes water but she blinked them away. She squeezed the queen's hand hoping she understood. She knew her sister. She was a warrior just like her. It was a great honor to die for those they were sworn to protect. They took their role seriously. Arezoo died in the most honorable way and she would hold that knowledge close to her heart.

When Nasreen overheard the soothsayer plotting her queen's death she knew it was time to go. The last time she'd been sent to feed her she tried to warn her but it seemed she was already aware. Nasreen would never forget the smile that graced her face. It was like she knew they would be free soon. It made Nasreen believe it as well.

"Do you know why your visions pale to mine?" Serenity asked Sho. Hearing her voice so strong startled him. "It's because my "power" is not my own. It comes from something greater than you or me. And you, Katsuo, and anyone who comes against us will always lose to it." Sho attempted to look defiant as she held the blade but the way his eyes kept shifting to it betrayed his true feelings.

"He will root you out and destroy you. I've seen his ascension," he desperately threatened.

"There's more than one type of ascension," she told him. A flicker of doubt flashed on his face before his angry expression returned. With a snarl, he used whatever strength he had left to lunge at her, only for Nasreen to step forward and trip him. As he came down Serenity met him with her blade, embedding it right in his heart.

"You won't live to see your vision fail to come true. But know that it will and Katsuo will never get his crown." Sho's ragged breath slowed and he slumped forward. Serenity let him fall in a heap at her feet. The dead soothsayer's vacant expression and glassy eyes would be her final impression of the man.

"Let's go, my queen. The hidden gate to the south is unguarded, we should be able to get through without detection," informed Nasreen.

Serenity nodded and wrapped the scarf around her head and pulled it up to hide her face, leaving only her eyes visible as Nasreen had done. She also put on the woman's outer robes. Nasreen tied her hair up to sit atop her head as many of the male soldiers did within the walls. They pushed the bodies out of the sight of the window of the cell door and headed out.

They walked the grounds without urgency so as not to draw attention. Nasreen had played her part well and in the dark, it would take thorough scrutiny to recognize she had been the servant. They used the darkness to their advantage, avoiding all the places Nasreen had already marked as having guards. With Katsuo taking so many of his men out, there were few left in the palace. They managed to avoid running into any of them. Since whatever servants or slaves were around feared the soldiers so, most of the ones they came across immediately averted their gazes and moved out of the way. Serenity's heart pounded the entire walk. The closer they got to the gate the more anxious she became.

So close to seeing her family again, the doubt that they would make it tried to creep in but she chased it away. Voices in the distance made her breath catch but neither of them faltered in their steps. They passed the entrance to the gardens and she was sickened to see the dying flowers in the distance. Her mother-in-law's favorite place would be restored along with everything else, she told herself.

Upon reaching the south wall Nasreen immediately began feeling for the latch on the hidden door while Serenity kept watch. A loud shout sounded making Serenity's blood freeze. She clutched at the dagger hidden at her side as Nasreen began feeling more earnestly. When another shout filled the air along with rambunctious laughter Serenity's whole body sagged in relief. Her relief was only enhanced by the sound of the door opening. Nasreen jumped back as the door began to swing open on its own. Both women took out their weapons.

Medhi's head came peeking out from behind the door. "My queen," he greeted, looking grateful to see her. Serenity breathed out a quiet laugh. Not wasting time, both women flew out of the palace with Medhi, towards the hidden path.

CHAPTER 44

Hai-In's leg had a large gash in it. Jung-Soo had used pieces of his shirt to stop the bleeding, but the poor soldier had lost a lot of blood. He'd lost consciousness just before they'd made it. From the shore, he could still see the enemy's ship floating in the same position which Jung-Soo found curious. If they suspected survivors this would be the obvious place to search but they seemed unwilling to get any closer. Once his bandage was secure and he was breathing steadily Jung-Soo sat back and finally took a much-needed breath. Some debris and chests had washed up with them. He would go through it for anything useful later. He still needed to find Rielle. The hard rain had lessened some making it a little easier to see. He stood and looked over the ocean. He could see more debris from the ship bobbing in the water. What was left of the vessel was only a small piece of wood peeking from the surface. One of the smaller boats had made it but it had crashed into the rocks.

Jung-Soo, after making sure Hai-In was safely hidden behind the rocks, walked the shore looking for a way up the bluff to get a better line of sight. This had not been their destination and he was unsure where they had landed. He doubted it was Anoeka given they had still been a day away. He found a slightly walkable path. He had to grab onto the trees to make it up. The heaviness of his drenched clothes made it that much more difficult. By the time he made it to the top, he was breathing heavily and hunched over. He took several deep breaths before standing. If this was an island it was large. Miles and miles of land stretched out endlessly as far as he could see. Looking behind him into the lush brush he couldn't see much past the trees. It wouldn't be wise to venture through them as he had no idea if and when it would end. His best bet was to keep to the shoreline. He slowly began a trek toward where the sun would be if not obscured by the clouds. He didn't want to go too far, having to leave Hae-In on his own, but he needed to find Rielle. The dark feeling started pressing on him, trying to scare him into believing she had not made it, that she was still struggling in the ocean or worse. He refused to entertain the lie. She had made it, she had to.

***

Rielle had only rested her eyes for a second. That's what she told herself she would do as soon as she made it to the sand. She probably was not safe where she was and finding Jung-Soo was going to be her top priority but after swimming so hard for so long, she just needed to rest for a second. Even the rain pounding on her back didn't bother her. Before she knew it, she was waking to no rain and clearer skies. She groggily dragged herself off the sand. She could feel it sticking uncomfortably to her face. She crawled over to the shoreline and washed off as best she could. The coldness of the water had no effect on her after nearly drowning in it. Once she felt a little less grimy, she forced herself to stand. Her legs were wobbly. She wanted to sit back down but having no idea how long she'd been asleep she didn't want to waste any more time. She looked around seeing the large bluff ahead of her. She didn't see herself making it up that. Instead, she walked sluggishly on the shore to see if she could find Jung-Soo. She dragged her feet, barely conscious, her eyes closing numerous times as she moved like a zombie. The sun had begun to make a subtle appearance behind the clouds. She walked towards it. Her mind was plagued with thoughts that shamed her for her stupid decisions mixed with genuine fear that she would never find Jung-Soo. She made a promise to God that if he helped her find him, she would gladly concede she should have just gone home. All she ever encountered in this world was misery and death. Why did she think for a second this time would be different? Except the thing was, she didn't think it would be. She understood exactly what she was getting involved in but it still wasn't enough to keep her from endangering herself. Before she'd done it for Serenity, an acceptable and unquestionable choice as far as she was concerned. This time though, this time she was risking it all for, she couldn't quite be sure. Her friend's friend? He was more than that. He needed to be if she was stranded in the wilderness for him. She walked for over half an hour before she saw the dock. In her exhaustion, it took her a minute to notice the people fishing on it. But the children playing in the sand noticed her first.

"Mama! Papa!" They shouted running up on the dock towards the two adults. Rielle's body wavered a bit and she blinked repeatedly, not sure if she was seeing things. The woman looked over first, with the girl clutching at her waist. Dressed in a sleeveless pale red gold print top with a matching skirt, the dark-skinned woman started walking towards her only to be pulled back by the man with her. He also was dressed in the same type of print clothing, only his head was wrapped as well. He was only slightly lighter than the woman. The woman looked back at him and said something Rielle was too far away to hear. Soon the woman was pulling from the man's hold and jumping down from the dock. The man was left with the kids. As the woman got closer, Rielle thought she almost looked like her mom before she finally collapsed.

CHAPTER 45

The news of the attack on the city had Kang-Dae isolated in his room with nothing but Blessing to keep him company. He refused to let her out of his sight, needing to hold onto something as it seemed he was losing everything he held dear. His mother attempted to comfort him but even she had been barred from entering. Blessing slept soundly on the bed after wailing nonstop for hours, wanting her mother no doubt. Kang-Dae felt the same. After his failed attack, his body seemed to rebel against him, making him feel like he'd lost some of the progress he'd made. He was tired all the time, and he felt as though his strength had waned considerably. No word from Jung-Soo. No word from Amir. He still had no idea where his neeco was. Kang-Dae felt defeated.

"My king, there's a problem in the tunnels!" someone shouted from behind the door. Kang-Dae jumped up, perhaps a little too fast as he immediately had to steady himself to keep upright.

He threw open the door to see a frightened young soldier and a few others. "Someone's made it inside."

"Get the guard and my mother and bring them here," he ordered as he grabbed his sword. It was heavy in his hand, something it had never been before but he pushed on.

Once outside in the courtyard, he found many of the soldiers facing the tunnel's entrance bows and swords drawn.

"What happened to the sentries we placed?"

"They were beaten back when they tried to stop them and one was taken captive," explained one of the captains. Kang-Dae rolled his eyes at the incompetence.

"They're coming!" One soldier called out. The men trained their weapons toward the tunnel. The first thing he saw was a frightened sentry being pushed in front, hiding the intruder from their eye line.

"Drop your weapons!" a surprisingly familiar feminine voice called out.

"Surrender yourselves!" The captain retorted.

Another figure came forward and Kang-Dae's eyes widened. He quickly bellowed, "Drop your weapons!" The men all did as they were told. The sentry was released and pushed forward revealing Nasreen in enemy armor but Kang-Dae's focus was on the one behind her. Kang-Dae stepped out from the line. Despite his dizziness, his fatigue, and his still-healing injuries, he sprinted at full speed.

Serenity took her cue from her husband and ran toward him. The two met in the middle with Serenity jumping into Kang-Dae's waiting arms. Tears fell and cries sounded and no one else was around as she clutched at him, burying her face in his neck. Kang-Dae only pulled back a little to inspect her.

"Are you hurt?" he asked, voice shaking. Serenity shook her head, taking his face in her hands as he held her.

"You?" she asked, her voice was raspy but it sounded beautiful to him. He shook his head. At that moment, he wasn't. At that moment, he was perfect. She rained kisses on him which he welcomed. They embraced again, squeezing one another even tighter. When they finally pulled away a large crowd had gathered. As soon as the couple noticed them, they all went to their knees. Serenity might've felt a bit embarrassed a few months ago but after everything, she couldn't care less. She reached for Kang-Dae's hand who wrapped hers within it.

"Our queen has returned!" Kang-Dae announced raising their combined hands. A round of cheers rang out echoing into the skies.

***

No one would look at him. Not his men, nor the servants. He thought maybe they'd heard what he had done and were rightfully fearful. The longer it went on the less he believed it. When he came to his hall and saw the soldier standing by the door waiting, already on his knees, he knew something was wrong. The soldier refused to speak of it, deciding to lead him to whatever the trouble was, not that it would save him. Katsuo had already made up his mind, whatever had transpired, someone would be paying with their life. He just did not know how true that statement was. When he was led to his dream walker's cell, he felt cold, empty. He tried to steel himself for what he was about to see, prepare for the worst but nothing, no amount of preparation could have helped. Katsuo stared down at Sho's lifeless body. It felt surreal, like he was outside his own body watching the whole thing like a play. He saw the bloody gold chopstick laying on the ground beside the body and felt his knees try to give out but managed to keep standing. Katsuo did not know exactly what he expected when he'd given it to her. Did he in the back of his mind mean for this to be the result? He didn't think so, but his mind had been so jumbled lately it was hard to tell. He knew he wanted to be sure no one could take her from him. On some level, he knew Sho's intentions. He just never imagined he would make the attempt himself. Katsuo walked over to the man who had been in his life for as long as he could remember. He placed a hand on his shoulder. Katsuo wondered if he had seen this in his vision.

CHAPTER 46

Someone was singing. Or chanting, Rielle wasn't sure as it wasn't in English. It sounded low and melodic. There was something fragrant in the air and she felt warm. Whatever she was laying on was soft. She opened her eyes. A ceiling of straw and thin wood beams was what she saw first. She struggled to turn her head feeling sluggish, like she'd been heavily medicated. A woman kneeled on the other side of the room or hut, as Rielle began to realize. It was large, with paintings covering the walls. The flooring was stone with colored rugs lying about in various places. The singing woman knelt by a structure adorned with colorful jewelry, and white feathers. Rielle realized it was the same woman she'd seen before. She was crushing something with a grinding tool in a small bowl. The woman kept working until whatever was in there had been ground to her liking. When she was done, she stood and walked over to the small table against the wall and poured the powder into a larger bowl. She mixed the bowl lightly.

Now that she was closer Rielle could see that though she was similar to her mother in skin tone and the way she carried herself, that was where the similarities ended. Her eyes were a bit lighter, her nose wider and her face a bit rounder. She was a beautiful woman, Rielle thought. Rielle tried to speak, to let her know she was awake but it was hard to open her mouth let alone form words. The woman came over with a tiny bowl in hand. She didn't seem surprised to see she was awake only giving her a comforting smile and putting the bowl to her lips. Rielle was not one to just accept what a stranger was giving her but she had no energy to fight or deny it. Also, for some reason she trusted her. It was a little bitter but not overly so. As she drank, she could feel her body warming even more and the sluggishness slowly dissipated.

"Your strength will return soon," the woman told her in a heavily accented voice. It sounded almost like she was from the Caribbean.

"How- how long-," Rielle tried to get out.

"You've been sleeping most of the afternoon. The sun set not long ago," she answered. "You can call me Safara. Do not fear, you will be safe in my village. Those who hunt you do not dare to venture here."

Rielle's brows furrowed in confusion. How'd she know? She wondered.

"Wh-where am I?" She managed to ask.

"Among the Umbala of the Assani."

'Assani" Rielle thought. She'd heard that term before. It was what the Anoekans who'd captured Serenity and her kept calling them. From what she could tell they did not have the greatest relationship.

"My," Rielle hesitated before finally getting out, "friends. We got separated when our ship was attacked."

"I've already sent out people to look for any others. You were speaking a lot about it in your sleep."

Rielle wondered what else she might have said and hoped she hadn't said anything that would make them suspicious of her.

"Rest some more. You are well looked after."

***

Jung-Soo had walked as far as he could until he feared he could go no further without leaving Hae-In in a vulnerable state. The sun had set and he could hardly see. He turned to head back, heart heavy with worry and defeat. She was alive, he kept thinking to himself. He'd lost too much. He could not lose anymore. A light among the trees caught his eye and he froze. It was moving. Not knowing if it was friend or foe he ducked behind a tree, only peeking out slightly to catch a glimpse. He was without his sword or anything resembling a weapon. Depending on how many there were, if it came to a fight, it could be over before it began. The light turned away going the opposite way, toward Hae-In. Jung-Soo had to think fast. He could follow them to make sure they didn't find Hae-In and hope he wouldn't be noticed. He could let them move off from him and just hope they never found Hae-In, or he could confront them now and possibly die. The choices were not good. He opted to follow them until he could come up with a better plan. He didn't move until they were a good distance away, judging from the light. He moved as quietly as he could in unfamiliar territory. The trees here were different than what he was used to and the ground more uneven.

He followed for less than half a mile before he heard it. Whispers. It was hard to tell which direction it came from. The light was still ahead but the whispers were much closer. Jung-Soo felt the need to hide himself but had no idea which direction he should hide. He tried listening for footsteps but heard none. But somehow the whispers were getting closer. Jung-Soo looked at the tree closest to him and found one of its thinner branches. He pulled and pushed until it gave way. It wasn't ideal but it was better than nothing. He looked ahead, waiting.

"Kimelea," a harsh whisper sounded from right behind him. Before he could fully turn, he felt something hit his head and he stumbled to the ground. He was about to get up and fight back when something fell at his feet exploding in a small cloud of smoke. The second he breathed it in he felt lightheaded and then nothing.

CHAPTER 47

Serenity was sitting in bed, leaning against Kang-Dae with Blessing asleep in her arms. The poor thing refused to leave her. If anyone attempted to take her, she let out a wail that could damage the ears. Serenity's absence seemed to have affected her greatly. It was almost as if she knew how close she had come to losing her forever. Kang-Dae tightened the arm holding Serenity at the waist. The action didn't bother her as she only leaned into him more. He looked down at her. The scar on her neck was fully visible to him. It filled him with hatred every time he saw it, knowing how she suffered, knowing how she could have been lost to him.

It was late. Most of the fortress was asleep save for those on guard. Kang-Dae hadn't had a full night's rest since he'd awoken from Rielle's surgery. Before, it was the restlessness of not knowing where his wife was and the worry and fears that came attached to it. Now that she was back in his arms it was a new anxiety, one full of constant fears that she would be taken from him again. That he would not be able to get back his throne. That his people would continue to suffer as he was forced to hide. The attack on the city had driven dozens towards the fortress. It had been a challenge to go out and bring them in without being detected. Also, the attack brought more unforeseen problems. Though built to be a hold out for the entire capital, supplies were running low. The more people that came the less there was to go around. They could not hold up indefinitely.

Serenity gently lifted Blessing off her chest and laid her on the bed. She patted her back softly when she began to stir but she was soon lulled back to sleep. Once she was satisfied she would not wake, Serenity turned fully into Kang-Dae's embrace, laying half her body onto his. She took his arm and wrapped it around the front of her waist and held it to her. She didn't speak much since she'd returned. Kang-Dae knew it was a side effect of her injury. Knowing it caused her pain to do so, he encouraged her silence, knowing her well enough to be her interpreter if need be. It was hard for her, especially when she tried to sing to Blessing to soothe her but was unable to. She had almost cried in frustration until Kang-Dae came and finished the lullaby himself. Kang-Dae kissed her shoulder, and then her cheek. She drew on his hand with her finger, writing out the word love.

"Saranghae," he whispered in her ear. They sat quietly just holding each other. He could tell when she began to fall asleep. Her head would begin to fall, then she would right it. It happened a couple more times until Kang-Dae laid them both down. He made sure they were facing Blessing as she would be the first one Serenity would want to see when she awoke. He ran the side of his hand down her face.

"Go to sleep, Neeco," he ordered softly. It only took a few minutes before her breathing evened and her body relaxed. He watched her and Blessing for half an hour before slowly disengaging from her and pulling himself from the bed. He placed the blanket over them both and left the room.

Kang-Dae walked the halls of the fortress. He walked through the courtyard with some sleeping soldiers strewn about who were forced to sleep on the hard ground when all the other spaces became occupied. Walking down the steps he made it to his destination. He pushed the heavy door open. It was dark, the torch he'd used the night before had long since burnt out. He raised his fresh lantern and set it on the hook by the door. The weapons rack was the first thing he went to inside the medium-sized room. He chose the staff this time. The first two swings were just to test the weight of the weapon. Once he felt comfortable, he swung harder, with purpose. He spun while jabbing at the invisible enemy on his left, before repeating the same action on his right. He spun the staff over his head and brought it down onto the floor mimicking the impaling he would do once he faced his enemies once more. He practiced into the night never resting or easing up. His head was starting to hurt but he pushed past it. He was so into his "fight" that he didn't hear the person opening the door or coming into the room. It wasn't until the door shut that he spun around, staff at the ready barely missing Serenity's nose. Guiltily, Kang-Dae dropped the staff.

"I'm sorry," he stuttered, rushing over to her to inspect nonexistent wounds. She shook her head to let him know she was fine and not to worry. She moved past him and picked up the fallen staff. She inspected it and turned to him, holding it out as if to offer it back to him. With a small smile, he reached for it but was confused when she did not release it. Instead, she drew him closer and bent down beneath the weapon to emerge on the other side between him and it. She looked back at him expectantly, and he knew exactly what she was demanding. He placed his hands on top of hers and guided the staff until it was upright. He started slowly, not wanting to cause her any discomfort. He stepped forward with his right leg and she did the same while moving the staff as if to block an incoming strike. He swung with minimal force, stopping at the middle of their eyeline, before sweeping it lower, showing her how to knock an enemy off their feet.

This was not something they'd done before. Arezoo had taken responsibility for showing Serenity ways to defend herself and Kang-Dae had been happy with it, feeling no need to interfere or add anything. He never wanted her to be in a position to have to defend herself. The shame of failing in that, along with the sadness and guilt of Arezoo's death started to fill him. He felt like he had failed her in so many ways. If he had only finished Katsuo when he had him. If he had checked the body himself to make sure when they reported his death. Maybe if he had focused more on securing the capital than rebuilding, maybe none of this would have happened. He moved without thinking, his mind being tormented. How much longer had she needlessly suffered because he failed to take back their home? Knowing she had been so close to death and he had failed her only made the shame he was feeling worse. Before he knew it, Serenity was leading him. He went through the motions as she swung and pushed at no one. Trapped in his thoughts, he was completely caught off guard when she raised the staff, spun underneath it, and pushed it back with so much force she rammed him into the door. He landed hard, an oomph escaping his mouth. He stared down at her, both surprised and impressed. She stared up at him with serious eyes and touched his head.

"Where are you?" she asked, voice just above a whisper. He tried to shake his head in denial but she held it still. He didn't want to put this on her, his fears, his doubts, his failures. He needed her to still believe in him. Because out of the two of them, she was the only one who did. She refused to let go so he eventually gave in.

"I didn't protect them. I didn't protect you," he finally said. She let the staff fall to one side. Serenity pointed at him and then herself.

"We didn't," she retorted. "We."

Kang-Dae shook his head again. "I am your husband. I am meant to keep you safe. I am the king, it's my duty to protect this land. I let the enemy come in and take our home, take you."

"It was my dream," she said, her voice rising. He wanted her to stop knowing she must be hurting herself.

"I saw it, saw the price of winning, and still let it happen. From the moment I helped him take Chungi I knew Xian would lose more than it's ever lost before," she stopped to swallow and take a breath. "We weren't going to prevent this. We couldn't. My dream wasn't a warning to stop it. It was to prepare for the victory that follows."

Kang-Dae wanted to believe that but he couldn't. They'd lost far too much. How could they ever truly recover in their lifetime? Serenity handed him the staff and went to grab another off the rack. She held it up in a defensive stance waiting for him. Kang-Dae let out an exasperated sigh.

"No, you should go back and rest," he told her, not willing to take the chance of hurting her. She didn't like the suggestion and came at him with staff raised. On instinct, he brought his up to block before the staff could connect to his face.

"Fight," she ordered him. Annoyed at her insistence, he lowered the staff once more.

"I said no. I'm not going to fight you."

She did it again, only this time aiming for his knees. He, once again, blocked it with ease but was getting more agitated. By the time she swung at his side, forcing him to move, he was borderline angry.

She repeated herself, "fight."

"Serenity," he said in a hard tone. She didn't appear to be listening based on the determined and angry look in her eyes. She just charged at him full speed, ready to bring the staff down on his head. He grabbed it out of the air and snatched it from her hands.

"Enough!" He shouted, not wanting to do this with her. He tossed the staff to the ground, wrongly assuming she would stop without her weapon. Instead, she charged at him once again with her shoulder pushing him back against the wall, her elbow hitting him in the stomach making him bend over in pain. He struggled to get a breath. Before he could right himself, she was pushing him up, and holding him trapped with the staff he had dropped.

"Fight. With. Me."

Still breathing past his pain, he tried to understand what she was saying. He repeated her words in his mind. As he stared down at her desperate watery eyes taking in her words, her actions, and he finally understood. He debated with himself, trying to respond. He knew what she wanted but it was hard, hard to forget, hard to believe. His hesitance made her angry all over again. He thought she might hit him once more. When her lips forced themselves on his he was frozen in shock. She kissed him hard, like she was desperate for him to understand. Full of adrenaline, anger, anxiety, a need to protect, and a need to prove himself, Kang-Dae grabbed at the back of her neck and brought her closer but didn't overtake her kiss. She reached up and wrapped her hands in his hair. She was kissing him to remove every dark night of their separation, every whisper of doubt of her trust in him. She was erasing every lie that tried to come and claim he no longer deserved her. She pulled back abruptly leaving him breathless.

Serenity jumped on her toes, pulled at his robe, and latched onto the skin on his collarbone. Kang-Dae let out a gasp as she kissed and sucked on whatever she could reach. Her hand trailed out of his hair and down his chest. When it snuck its way into his loose pants he almost fell over. She didn't stop her assault on his neck as her hand moved indecently inside his clothes.

"Serenity," he moaned, unable to stay silent. This was a side of her rarely seen. In fact, he would have a hard time remembering her ever behaving so wantonly as he was used to being the aggressor in their bedroom. When she pulled back and removed her hand, he felt immediately bereft but his disappointment didn't last as she quickly shed her outer robe and the pants beneath her skirt. Following her lead, he started to remove his robe. She was back fast, helping him push the material down and tossing it across the room. Neither bothered with his shirt, both going for his pants at the same time. He worked at the belt while she pushed them down just far enough. He pulled her to him, grabbed her by her thighs and hoisted her up. He spun them both around and pushed her until her back hit the wall. She held herself up by his neck as he balanced her with one arm grabbing hold of himself. When he thrust into her, he felt better than he had in weeks. No pain, no weakness or dizziness. Just perfect love. Serenity's mouth formed a silent oh as she clung to him, her nails pressing into his neck.

"More," she begged with a whisper. Kang-Dae was more than happy to oblige. He pulled out almost completely before joining them forcefully. They both cried out. She moaned, he gasped. He did it again, and when she took it upon herself to start moving against him, on him, he almost disappointed both of them but he managed to keep his control. She kissed him like she had before, matching his rhythm with her mouth. When his knees could no longer take it, they buckled and the two fell to the floor. Serenity didn't let that distract her. She pushed him onto his back, straddled his lap, and joined them intimately once more. He grabbed hold of her waist as she rode him with vigor. Her hand took hold of his shirt, crumpling the material in an unyielding grip while she used her other hand that lay on his thigh for support to push herself harder and faster on top of him. She was saying something, something he couldn't catch. He was almost too into his own pleasure to notice. Needing to hear it he sat up taking control of her rhythm with his hands while he kissed her neck. "Yours, I'm yours," she was chanting over and over. The impact of those words, the reassurance, and the utter trust she still had in him drove him to the edge. He cradled her head and rolled them over until he was on top thrusting even harder than before. He raised her leg, gripping her thigh, going faster, deeper. He heard a dark rumble building from his own chest. This was the only heaven he would find in this world. That's what she was, what they were. Her gasps became full on cries, only getting louder and higher. She was close and so was he. Like they always should, he was going to make sure they went over together. He pressed his pelvis into her in just the right way and he felt her body react viciously triggering his own release. Her scream was anything but quiet and it was only drowned out by his own shout.

He was weak again, but now he welcomed it. They lay entangled, sweaty, and struggling for breath. He knew he was probably crushing her and knew he should move but everything in him wanted him to stay, stay with her, in her, to never lose this connection again. She didn't seem to mind as her arms wrapped around his neck holding him close. Eventually he figured he had to make the hard choice and do what was best for her still recuperating form. He slowly moved off her and plopped onto his side next to her. Not ready to stop touching her he grabbed her hand in his. With what seemed like great effort she rolled onto her side to face him. She didn't say anything at first, only regarding him with eyes he knew so well, so much so he knew she was not only thoroughly satisfied, but determined as well.

"Together. We have to be together," she said once she could. "We have to fight together. We have to believe together. You can't doubt you, or us or we really won't make it." It may have been the aftereffects of what they'd just done. Or the sincerity in her eyes, or maybe she'd done what she set out to do and used her body to force him into submission. He didn't know which but he felt like he could believe what she was saying. He raised her hand to his face and kissed it.

"I understand," he told her and he knew he meant it. These past weeks locked in the fortress being told over and over that he was losing, not having her, his health, his friend, his home. It was easy to slip into a defeated state. He stupidly allowed himself to forget all they'd faced and came through before. Without her by his side he started to let go of all the things she'd taught him and all the hope she'd brought him. Serenity once told him that her God's promise was like a mandate over one's life. If you followed the rules it had to come true, even when it looked like it couldn't possibly happen. 'That was the miracle of him,' she'd said. He'd forgotten the promise, the dream they held onto in any moment of doubt. If he believed they would come through this, they would.

CHAPTER 48

"Kimela! Kimela!" Rielle could hear someone shouting from outside. She had finally managed to sit up and was eating a small dish she had been brought. Like Safara had promised, she was feeling much stronger.

"Mama, they caught one!" The young girl came running inside yelling. No older than ten, she wore her hair in pretty braids with gold thread intermixed within the hair. She had white markings similar to Safara on both her cheeks. Safara caught the girl before she could fall over her own feet.

"Careful," she admonished. "What is it?"

"An Anoekan, they found one near the village."

Panic filled Rielle and her bowl slipped from her unsteady hands. Safara came over quickly and laid a comforting hand on her shoulder.

"Do not fear. We will not let them harm you," she assured her. Rielle wanted to believe her but having dealt with them so recently had her doubting. Especially since she was told they wouldn't step foot on this land. The thought gave Reille pause. Had they?

"Can you take me to them? She asked, needing to see if her hunch was true.

Safara looked unsure for a second before nodding. She helped Rielle up and they stepped out. It was the first time she was seeing the village. Even though it was night, there were numerous torches and lamps hanging up. There were dozens of structures and huts if you could call them that. They were much larger than the ones she'd seen in movies or commercials. Some even interconnected, making them into an even larger structure. All of them were painted with intricate and unique designs. The path was lined with jasmine flowers bringing a pleasant smell with the breeze. Rielle was led through the village to the largest structure. Its triangular shape reminded her of old school churches.

The similarities continued inside with rows of long cushions evenly spread to face the front where an altar stood. Before the altar were two very large, intimidating men. One wore his thick hair in large locs while the other was bald. They stood facing something on the ground but Rielle couldn't see what. "Move aside!" Safara spoke in a voice so commanding Rielle flinched. Even the large men seemed to shrink at the tone, moving without question. On seeing a kneeling Jung-Soo Rielle, got a burst of energy and ran toward him.

"Hey," she said softly, putting her hands on his shoulders. He slowly looked up at her. It seemed to take him a second to register who she was. When he did, Rielle could see it in his eyes. He immediately started trying to get up, even though he was bound. One of the men stepped over threateningly. Rielle blocked him with her arms spread wide.

"He's not Anoekan," she said pleadingly. The man's lips curved and the other sucked his teeth. Rielle turned to Safara for help. "He's not.

He's one of the people I came here with. He's from Xian. They're at war with the Anoekans."

Safara's jaw clenched as she took in Rielle's words. "Then why is he here if they are at war?" The male asked.

Rielle realized she had to choose her words very carefully.

"We were on our way to find the Anoekan king to get him to stop the attack on Xian."

"Which one?" the bald man asked.

"What?"

"There are three. One in the west, South and east," explained the one with the locs.

"He would have only just been appointed a couple of years ago," Jung-Soo spoke up.

"The South. There was a time we saw many of their ships leaving. We had hoped they were finally abandoning the land but many stayed."

"I would not bother with the Southern king; their people do not know anything of honor or peace. The Western king may be of more help."

"It is true he is more…reasonable than the others."

"Enough," Safara said. Both men went quiet. "Leave us," she ordered the other men. They hesitated for just a second before complying.

When the men were gone, she untied Jung-Soo and together she and Rielle helped him stand.

"There's another, Hae-In, one of my men, he was hurt. I left him hidden on the beach," Jung-Soo said.

"I'll have someone bring him. Come," she beckoned. "You can sleep here for the night."

Rielle helped Jung-Soo up and the two followed Safara. She took them into a small empty hut. There was a small but comfortable-looking bed in the corner and a little wooden table on the other side. Rielle helped Jung-Soo into the chair. She immediately began checking him for injuries, looking over his body and head as she kneeled in front of him. He tried to wave her off, claiming he was fine but she just needed to be sure. Safara left them, saying she would be back with food for Jung-Soo. Rielle thanked her and turned her attention back to him. She felt the back of his head and when her fingers touched a small but noticeable knot, she pulled his head toward her. Jung-Soo fought against her, jerking his head back.

"You're hurt," she argued.

"The wound will heal. Their powder did more than anything."

'Powder?' Rielle questioned in her head.

She went to call for Safara hoping she'd have something to help with the swelling but Jung-Soo pulled at her wrist. "Stay," he said. Now Rielle was really concerned he may have brain damage because she could not believe her ears. She kneeled back in front of him.

"Do you feel dizzy? Nauseous?" she rattled off symptoms trying to determine if he was concussed. He denied them all. He let out a yawn and looked to be closing his eyes but Rielle needed to know the extent of his injury before she let him sleep.

"Jung-Soo," she called out but he didn't respond. She tried again and still nothing.

"Hey General!" she shouted and his eyes fluttered open. She felt bad seeing how tired they were but not that bad. She forced him up out of the chair and made him walk around the tiny hut with her. She asked him things about recent events, testing his memory. He seemed to recall everything so she went back further asking about their first meeting.

"What shoulder did I stab you in?"

"You barely scratched me and it was the left," he answered, coming to a stop. She looked up at him trying to determine if she was comfortable with his answer and his health.

"Fine," she acquiesced, leading him to the bed. He collapsed into it, his eyes closing as soon as his head hit the pillow. She went to sit at the table.

"Stay," he said again. This time it was softer. From how calm his breathing was and the fact that his eyes were still closed she might've thought he was asleep. She lay her hand on his shoulder.

"I'm right here," she told him. She patted his shoulder until his breathing became deep and she was sure he was sleeping. Even then she just sat down with her legs beneath her and lay her head on the bed near his face, watching him, just to make sure he kept breathing, so she told herself.

CHAPTER 49

Serenity had gathered some of the children in the courtyard to get them some fresh air. The parents and civilians were off helping to keep things sorted and take inventory. The last group sent out for supplies had yet to return. It could be something as simple as a delay, maybe they had to take a longer route to avoid detection. Or it could have been the very worst-case scenario. They had no way of knowing until they appeared, or didn't. Blessing was crawling around from child to child as they took turns playing with her. She was glad the younger children didn't have a strong grasp on what was going on. Their playground being a literal fortress was a depressing fact but they didn't seem to be very phased. People say kids are resilient and she hadn't known how true that was until now. By the wall, Kang-Dae was meeting with his soldiers, designating their tasks and positions. By now Katsuo must have realized she had escaped which meant he would be scouring the whole world to find her and most likely kill her for Sho.

"They're returning!" The man on the high lookout reported from his post. Kang-Dae and her locked eyes and she smiled at him. Their problems could be pushed off a couple more weeks. It took a while for the men to make it up into the fortress. When they came spilling out into the courtyard with their sacks of food and supplies, they looked exhausted like they'd been running for days.

"They spotted us, on the way back," one panted out.

"We thought the east path was clear but they were there. Dozens of them. Like they were searching for us."

'Not them,' thought Serenity grimly.

"We ran with as much as we could. We had to abandon the rest."

Someone came up to them offering them all water and they drank heavily.

"We had to go through the city to lose them. It was destroyed. They burnt so much of it."

Serenity went to take Kang-Dae's hand knowing that news would be hard for him to hear.

"Are you sure you weren't followed?" he asked them, voice tight, trying to hold back his anger.

"We lost them. We had to have. They wouldn't let us go," one of the other men reasoned. Serenity and Kang-Dae shared a look.

There was another reason they were able to make it back. A horrible one.

"Gather every soldier, along with every able-bodied man, and bring them inside the walls. Clear out the armories and prepare all the weapons!"

"My king?" one soldier questioned.

"We need to be prepared for an attack."

***

Katsuo sat on his throne with his legs hanging over the side. The room was empty, no guards, no servants. He didn't want to see any of them. Just seeing their faces made him want to run them through. They were useless, all of them. Only able to betray him or cost him everything. That's what it felt like. He looked over to the empty space where Sho used to stand. Even he had betrayed him. His stupidity and disobedience got him killed and now he was all alone. He missed his home. It had been so long, he had forgotten the smell of it, the feel of its air. This was the cost of his destiny, Sho's voice whispered in his mind. He was told he had a greater role than to be a partial king of one nation. The world was to be his kingdom. That was what he said back when he had just been a child of 8 years. He reminded him, when his mother returned to the palace with his little brother after so many years. He told him that when his father's mind began to decline and the healers could not figure out why. He told him when he took the crown. He told him when he made him orchestrate the death of his own brother. He told him when he set him on this journey despite everyone else's warnings and objections. Even when they'd threatened to take his crown he didn't care because Sho told him he'd have a greater one. He had assured him he would return one day as the hero who united the world.

He didn't feel like a hero. He hadn't felt like one in a very long time. Katsuo tossed his cup across the room. Who said this world deserved to be saved? He thought bitterly. Look what trying to save it had gotten him. A disgusting face, treacherous people all around him, the loss of the woman he was to marry, their child, his brother, his mother.

He sent his men out to bring his dream walker back, not to punish her as he initially thought. Try as he might he could no longer raise any emotion over Sho's murder after all he'd done to his life. If he were to grab even a piece of what he was promised he would need her. If all he had, if all he could have now was this throne, this piece of the world, he would keep it. With his dream walker queen at his side the people would have to submit.

After everything they would have to take it from his corpse before he gave it up.

"My king!" one of his soldiers came running in. Katsuo turned his narrowed eyes toward him. The soldier quickly went to his knees. "We found where they are hiding."

Katsuo smiled at the news and slowly sat up. "Prepare the men."

CHAPTER 50

The first thing Jung-Soo thought when he
woke up was that he had to get to Anoeka. It took a
few seconds to remember where he was. He opened
his eyes to remind himself but saw a mass of
familiar black hair. He recalled his injury and
Rielle's insistence. He felt a small twitch of his lips.
She must have stayed with him all night. He wanted
to touch her. The thought came out of nowhere. It
was a ridiculous notion, but the urge was so strong
he already felt his hand reach out to touch one of
the pieces of hair closest to him. Luckily, he
realized what he was doing and practically slammed
his hand back down. Maybe her concern about his
head had merit, he thought. He wiped his face in an
attempt to remove any trace of lethargy left in him.
He'd wasted more than enough time. He still
needed to find his way into Anoeka lands. He stared
down at Rielle who had yet to stir. Maybe he could
convince these people to let her stay as he went on.
He would never have told her before but he never
had any intention of bringing her into enemy

territory. His original idea had been to leave her waiting on the ship, with that plan now scattered across the sea, this seemed a good alternative. Despite their hostile meeting they didn't seem to bare Rielle any ill will. That Assani woman seemed kind enough and was possibly willing to look after her considering all she had done for them already. Perhaps he could speak to her before Rielle awoke and make a deal.

That plan was instantly forgotten when the woman herself came through the door. Rielle began to shift and frown like she was insulted because she'd been woken out of her sleep. Her eyes opened and fell on Jung-Soo. He didn't know what to say or do so he did nothing. Her eyes shifted, taking in their surroundings and she slowly lifted her head. Trying to avoid looking at him and failing awkwardly, adorably.

"El Eloah bless you," Safara said. Jung-Soo assumed it was some kind of greeting amongst their people. He nodded in return. Rielle looked like she was struggling to get up. Jung-Soo reached out to steady her. Like a switch, her eyes went from awkward avoidance to concerned healer.

"Is your head okay? How'd you sleep?" She asked suddenly. Jung-Soo almost laughed at the shift in her.

"I am fine," he told her.

"You both are welcome to join us for breakfast or I can have something brought," Safara offered.

"Where's Hae-In?" Jung-Soo asked, remembering the state in which he'd left him.

"Your friend is resting comfortably in our healing room. He has been well cared for."

Jung-Soo wouldn't feel settled until he saw him for himself. He started to move to do just that but Rielle stopped him. "Just wait a few minutes," she advised. "Give your body a chance to catch up with your big head."

"I've discussed with my people about your intentions. If you still wish to enter the Anoeka lands we may be able to help you," Safara stated. Both Rielle and Jung-Soo looked up at that.

Safara approached Rielle and gently pulled her to her feet before taking Rielle's place in front of Jung-Soo. She stared at him for an uncomfortably long time. Jung-Soo never let his gaze waver but he wanted to look away. Something in the woman's gaze was too much. There was wisdom there, wisdom that seemed well beyond her years. There was knowledge in them, supernatural otherworldly knowledge, like she could see straight into his mind and beyond.

"You are a great warrior," she stated it as if it was a fact she'd known for years. Her gaze went to Rielle, lingering only a second before she turned her attention back to Jung-Soo. "and you have a leader's blessing." Jung-Soo felt as confused as Rielle looked. "I can have you escorted to the East king's lands. There will have to be a price."

"What do you want?" Jung-Soo asked, willing to agree to anything to achieve his mission.

"There is a place I need you to go, and someone I need you to bring to me," Safara said.

"Where is this place?" Jung-Soo asked, becoming more hesitant to agree.

"It is not as far as it seems but further than you'd like." Jung-Soo was losing his patience.

"We do not have time to waste. Our people need help now," he told her, trying to express the urgency of their situation but Safara's face never changed.

"If it helps, time may not be an issue," she offered mysteriously.

"What does that mean?" Rielle asked. Safara didn't answer.

Jung-Soo shook his head. "No, I cannot. This must be done now. I cannot waste any more time."

"We *could* do this favor for you now, if you wish, with the promise you will return to pay your debt."

"I'll do it," Jung-Soo quickly accepted without a thought.

"Wait a minu-," Rielle began.

"We need to leave as soon as possible," Jung-Soo said, effectively cutting off Rielle.

"In order for me to convince my people to help you must give some assurances," Safara said.

"I've already agreed."

"What guarantee will they have that you will return?" She asked seriously. Jung-Soo hesitated before responding.

"My word."

"That will not be enough," Safara told him.

Rielle felt her chest constricting and her stomach felt tight.

"It's all I have."

"They won't trust you."

It was getting a little hard for her to breathe.

"Just point me in the right direction and I will go on my own."

"I'll stay," Rielle said it so quietly because she secretly hoped she wouldn't be heard. Two heads turned toward her. "I can stay, be your leverage, until he can come back. You have my word."

"No," objected Jung-Soo.

At the same time, Safara responded with "done," a hint of a smile on her face.

"I said no." Jung-Soo's voice rose, but it seemed both women were determined to ignore him now.

"I will inform my people. You will leave with the rise of the sun."

Before Jung-Soo could object anymore, she left them alone. "You are not staying here," he stated as soon as she was gone.

"Let's be real, taking me through their lands was always going to be a huge risk. This is better."

"We do not know these people," he said, completely ignoring how he had planned to do almost the very exact thing only a few minutes ago. "You realize it could be months. If I am to seek the new king's aid, to get him back to Xian in time, I would have to leave with them. I won't be able to return until Katsuo has been dealt with."

"You're the one volunteering for secret missions for people you don't know. I'm just following your lead," she responded defiantly.

"We're leaving. We can sneak out and be gone before they know," he said, grabbing her wrist and heading toward the door. Rielle twisted her arm until she was free.

"No. You gave your word and I gave mine. This is happening. If you're that worried, just make sure to come back," she said nonchalantly.

"You have no idea what could happen," he attempted to reason with her.

"Please! I was on the same ship as you. And in case you forgot I spent days being held as a slave by those people as well as almost being killed by them multiple times. I'm not stupid. I know the risks. I knew them when I came."

"Why did you come?!" he demanded.

"To make sure you made it back!" She snapped. "I didn't want to be back home or even in Xian waiting to hear word you were dead or alive. I needed to see for myself. I needed to be with you." She said the last part so softly it could have been a whisper. She didn't look at him. Her eyes were purposely downcast trying to keep him from determining the truth of her words but he didn't need to. He could hear it in her voice.

Rielle could hear him releasing a frustrated breath. Before she knew it, she was in his arms as he wrapped one arm around her shoulders pressing her into him. So shocked by the action she stood frozen for a few seconds before she slowly returned the embrace.

"I can look after Hae-In while you're gone," she said in a lighter tone.

"You think they would accept him as their leverage," he asked in a tone that had the barest hints of joking. Rielle let out a short laugh.

"Damn, I should have thought of that."

CHAPTER 51

Outside the room Serenity could hear all the heavy footsteps of people and soldiers running around. The shouts and cries of fearful citizens tugged at her heart but did not distract her. She watched Kang-Dae tighten his armor. He looked down for his sword, but it was already in her hand as she held it out to him. With an appreciative grin he accepted it and put it into his sheath.

"They're about to breach the walls!" Someone yelled from behind the door, drawing Serenity's gaze. With a gentle hand, Kang-Dae turned her face towards him. Refocusing, she cradled his face in her hand.

"Make it quick," she demanded, refusing to show any fear or doubt. Surprise entered his eyes for only a second before a confident smile spread across his face. With a quick movement, he grabbed her by the back of her head and brought her lips to his for a passionate, almost overwhelming kiss. He pulled away leaving her breathless.

"They are already dead," he promised. And she believed him.

With a final kiss on her forehead, he headed out into the fray.

***

The citizens all gathered in the deepest part of the mountain. The children had been pushed to the back near the only other way out through the tunnels. Serenity did as best she could to keep the people calm while helping out to ensure their safety. Blessing was with her grandmother in the safest part of the mountain. Serenity trusted her to protect her with her life. A small rumbling had the space going quiet. The few soldiers assigned to protect the people stood rigidly by the entrance, no doubt wishing to be a part of the battle.

"You should join the others in the back, my queen," the captain suggested. Serenity shook her head.

"Someone needs to keep order in here. If we lose it in here, it makes it harder for those out there fighting," she insisted.

The captain gave a nod of acceptance and directed his men to keep their composure. A couple of servants came by with a bucket of water but a rumble had them skirting to a stop which spilled half the water.

"Watch what you're doing!" one of the soldiers snarled. The young woman began stuttering out an apology but Serenity stopped her.

"It's alright. Go on, and make sure those in back have enough to go around." The woman bowed nervously and the two shuffled off. She turned her attention to the angry soldier whose eyes still held sharp anger, but Serenity wasn't fooled. The anger was a mask for the fear he refused to acknowledge.

Serenity turned to the captain and though she appeared to only be speaking to him, she made sure to speak loud enough that everyone in the vicinity could hear.

"When the enemy retreats we have to make sure the storeroom is restocked. If years down the line our children need this place for refuge, we must make sure it's still sustainable."

"When, my queen?" he asked curiously because of the word she chose.

"This is just a storm that passes and leaves clear skies in its wake. The dreams already assured me of it. Where there is war there is victory, and ours is already guaranteed. All the enemy can do is make it seem as though they have a chance, but it's a trick, a threat meant to make us falter. But we won't, they will." The room had now grown quiet for a different reason as those around hung on her every word. The soldiers stood a little taller and the people's postures eased ever so slightly.

***

"Second wave!" Kang-Dae screamed. A new line of archers stepped up to the front and pointed downward. The men attempting to make their way up their unsteady ladders tried in vain to press themselves as close to the mountain as they could. To even have a chance, the enemy had to bring their ladders half-way up the mountain on a very narrow ledge that could only hold so many people. The way the fortress was structured Kang-Dae and his men had the perfect view and angle. As the arrows were let loose multiple enemy soldiers cried out and fell to their deaths. Luckily, they had yet to stumble upon the entrance to the fortress so they continued with these useless methods to get over their walls. Kang-Dae had men ready at the tunnel just in case they made it through but it was barricaded and camouflaged to look like a part of the mountain.

"It's ready, my king!" A soldier shouted.

"Pull back!" Kang-Dae ordered the archers. As soon as they did, a new line of men holding steel pots took their place. One by one they began pouring. He heard some shrieks as hot oil must've hit more than a few of them. Once all the pots were empty Kang-Dae called for the next wave of archers. As they came forward, they took time to light the tips of their arrows before unleashing another slew. More screams sounded below. Kang-Dae looked over to see half the ladders had caught fire along with the men on them. As more of the enemy fell Kang-Dae could see the line of men waiting at the very bottom of the mountain, attempting to stay away from the falling bodies and debris.

Katsuo barely flinched as a flaming body fell only a few feet from him. With a sneer he turned back and moved a safe distance away while the men around him ran for cover. "Fire the catapults!" he commanded. He needed to cause damage.

"We can't get any to go over the wall," one of the soldiers responded. Katsuo glared at the man. He quickly cowered and went off to do as ordered. Katsuo watched as another bolder hit only about halfway up the mountain causing very little to no damage to the structure. They had used their most powerful explosives on the attack on the palace and what they had left was not strong enough. He secretly cursed Sho for his insistence on using so much of it.

"My king we are only losing men here," one brave man spoke up. Katsuo's first instinct was to cut him down. The need to get blood on his blade riding heavy on him but he held back. The soldier wasn't wrong and he was no fool. He could see their attack was futile, but the idea of falling back, knowing Kang-Dae would be watching with his smug expression thinking he'd bested him was not something he could tolerate.

"Find me another way in!" he ordered. There had to be a way in. There was no way they'd carried all their people up the mountain into the fortress. There was an entrance hidden somewhere and when they found it, he'd wipe the smile off of the weak king's face. Another slew of bodies fell, a mass of flesh and bone.

"Bring them down," he said in a softer tone, defeated. The horn sounding may as well have been the bellowing laugh of the enemy. A laugh at his failure, at his weakness. This had been a foolish endeavor fueled by his own rage and need for retribution. He could no longer afford to allow his feelings to rule over him. Without Sho, he needed to be careful and think through his actions. He knew the outcome of everything, he just had to get there.

CHAPTER 52

The sun had barely risen. They all stood at the edge of the village. Hae-In was still too weak to stand, so he had left him behind bidding him farewell as he lay in their so-called "healing room." He made the soldier promise to do what he could to keep Rielle safe, to which he agreed.

The guides he was setting off with, the same two who had attacked him, were waiting up ahead. Safara stood with Rielle who'd been given some of their clothing. A gold and blue skirt wrapped in such a way it left half her leg visible and a short blue top that left her shoulders and stomach bare. He did not like the idea of leaving her, even more so leaving her looking like that with men around, especially men with eyes.

"I pray your journey is fruitful," Safara said. Jung-Soo nodded to her. He turned to Rielle.

"Be quick," Rielle said, trying to sound casual but he could see the stress in her posture.

"I will return," he assured her and he meant it. If he failed or succeeded, he would not abandon her here. Probably sensing their discomfort, Safara smiled and began walking back to the village.

"Keep Hai-In alive as best you can."

"I will," Rielle promised.

"And yourself. Keep yourself alive. No matter what." Rielle nodded. She stepped forward and he braced himself for a hug but was even more shocked when she placed a kiss on his cheek.

"Come back," she whispered in his ear before pulling away. Jung-Soo had never been struck dumb in his life but at that moment, he forgot how to breathe.

"I-I will." He cleared his throat trying to clear away the embarrassment of his stutter. Not wanting to add to his shame he turned and walked off refusing to look back even for a second.

Rielle watched him walk away. She didn't doubt he would do everything in his power to make it back. Still, she would pray, daily, until he did.

CHAPTER 53

"This is as far as we go," the one called Tutoa spoke.

They'd made it to an opening overlooking a vast city. The buildings looked very much like Xian with subtle differences. Many of them sat high, built atop high elevations. "Over there," Fusi pointed to the highest and most impressive building. "That is where you'll find the Southern king."

"May El Eloah be with you," Tutoa told him. Jung-Soo thanked them for their help and set off into the city.

Jung-Soo was able to blend in easily. Their clothing styles were not unlike Xian. The city was bustling. They didn't appear to be lacking for much. Which made Katsuo's actions that much more deplorable. Was this kingdom not enough for him? According to Tutoa, he shared his throne with two others. Perhaps he got tired of sharing and sought a whole kingdom of his own. It didn't matter the motivation. He'd been a plague on his home for long enough. Jung-Soo prayed the new king would want to hold onto his title enough to help them.

The walk to the palace took hours. On the way he began to see more than a couple of abandoned homes that looked to have been damaged beyond repair. There were some houses still habitable as he could see from the people going in and out. But they were few and far between. No markets or stalls were in this desolate part of the city, Jung-Soo passed by more than one "Beware the Dogs" message painted on walls and broken doors.

As he made it back to a much more lively part of the city he finally came upon the palace. Built on a massive hill Jung-Soo had to crane his neck to see all of it. Extravagant, over the top, indulgent, those words all came to his mind as he stared at it. It was built to impress, that was clear to him. He approached the many steps leading up to the place. There were two rows of five guards standing in front of them. Behind them there was one guard on every other step leading all the way to the top. They were all armed, and they all looked decently trained. Jung-Soo approached the one on the end, dressed in golden armor.

"I have urgent news for the king."

The guard didn't even look his way. "The king is not taking supplications today. Come back next month."

"I don't have a request. I have a warning. From King Kang-Dae of Xian." Jung-Soo corrected. The man finally looked his way. For added effect Jung-Soo removed the letter from his shirt and showed the seal. The guard's eyes narrowed for a second before he replaced it with false indifference.

"Hase!" he called out. One of the soldiers on the lower step came forward.

"Escort him to the assembly hall. I will speak with her majesty."

'Her?' Jung-Soo questioned in his mind. The guard tried to grab Jung-Soo's shoulder but having enough of being detained he quickly slipped out of his hold in the most non-threatening way he could. He just gave the guard one look of warning not to try that again and began to walk up the steps as the other guards made an opening for them.

The inside of the palace was even grander than the outside. The large oversized double doors led into a massive room. There were stairways on opposite sides and one just ahead. He was taken behind the middle staircase down a very long hallway. They passed a few doors on the way and several entryways leading to various rooms. One seemed dedicated to just music as he saw a type of zither in the middle of the room. They walked until they reached another hall perpendicular to theirs. They traveled down the left side for another few minutes until they reached a room tucked in a back corner. The guard had him stand behind him but did nothing else. He stood waiting for something but Jung-Soo had no idea what.

Seconds rolled into minutes and Jung-Soo began to wonder if it would take hours. A muffled sound came from the other side, something akin to a gong. Once it did the guard opened the door and stood by for Jung-Soo to enter. Jung-Soo moved with urgency, not bothering to wait. He didn't let the opulence of the room slow his stride or the numerous eyes of staring men in noble attire. What gave him pause was the two thrones ahead of him. One seated a middle-aged woman in a fancy pink dress and a small gold headdress on her head. The second, a young boy dressed in green and black with a crown on his head clearly too big for him, with gold beads hanging low obscuring his face. The throne itself swallowed him up.

"Do Xians not show respect to royalty?" The woman spoke first. Jung-Soo bit back a response and went to his knee.

"Your majesty," he greeted.

"You have a message for me, pertaining my son?" The conqueror's mother. 'Perfect,' Jung-Soo thought sarcastically. Katsuo's replacement was a mere boy clearly under the influence of the woman beside him, a woman who happened to be the mother of their greatest enemy. Now he had to determine if revealing Katsuo's return would be a benefit to him. A new king would have been easier to reason with, but a grieving mother? Jung-Soo did not see this ending well.

"It would be best spoken without so many ears," Jung-Soo tried, not wanting to reveal such a thing to a room full of strangers when he had no idea where they would fall.

"These men are staples of our city. Without them we would have fallen years ago. They are privy to as much as I am."

"Your armies have been raging war on us and it needs to end," Jung-Soo announced, figuring that was as good a place to start.

"That war ended when you killed our last king. Whatever war is happening is among your own people. We have no responsibility to relegate your country," she spoke coldly.

"Your majesty, there *were* quite a few ships that failed to return," one of the men spoke.

"Killed by them no doubt. Unwilling to allow them the courtesy of returning to their home," she scoffed.

"They were enemies trying to overtake our lands," Jung-Soo gritted out, trying to keep calm, keeping his head bent not in respect, but to keep from rushing the throne.

"We find the actions of our previous king regretful," another man spoke out, causing the woman's head to snap towards him. He didn't seem fazed by her glare. "The campaign of King-, of *former* King Katsuo, was not approved by us, nor the other kings."

"Yet you did nothing to stop him," accused Jung-Soo addressing the old man. A couple of men shuffled in their seats and one cleared his throat.

"Our king was quite forceful," another spoke from the opposite side.

"With the backing of one of our most influential spiritual leaders, many of our military chose to follow him," a man with short hair and dressed in blue added.

"We did not want to make an enemy of Xian then or now."

"So, we will not interfere in any way," the mother of Katsuo said forcefully, voice tight. "Until we have proof it is our soldiers intruding on your lands."

Jung-Soo, having enough, finally stood and removed one of the signs he'd managed to salvage from the wreck. He walked up to the steps. He could hear the guards rushing over with the intention of stopping him. He tossed the parchment at the woman's feet.

"Stop!" It was the first time the boy had said anything and his small voice echoed throughout the room. The boy stood and reached down to pick the paper up. He removed the headdress as he read. Jung-Soo blinked.

"Ami?"

A Year Ago

Ami was sweeping out the small room. The small house he had once lived in with Iko, now only housed him. While many of the others who had lived in the town before Katsuo's invasion had left to move further into Xian, Ami had wanted to stay in the home he'd experienced most of his fond memories. It had been Iko who he'd been entrusted to after being smuggled out of Anoeka. At the time he had no idea what was happening and why he was being forced to leave his home. It wasn't until he was a few years older that Iko told him the truth so he could keep himself safe and understand the magnitude of danger they'd both be in if the truth was ever discovered. A letter a year was all he received from his mother in all the years he'd been in exile. He started having a hard time remembering the faces of those he left behind. Iko was good to him, and treated him like a real son. It was the only reason he had not grown up in despair and bitterness.

*Ami finished sweeping and went to prepare
something to eat. He would fish early in the
mornings and sell what he could while keeping a
little for himself. He slept very little. Every time he
closed his eyes he was haunted by his brother's
pleading and screams the last time he'd seen him.
He tried telling himself he should not feel guilty. He
had tried to kill him after all, he was not obligated
to save his would-be-murderer. But it did not stop
the screams from penetrating his nightmares. His
brother earned his fate, he knew that. His evil deeds
had just caught up with him. That darkness was
shared by their father as well. He wondered if he
too would eventually fall into those dark ways of
thinking. It was one of the reasons he'd declined to
stay with Serenity in the capital. What if the evil
soothsayer had been right and he became just as
power hungry as his brother? It was best for him to
stay far from any throne.*

*He checked on his fish, the pleasant smell
filling the room making his stomach growl. A knock
on the door put him on alert. He didn't get visitors,*

ever. No one visited the strange boy who lived by himself. Ami wanted to hide himself away, ignore them until they left.

"Prince Akimitsu! Please come out," a commanding voice called out to him, making Ami's heart stop. He'd been found but how? Katsuo was dead, who else could know of his existence? Had his followers come for revenge? He took off for the back of the house hoping to sneak out. He managed to open the back door without making much noise. He stepped out prepared to take off through the surrounding homes. Maybe he could get to a boat and barter passage south. He made it a few steps before two pairs of large boots entered his eyeline. Ami looked up into the faces of two big Anoekan soldiers, defeated.

The one on the left stared at him menacingly, while the other looked relieved to have found him.

"Prince Akimitsu, we've come to take you home, by order of the queen."

'Mother?' He had not heard from her since before his captivity. The urge to run away was heavy on him, though he doubted he could get far. His mother wanted him to return, but he didn't want to. Returning meant facing what he'd done, accepting all that had happened, and giving up who he'd been for most of his life. Ami would disappear, the boy Iko raised would be no more. He didn't want that, he didn't want to forget, he didn't want to be a prince again. Because he knew exactly what would come next and then he'd be back on that path his brother had sought to keep him from all those years ago.

***

The clothes they'd made him change into were heavy on him, not as heavy as the invisible weights he could feel cementing him in this place. He was led to the large doors of what he believed was the throne room. It had been so long he could hardly remember. He had yet to see his mother. Having been forced off the boat after days of travel, he had been taken straight into the palace and sent into a bedroom bigger than his and Iko's home. He slept off the travel and was awoken to several servants trying to feed and clothe him.

The doors were opened and Ami couldn't move. There was a group of men standing and staring at him, waiting on him. At the end, he could see a woman standing in front of the throne, his mother. The need to flee was on him again. Instead, he forced his feet forward keeping his eyes down, unable to look anyone in the face. Did they know? Were they angry about his return? He moved until the steps came into view. He saw her feet first and the hem of her pink gown. He felt her hand on his cheek next trying to force his eyes up but he resisted, still not ready to face it all. She finally won the battle and raised his face to meet hers. Staring into the familiar face of his mother after so many years was too much. He pulled back, having trouble breathing. He needed to leave, to run, go back to his real home. Before he could turn and run for the door his mother's hand was on his arm pulling him to her. She wrapped him up, holding him. He refused to cry, not wanting to show even more weakness in front of so many but he could not stop the tears especially as he heard his mother's voice for the first time in years.

"Welcome home my son."

The woman jumped from her throne.

"How dare you address our king in such a way!"

Ami finally looked at him. His eyes widened with recognition. "General Jung-Soo?"

Ami approached him despite the woman's attempt to hold him back.

"Is it true?" he asked, tears in his eyes. Jung-Soo nodded warily, still unsure as to what was going on.

"Everyone out!" the woman screeched, finally reaching her limit. The men took their time filing out. When the guards didn't move, she shouted at them as well and they too exited.

"Is Ser-," he paused. "Queen Serenity, okay?" Jung-Soo felt that tight feeling in his gut once more.

"The palace was attacked. Many were killed and the survivors were forced to seek refuge. Our king survives. We have not been able to locate our queen. If she survived, we fear she is in enemy hands," he informed the boy or king.

Ami's eyes darkened. The woman began tugging Ami harder. Ami turned to her.

"We need to do something," he told her. The woman looked indignant.

"This," she gestured to the paper, "means nothing." She snatched it out of his hands and threw it to the ground. "It's not proof. Even if it is," her voice faltered just a bit. "The moment he left this land against the advice of the assembly he forfeited his title and cut ties with our city."

"He was our king, your son, my brother. He wreaked havoc with our armies and he still is. It should be our responsibility," argued Ami. "He never should have been allowed to do so."

"We cannot spare the men. Your brother left us in a vulnerable position when he chased his so-called destiny. There are still those out there who would flock to him if they find out he's alive. You may cause more harm than good," she warned.

"We can ask the other kings for help. Their men have no allegiance to Katsuo," suggested Ami in a hopeful tone.

"You would have us lower ourselves and beg the other kings," she countered. Jung-Soo wanted to throttle her.

"I don't care about that!" shouted Ami, wrenching his arm from her hold.

"Serenity saved me. She helped Iko." The woman flinched at the woman's name.

"Katsuo's actions killed her. He tried to kill me. I'm going to stop him," Ami declared. "If you won't help me, I will not make you. But I am going to do this."

"I do not want to lose you again," she whispered, grabbing his hand this time. Ami looked at her, already tall enough to look her in the eyes.

"Then let me stop him. As long as he's out there you know I won't be safe, whether from him or those who support him."

The woman's harsh expression dropped momentarily. She touched Ami's face.

"Send word to the other kings," Ami told her. The softness slowly melted and the harsh look came back. She dropped her head and released his hand. She turned to Jung-Soo.

"Anoeka will hold Xian responsible if we lose another king in your lands."

Jung-Soo didn't respond. The queen mother stomped off leaving the two alone.

"Do you think she's, Serenity, do you think she's alright?" Ami asked, turning back into the young kid he'd met back then.

Jung-Soo answered truthfully. "I do not know."

"I wanted to tell her, but I was afraid she'd look at me like she looked at him," he confessed.

"She wouldn't. She cared," Jung-Soo corrected himself, "cares for you." Ami nodded and wiped at his eye.

"I can have my personal troop prepare to sail in a few days I think," he said as if he weren't entirely sure. The young king did not seem to be used to making orders. From what Jung-Soo saw of his mother, he could imagine why.

"Will the other kings be willing?" Jung-Soo asked.

"They never got along with my brother; I'm told. What he did in Xian only angered them more.

If they can help stop him for good, it would only make things easier for them."

Jung-Soo hoped he was right. And he prayed they could get back in time.

CHAPTER 54

Serenity, along with her mother-in-law were giving out the last of the bread along with some volunteers, a couple of noble women who had probably never even dressed themselves, and a few palace servants. It was a warming sight to see people of completely different statuses working together to help those who needed it, especially as they were all in need. Serenity had been on her feet all day and would kill to be able to just curl up in her old bed and pass out but she kept going. The reserves had some grain and dried meat left but it would probably only last another few days. Katsuo's men stayed posted a safe distance from the mountain, to keep anyone from being able to go out, at least not without alerting them to the entrance.

Kang-Dae and Serenity had been brainstorming with some of the others to come up with a solution. So far everything they could think of had very small chances of success and survival. Their most promising idea was to try and find the forgotten tunnel that ran under the mountain and supposedly led to the river. Unfortunately, no one living knew where the tunnel could be or the condition of it.

As she was giving a young girl her ration, she heard murmurs of objections in the crowd. Serenity frowned as she looked over to see a group of large soldiers barreling their way through the people without apology or remorse. The largest of the men came to them first. He reached out to snatch the bread out of the servant's hand. Serenity was faster as she snatched it herself. Looking him straight in the eye she handed the bread to the older man behind him who he had cut in front of. The man seemed to hesitate when he realized she was in the serving line but perhaps his bravado was too strong because he regained his attitude.

"We worked all night keeping the walls safe. We want our food now." His buddies behind him murmured their agreement. Serenity didn't bother looking up. She knew Kang-Dae was probably already looking down at her from over the second-story wall, where he was meeting with his military leaders. He might already be on his way down but it wouldn't be necessary, she decided.

In the back, she could see the other soldiers stationed on their floor about to come over to diffuse the situation but Serenity held her hand up to stop them, not wanting things to turn into a fight they could not afford.

"I appreciate what you're doing for us, we all do. Once everyone who has already been waiting gets their share, I will gladly give you yours. I promise we won't run out." She never raised her voice. She even managed to smile a bit. The leader almost took a step forward but then he must have remembered his place and went back to the young servant who had already made herself as small as she could.

"Give me it now!" he growled at her. She reached with a shaking hand to give into the man's demands and once again Serenity took the bread from her.

"I know things are dire. Many of you are scared and unsure of what will happen." The man's nostrils flared and his eyes flashed at the indication that he could ever be frightened. This time he did step to her. Serenity didn't move an inch.

"If it weren't for you, we wouldn't be here," he spat.

Serenity handed the bread to the child behind him, not acknowledging his words for the moment.

"Gyuri, make sure the people also know where to get their water rations for the day." The longer she ignored him the more rage he radiated.

She turned back to him. "If it weren't for me, Katsuo would've wiped you lot out over a year ago. If it weren't for me, your brothers in arms, your families, everything you swore to protect would be dead or slaves living only to cater to the whims of the Anoekans. If it weren't for your king that armor you so disgracefully represent would litter the ground as a trophy of the enemy's victory over you. If not for me, you would already be tossed over that wall showing your men what happens when you attempt to take advantage of an already bad situation while looking down on those you were meant to protect." His eyes displayed a trace of fear at this. "These are my people. Xian is my home. I have done and will continue to do what is best for everyone even when things are dark like they are now. If you refuse to be a part of that. If serving under a queen like me is not to your liking that's fine. But you will not disrespect these people, your king, or me and think you will continue to enjoy the safety and shelter within this fortress. So, either get in line, take your chances outside the fortress, or I will personally toss you over that wall myself!" He balked for a second, like he was considering if she were capable of doing it. She never faltered nor broke eye contact just so he could see how dead serious she was. She may be smaller but she had plenty of anger built up over the last few months and that was all the motivation she needed to pull it off. She could see that Kang-Dae had arrived.

Judging from the smirk on his face he had heard her little threat. The soldier turned to his men, probably to get their support but none of them were willing to even look at him. Like a beaten dog the 6'3 man slunk back into the crowd and walked away. He must've caught sight of Kang-Dae cause out of nowhere he picked up speed and did a ridiculous race walk into the fortress.

"Let's keep moving," she told the ladies and the line continued, like nothing had happened.

Kang-Dae made his way over along with Captain Kahil and the two grabbed some bread and began handing some out. Serenity smiled up at him and he did the same. Things weren't necessarily good, in fact, they were probably in the worst positions they'd ever been in, but they were still standing and they knew they would continue to do so.

***

Pounding at the door of the room he'd been given, awoke Jung-Soo. He looked over at the window and saw the moon was still out. He shook off his slumber and went to the door.

"The king ordered you to dress and for us to escort you to the docks."

Jung-Soo squinted, still trying to comprehend what was happening. They weren't meant to leave until tomorrow when the Western king's men would arrive. Still, he did as he was told and dressed. After riding to the dock, the sun was starting to rise in the distance. He came upon Ami who was watching as men loaded the ships in a rush.

"What's happening?" he asked.

"Katsuo's return has reached the people."

"How?" Jung-Soo demanded. Ami shook his head.

"I don't know. Two ships snuck out late last night."

Most likely full of Katsuo supporters, surmised Jung-Soo.

"I figured we needed to leave as soon as possible even without the other men."

"You made a wise decision," he assured the young king. He didn't want to dwell on the how of the situation especially if it turned out his own mother was involved of which Jung-Soo had his suspicions but it could have easily been anyone else. There was no way to know and they had no time to figure it out. Xian could not fight off another wave in its current state. Their best bet was to defeat Katsuo for good, eliminating any other options for the supporters and placing the crown firmly on Ami. Though they had a head start Jung-Soo had the benefit of knowing exactly where to go. He helped them load up and surprisingly Ami did the same. The king liked to get his hands dirty it seemed.

CHAPTER 55

Rielle checked on Hae-In's wound; the big baby wouldn't stop squirming. She popped him on his shoulder for the third time. He had the nerve to pout and rub at the nonexistent bruise. "Then stay still," she scolded. "I'm almost done." Only a couple of days had passed since Jung-Soo had left them. There was a small part of her that regretted her decision but she couldn't find it in her to completely lament it. She believed he would succeed in his mission. If anyone could, he would, she knew that, knew him. The doubts would sometimes creep in reminding her of her obligations back home and what she would be missing but when she really thought about it, she realized she didn't have much to return to. A job she hated and was overqualified for? A nonexistent boyfriend? A home that was never hers? The only family she had who'd even notice her absence also belonged to Serenity. It led to a sobering and depressing question. 'Who was she without Serenity?' Had she really built her life around her one true friend? The thoughts threatened to send her into a slump so she had to repeatedly push it out of her mind, never wanting to dwell on it. Or deal with it.

After she was done, she moved to rewrap Hae-In's leg. Safara, who'd been on the other side of the room, came over. Rielle had the feeling she had been watching her the entire time.

"Here, this will help," she told her, handing her a bowl with a red paste.

"What is it?" Rielle asked skeptically. She didn't distrust Safara. She believed she wanted to help but from what she knew about medical practices without modern medicine on her Earth she didn't know if she could accept something that could be completely useless or harmful to Hae-In.

Safara knelt down next to her and dug her finger into the paste. "Bani plant root. Good for pain and it protects the blood. She smeared some on his stitches which Rielle had done with Safara's guidance. Hae-In flinched in a more believable way. Rielle winced in empathy. She did it until the wound was covered. Rielle couldn't help noticing he'd stop jumping at the third swipe and he didn't appear to be in any discomfort.

"What is it called again?" Safara let out a breathy laugh.

"Here," she handed her the bowl. "We will go out later and I will show you where it grows and how to prepare it."

Rielle accepted the bowl and nodded. "Okay." Safara stood and went back to where she had been. Rielle could hear her washing her hands in the basin.

"How do you feel?" She asked Hae-In. She pointed at his leg. "You okay?" He nodded enthusiastically.

He gestured to his leg. "No pain," he told her.

Rielle's brows raised in astonishment. There was a lot about this world she still didn't know. Before, any curiosity she had was stamped down from trying to survive. She was starting to let her curious nature surface. If she was going to be stuck here, it wouldn't hurt to learn some things, she reasoned. She rewrapped his leg and helped him up. They hobbled out of what was known as the healing room and went just a couple of huts down to the community hut. The tribe used it for their meetings and gatherings when the weather wasn't great but they had been allowing Hae-In to take up residence there for the time being. Safara had allowed Rielle to stay in the healing room, something that must not have been normally done as people gave her strange looks every time they saw her come out. Maybe it was because she was a stranger but Rielle just felt there was more to it.

After helping Hae-In sit on one of the two benches they'd pushed together to make him a "bed" she went to grab his woodworking tools. Hae-In was a very talented whittler, she learned. When Safara had complimented the wooden figure on his necklace he'd confessed to making it himself. To keep his mind occupied, as Safara put it, she had sent him some tools and blocks of wood. He spent most of the day doing it. She turned back to see Hae-In smiling and waving at someone. She looked toward the entrance and saw a small boy, no older than four, peeking his head in. The boy shyly waved at him before Safara's daughter Niobi, pulled him away. It was her first time seeing him. She'd seen many of the children running around during the day, all very young. The older ones only seem to appear after sunset. She wondered if they went to school. From what she heard there were several other villages within walking distance of the Umbala. Rielle handed Hae-in his tools. She told him she'd check on him later and stepped outside. Women walked by with large buckets on their heads with ease. There was a small group of men sitting in front of a hut talking and laughing. Up ahead the children were running around chasing Niobi, who was the only older kid around at the moment. She wondered why that was. She could hear singing coming from the edge of the village. Harmonious voices rang out as the women hung up and beat at clothes. Of all the places to be stuck in, Rielle felt she could do a lot worse.

CHAPTER 56

Everyone was in a tizzy as they prepared for a full attack inside the fortress. When the first line of soldiers that had been left to keep them from escaping the fortress disappeared, they thought it was strange, but figured they would once again return after failing to find a way in as they always did, but when they didn't and the second line disappeared it raised alarms in the lookouts. When the tunnel guards announced movement from inside everyone sprang into action. Citizens were sent into the mountain, soldiers took positions. Men stood at the entrance with large sledgehammers ready to try and bring the tunnel down, a last resort they hoped not to enact. Kang-Dae waited in front with his men. He had been dreading this moment and still was wondering how they found a way in. Whether it was just bad luck or something more sinister at play. It didn't change what was heading for them right in that moment so he put it in the back of his mind. Crossbows and arrows were already aimed toward the dark entrance in case they made it through.

Light from a flame could be seen approaching in the distance.

"Men!" Kang-Dae shouted, ready to give the order to collapse the entrance.

"General Jung-Soo reporting!" A voice shouted from within the tunnel.

"Hold!" Kang-Dae screamed. He slowly went forward. "Jung-Soo?" he questioned, hopeful yet cautiously.

"It's me! Stand down. I've brought some help." The collective relief was felt among everyone present. It took some time for Jung-Soo to finally appear. When he did, Kang-Dae clasped his hand and gave him a hug.

"You made it back," he said jovially.

"And you're looking a lot better," Jung-Soo remarked as they pulled away.

"My king!" One of the men shouted, pointing his bow back toward them, except it wasn't them he was pointing at but those emerging behind them. Men in Anoekan-styled armor were coming out. More of his men followed suit ready to fire.

"Stand down!" Jung-Soo repeated. "They're not with Katsuo," he explained.

When a familiar face came out, Kang-Dae did a double take.

"Ami?"

Ami almost went to his knees but seemed to remember something and only gave a short bow of the head.

"King Kang-Dae," he addressed him in a deeper voice since the last time he saw him. He'd grown a couple of inches and had put on a little more muscle but he still stood as a child to him.

"Meet the new king of southern Anoeka," Jung-Soo said dryly, gesturing to the boy. Kang-Dae looked to Jung-Soo, back to Ami, and back to Jung-Soo. Jung-Soo nodded, confirming what he said was true.

"Wh-How?"

"Questions best saved for later," Jung-Soo said. "We've brought more supplies and taken care of the men down there, but we need to set up a perimeter to keep them from trying to block us in once more."

Now that they had more numbers it would be possible, Kang-Dae thought. He gave the order and the men went off.

"Come, there's someone you both should see. And you," he stared pointedly at Ami. "have a very important story to tell, I imagine." Ami's cheeks pinkened slightly and he gave a little nod.

When Kang-Dae sent for her to come out, Serenity wondered if the fighting was already over. She rushed through the halls to the courtyard. There were many men still standing in position but others seemed to have moved elsewhere. She saw the back of Kang-Dae's head and headed toward him as he was engaged in a conversation with someone in front of him.

"What's going on?" She asked. Kang-Dae paused mid-sentence and turned to her with the most mischievous smile she'd seen him give in weeks. With her head tilted she came closer. As he took a step to the side she gasped and her hands went over her mouth.

"Serenity?" Two sets of voices whispered. Jung-Soo stared at her like she was a ghost. Little Ami was already rushing toward her. She barely had time to open her arms as he launched himself into her. Serenity wrapped her arms around him.

"Hi!" she said, trying to keep her voice from cracking. Ami just held her tighter.

"I was afraid you were dead. That he'd taken you," he whispered. Serenity rubbed his back soothingly.

"I'm okay. I'm here. He'll never have me again," she swore.

"I won't let him," Ami declared once he pulled away. Kang-Dae let out a short laugh.

"We appreciate that King Ami," he said amused.

"King?!" Serenity shouted so loud her throat throbbed. Ami looked down sheepishly.

"There's some things I never told you," he said. Serenity stared at him.

"Is that so?" Serenity looked up to tell Kang-Dae he had been right in his assumption she had no idea what Ami was going through when she noticed Jung-Soo still frozen, staring at her. She left Ami and went over to him. She took his hand in his. "I'm here. I'm real." Then she pulled him in for a hug. He continued standing unmoving. It was when she moved to pull away that his arms finally wrapped her up so tight she was finding it hard to breathe but she didn't complain.

Later Ami filled her and Kang-Dae in on his origins and how Katsuo had tried to have him killed as a child to "protect" his throne. She remembered Katsuo confessing to her vaguely about things he'd done to ensure his "destiny." She realized that was what he was alluding to. It was one of the few times she saw genuine remorse in him. She felt so bad for Ami, having to live with that knowledge and now being forced to rule at such a young age. No wonder his communications were so few and vague.

Jung-Soo informed them of the cadre of soldiers making their way to throw in with Katsuo. Serenity tried not to become worried and she remembered the dream she'd had over a year ago when she'd been forcibly held by Katsuo and the spectacle she saw that took place before both Xians and Anoekans. Maybe this was just the stage being set.

"How long do we have?"

"Not long. Could be a day or several. We only got here first by cutting through Queen Prija's waters."

"Amir and her people will delay them if they or any others attempt the same. I sent word to General Wei of our situation and he should be able to intercept them if needed, if only for a short time."

"My king, my queen. A fight has broken out in the courtyard." Hearing this everyone rushed out.

In the courtyard mass of fighting limbs filled the grounds. Some of the leaders were trying to separate the men but they were only sucked into the skirmish themselves. Serenity stepped forward but both Kang-Dae and Jung-Soo held out their arms to keep her back. Kang-Dae went into the weapons bin brought by Ami's men and pulled something small out. "Do you mind?" he asked the young king who quickly shook his head. Using one of the lit torches, he held the thing up to the flame until it began to smoke and tossed it in the center of the brawling men. It took seconds for the coughing to start. One by one the men withdrew from one another trying to escape the rising smoke.

"We could be under attack at any moment. This is how you would defend us?!" Kang-Dae scolded. Most of the Xian soldiers who were involved hung their heads in shame with the exception of a few. Serenity had a good guess who'd started the altercation. It was the same rude soldier from before. The Anoekans who'd arrived with Ami stood defiantly, ready for an opportunity to begin again.

"We refuse to work with the enemy," the nasty soldier scowled. The men around him nodded in agreement.

"Katsuo and all who support him are our enemy. The Anoekan people are not. They've come to aid us when they didn't have to. You will show them the respect and honor due them as fellow soldiers," Kang-Dae's authoritative voice rang out. He approached the one soldier. Seeing the large man looking like he wanted to hide was a funny sight. Kang-Dae leaned into the man's ear and spoke softly, leaving everyone around ignorant of what was being said. The man's face got progressively paler and his eyes were wide with regret and fear.

Kang-Dae pulled back and said out loud, "am I understood?" The soldier fell to his knees bowing over and over, hitting his head on the ground so hard she knew it would leave a mark.

"Forgive me, forgive me," he repeated over and over. The men around him stared at the crying man in shock. Soon they all took the same posture.

"There is still work to be done. Get back to it!" Kang-Dae ordered and they scurried off, dragging the still-bowing soldier with them.

Serenity looked to Ami who looked at the men he'd brought with him, unsure. Serenity understood. Such a young boy having to give orders to grown men was not an easy thing to do. Even adults would struggle with it. With these men mainly being loyal to his mother and another king, it only made it that much more awkward for him. Serenity gave a small tug on his sleeve, getting his attention. She gave him an encouraging look and nodded toward the Anoekans. As much as she would love to take the burden from him even just for the moment, she felt like it was better for him to start getting used to taking charge. It was clear he

was not given much opportunity to do so back
home.

Ami cleared his throat and opened his mouth
but only a weak "men," managed to escape. She
gave an encouraging pat on his shoulder. He took a
breath and tried once more.

"Men!" He called out. "We came here to
help. Not fight each other. If you aren't here to help,
maybe you'd do better to take your chances with
Katsuo." That must have struck a nerve for many of
them as they straightened up in posture. Serenity
kept her pride-filled smile to herself. "Help our new
brothers in arms," he finished and they too
dispersed. When they were gone Serenity clasped
his shoulders and playfully shook him side to side.
"That's how you do it," she praised. A shy but
satisfied smile slid on his face.

CHAPTER 57

"He still has not made a move to attack. We must assume he has other plans," surmised Kahil. The men sat around the table after another day of waiting for an attack that never came.

"He could still be holding out for his reinforcement," Captain Lee said.

"We still have no word on them on any fronts," Jung-Soo brought up. Kang-Dae kept his mind from going to the unthinkable. He prayed Amir and Tae-Soo were fine.

"Maybe we should take the fight to him. We have enough men," another suggested.

"We still have no idea of his full numbers. Until we get word on where those reinforcements are, I do not want to risk an attack," Kang-Dae countered.

The men around the table agreed. Ami sat silently, listening but with his lack of experience was unable to contribute much. Kang-Dae didn't fault him. He was grateful he had come. As far as he was concerned, he had done more than enough.

"Has the queen had any other visions?" asked one of his generals. Kang-Dae shook his head.

"Not since the last."

Kang-Dae recalled the dream Serenity told him about.

Serenity walked through the palace garden. It was spring and the flowers were in full bloom. At every turn she was met with an array of colors and sweet fragrances. She arrived at the center of the garden; a large flower bed lay before her. She approached them eager to smell them but stopped when she noticed the weeds. There were a lot of them, all clinging to every flower. Serenity hated to see it and decided she would remove them herself. She got on her knees and started pulling. Once she reached out to pull, she noticed she was wearing armor. It seemed normal so she continued without pause. The weeds came up with ease. Some tried to stay attached but they were forced to let go with every yank. Once she'd plucked them all, she looked over the bed. It looked much brighter and the flowers stood straighter. Satisfied, she decided to continue her walk. She went through the arch but something told her to turn back around. She did so but found nothing out of the norm. She went back to the flower bed. She couldn't see anything wrong. So, she bent down to look closer. One of the flowers had a single thorn sticking out drawing her eye. As she moved to get a closer look she saw it. Another tiny piece of weed sticking out. She had to use her thumb and index finger to pick it. Once she got hold of it and began to pull it, it came out with a little resistance but she kept pulling and it kept coming. What looked like a small weed was at least two feet long. Once it was out the flower it was attached to grew an extra two inches revealing more thorns. Suddenly the thorns were on all the flowers as they stood taller. Blooming proudly.

Serenity and he had attempted to decipher what it could mean. They'd been able to ascertain that the weeds were Katsuo's supporters. Their overgrowth showed there was more than they realized.

"Could the garden mean good fortune? Perhaps it is an auspicious omen," one lord brought up, hopeful.

"Wearing armor may suggest a necessary battle," said Jung-Soo.

More men spoke up offering their opinions and guesses as to what the dream could mean. Kang-Dae listened to them all but did not feel any of them were correct.

A small noise had him looking over at Ami. His mouth was moving but hardly anything could be heard over the loud men speaking to each other.

"What is it, Ami?" Kang-Dae asked, silencing everyone. Ami slightly jumped at his name. He gave a quick glance around the room and looked back down at the table.

"Sometimes when you garden you miss things. The weeds are things that were hidden in the dirt. Even if you already checked. The weeds may have been able to grow back because you're overlooking a place you thought was already clear."

When Ami said it, it was almost as though it clicked in not just Kang-Dae's mind but everyone in the room.

"One of the cities he'd occupied before perhaps?" Kahil brought up.

A couple of the men nodded. "Somewhere we wouldn't consider."

"Because we'd already chased them out."

The options weren't many but it left more than a couple of possibilities.

"When was the last time Senoia reached out?" Kang-Dae asked suddenly. The room got quiet.

"I believe they sent their taxes at the normal time."

Kang-Dae's frown deepened. Jae-Hwa and Serenity were not on the best of terms. Their strange relationship still confused him to this day. The sporadic letters where they would only seek to check in on the other, where no pleasantries or kind words were exchanged was a mystery to behold. He tried to remember the last time she'd gotten any type of communication from her. They had been so preoccupied with the rumors and the people that it may have slipped Serenity's mind she had not heard from her.

"They'll come from the west," he stated. "That's where they'll come from."

"Are you sure my king?" No, he wasn't but he felt it. As Serenity would say, you should never ignore your spirit.

"We can intercept them. Stop them from ever arriving," one of the East Anoekan captains volunteered.

"They need to arrive," Kang-Dae blurted out, confusing the man.

"Katsuo will not emerge without his support. So, his support will come. The enemy is good at infiltrating. We need to be the same." Realization came on the men's face and they all began making their plans.

CHAPTER 58

General Yutaka walked along the deck of the ship. Some men were huddled together in conversation. Some played a spirited game among themselves. Others took the time to practice their combat skills. To the left of their ship in the waters their sister ship sailed alongside them just slightly behind. They were making good time. They would be in Xian waters soon. The wind was on their side, a blessing from the gods, he surmised. A gift to honor their loyalty to their true king, Katsuo. He'd received the news of his victory in Xian and hadn't hesitated to go and join him. He wanted to make up for his failure to join him when Katsuo sailed off back then. He hadn't been brave enough to disobey the assembly and other kings and risk losing his position. He'd heard the prophecy over Katsuo as many had. It had been a cause for great celebration during that time. When he had the chance to witness its fulfillment he hesitated. When word came that he'd not only failed but was killed in his journey Yutaka thought the soothsayer had been wrong and praised his smarts for not falling prey to it. Hearing that he'd been resurrected and now sat on the Xian throne, it was all he needed to know before he and others who now believed, took it upon themselves to join the cause before it was too late. Hopefully, Katsuo would appreciate their help so much he would overlook their lack of faith.

"Ships inbound!" The lookout yelled while pointing to the east. Sure enough, there were a string of ships sitting in the water, a battalion in wait. They were too far to see who they belonged to. He hoped they were his brothers awaiting their arrival. They'd left so fast they were unable to send word ahead they were on the way. He ordered the flag to be drawn up so they could see it and know they were there to help. With Katsuo on the throne, he must have sanctioned the waters off to claim the coast as his. They drifted closer towards the ships. As they did, two of the smaller but fast-moving ships started moving toward them. The design of them did not look like one of theirs. They were very colorful and where the mast would normally be, a temple-like structure protruded from the ship. They were built in a way he'd never seen which may have counted for their speed. Yutaka began to get nervous the closer they came. He finally was able to see the colors they were flying. They weren't Xian which caused him to relax just a little. They still weren't Anoekan. The ships split up sandwiching both ships between them. Pulling out his monocular he spied on the ship closest to him. The crew running the ship were not dressed like Xians from what he could tell. Their armor was not like theirs either. The people had very tanned skin and dressed lightly. At the ship's railing he could see a foreign woman in gold and red. A man was standing beside her in the same armor only his clothes were different from the others.

Just as he was wondering if he could be Xian, shouts from the other ship sounded. He watched in horror as arrows rained down on the men topside. He turned back to the other ship just in time to see a group of men line up along the side of the ship drawing their arrows back.

"Get down!" By the time he said "down," several of his men were already hit. Throwing himself on the floor, he tried crawling to get below deck. Hearing the commotion more of his men came onto the deck to investigate only to be instantly struck down. Fearful, he continued to crawl. If he could get below, he and his men could regroup and get their weapons to fire back. They had blasting powder. It would only take one shot to bring them down. Something pierced his leg. The pain was dull before it became searing. He turned to look at it when two more arrows whizzed past him embedding into the ship's railing. Seeing the flames, his eyes widened. It appeared they had the same idea as him. More arrows flew onto the deck igniting everywhere they landed. He tried to move but could only cry out as the arrow had him pinned to the floor. The flames began to eat at his skin slowly traveling up his leg. He tried to turn over so he could get it out but he couldn't reach. As the flames continued to spread, he could only scream.

Tae-Soo watched as the fires spread on the boats. Queen Prija stood regally as she ordered her men to fire more. Amir was on the other ship with her military commander Su. When he and Amir had arrived on the island, they were prepared for resistance, even a straight refusal to get involved given their history with Katsuo. To their surprise she had been not only willing to help but was eager to, especially after hearing about the possible queen's demise. They were planning to sail back toward the capital when a message from Jung-Soo surprised them with a request to intercept the enemy before they could reach the land. They'd made their way to the north knowing it was where Katsuo first landed. They were lucky they had gotten there just a day before they arrived. As the fires spread, he could see men on the deck running around trying to put it out while trying to avoid getting hit. Some men gave up and took their chances in the water. Once they were through here, they would sail back south and join up with his king. Now that Katsuo's reinforcements were gone, they could confront the bastard head on.

CHAPTER 59

"Come!" One of the men left in her city rudely ordered. Jae-Hwa had not left her room in weeks. She had no idea what was transpiring outside her city or in it. After Katsuo's departure she'd hoped to find a perfect opportunity to escape or at least send a warning but the ones he left in charge were even more ruthless than him. On orders from Sho, she assumed. Her men were no longer allowed around the estate. They'd been forced to work in the city as the enemy's distraction to fool the people into thinking everything was as it should be. Jae-Hwa stared at the intruder from over her book. Reading was all she could do so she did, all day.

"Our reinforcements have arrived. You must give your permission to open the gates. Jae-Hwa scoffed and turned to the next page. The guard stomped over to her and hit the book out of her hands sending it sprawling to the ground. She gave no physical reaction, though her heart was racing.

"Now, or this charade ends and we do what we have to." That was code for revealing themselves and intentions to the people. Which would involve a more hostile takeover. Jae-Hwa glared at the man. She was not a violent person by any means but she wished she'd been given a sword instead of embroidery needles as a child. The man attempted to pull her out of her chair but she avoided his hand and got up on her own.

Stepping out into the streets felt like a dream as she'd been kept inside for so long. Looking at the people and seeing them move about without care, did comfort her some but knowing it was all a lie just made her feel worse. Maybe if she hadn't been preoccupied with keeping only her people ignorant, Xian would have been more prepared for Katsuo. She still had no idea if Katsuo had succeeded in his ploy or not. No one would inform her of anything. But if they needed the men, he clearly was not dead. They walked her to the gate acting as though they were there to protect her instead of holding her hostage.

It was still her people at the gates. Something they did to keep up the appearances in case any Xian soldiers came by.

"My lady, they just arrived," the gatekeeper informed. Jae-Hwa forced a smile on her face to reassure the man.

"Did they say what they wanted?" she asked. She could feel the guard to the left of her shifting impatiently.

"They say they were invited. A gift from the king?" Jae-Hwa stepped up to the gate and looked out the open window. Rows of armed men stood right outside. Jae-Hwa felt dizzy. Would this never end? It was all becoming too much. Sometimes she wished it would all just stop even if it meant her death. At least then it would be over.

"Open the gates," she forced herself to say. It made her feel sick at the trusting look from the gatekeeper as he signaled the man on the other side. The men in front came through first with his second trailing behind him. The leader only spared her a quick glance before heading to the guard. The second seemed to slow as he passed her but then pushed on. Jae-Hwa thought it odd at first but figured he wasn't expecting someone like her. The two men conversed among themselves quietly.

Jae-Hwa watched them closely. The one she'd been dealing with spoke fast and aggressively as the other remained calm. Whatever he'd said was riling the man up. He nodded emphatically and summoned her over with a harsh wave of his fingers. Jae-Hwa took her time making her way over.

"Have your men see to everyone out there. They need to be well taken care of."

Jae-Hwa clenched her fist while pulling at her dress, bunching up the material in a tight fist.

"Now!" he whispered harshly. Another guard came to escort her away. She reluctantly followed.

Seeing Captain Chung-Su after so many weeks was enough to make her want to weep. He and many of the men were forced to reside in the storehouses that were still under construction, so they could be kept under watch. Upon seeing her, the captain almost rushed toward her but she stopped him with her eyes, not wanting to see him hurt as the guard was already palming the hilt of his sword. Katsuo's men were stationed all around the building inside and out. They were given zero privacy to keep them from planning anything. The conditions were egregious. Many of the windows had no covers leaving the men vulnerable to the elements. Their armor was taken from them and only given to them when they were being forced to walk the city. All they had were thin underclothes while their captors sported warm leather padded armor. There were no beds or anything that could even be called a cot anywhere. Most of the men were sleeping on the ground. The very desperate lay on top of each other for some warmth and comfort. A lot of them looked underweight. Dark shadows painted their eyes. Jae-Hwa choked back tears and guilt at what was being done to once proud and strong men.

"I am told that things are ending soon," she said, her voice had a tiny tremble in it.

"After today they will leave our city for good." The men sat up as she spoke, taking in her words with uncertainty and suspicion. "We just need to supply them with some things and send them on their way." She tried to make it sound so simple though they all knew it wasn't. It was in their eyes, their bodies. They did not believe it for a second. "I ask just this final thing of you," her voice broke as she spoke. The men silently looked at her.

Captain Chung-Su was the first to step forward. "We will do as you wish my Lady, always."

Knowing what she was asking without asking, knowing the danger in it, seeing every one of them stand and step forward was almost too much to bear. This could only end a couple of ways. If the enemy did leave, they would not leave them with the ability to regroup or come after them. They'd either be forced to join them on their siege, acting as slaves, or they would be eliminated. She knew it, and so did they. The tears that rolled down her cheek could not be stopped.

"Thank you," she breathed out. Unable to take it anymore, she rushed over to Chung-Su and took his hand in his.

"I'm sorry," she sobbed. "It is my fault. I am so sorry." Chung-Su squeezed her hands back. The guard who'd brought her was already pulling her away.

"It's alright, my lady. We will do our duty."

Jae-Hwa had to watch as the men were given their armor and dulled blades in too small sheaths just big enough for the sword to fit but harder to remove. One by one each man bowed their head towards her as they exited. Jae-Hwa cried even as the last men left.

The guard was waiting for her as she entered her home. He was speaking about how he would be leaving his men in place and warning her not to try anything when they left. Jae-Hwa wasn't listening, too consumed by her own guilt and grief. Would her punishments for her past misdeeds never stop? Was she to continue to lose until there was nothing left? The guard must have gotten tired of her not listening and roughly grabbed her by the shoulder. The combination of her imprisonment, her guilt, the fate of her men, the loss of Chung-Su, and the possibility that Katsuo could succeed was too much. Reaching for her hairpin she brought it down forcefully on his hand, piercing flesh. The guard let out a shout and smacked her, sending her stumbling.

"Take her to her room and keep her there!" He ordered holding his hand. Jae-Hwa mindlessly went to her room ignoring the men escorting her. She held the bloody pin in her hands and felt an odd mixture of satisfaction and fear. Satisfaction because she knew what was going to befall that guard and fear because she knew she would have to pay for it once her actions were discovered.

CHAPTER 60

Kahil walked among the men, shifting in the armor he wore. It fit him well enough but it was nothing like his own custom armor. As long as it did the job, he would deal with it. It had clearly fooled the men in Senoia. The East Anoekan leader, Iaki, was good. He was impressed by the commander's cool demeanor. He didn't falter at all when confronted with Katsuo's men. Every question was answered with ease, giving them the false security that things were going to plan. Now they just had to wait for the Senoian men to enact the next phase.

They only waited an hour before Katsuo's men brought them. Seeing his fellow soldiers in such a state made him want to attack them now, plans be damned but he controlled himself. He would not be the reason they failed.

The men were made to stand before them like horses on display. Iaki met with the head guard. Kahil went up to the one with the captain's insignia on the shoulder of his armor. "You men get to work feeding the horses. Then pack up all these weapons into the wagons!" Kahil shouted out loud before leaning into the captain's ear.

"We are here, brother. Do not fear." The captain did not react outwardly at all, almost worrying Kahil that he may have been mistaken to open his mouth. The captain's subtle move of rubbing his closed fist over his heart was masterful and Kahil knew he got the message and he and his men would be ready when the time came. Kahil secretly drew his finger over the well-blended red markings in the armor that were only present in the Eastern soldier's. The man looked around at the others, noticing the similar markings on their armor as well. He gave a slight nod as he grasped Kahil's meaning. The men were sent off with a "guard" to do the work asked of them.

Katsuo's men ordered the men about as Kahil watched. Soon, he kept telling himself to keep himself under control. They were getting more and more hostile as they finished the task, most likely anticipating what they believed would be their final act in Senoia. The word had already been spread among the Senoia warriors. The guard who'd brought them was particularly vicious. Kahil wanted to take him out personally.

"It's loose!" he shouted, pulling at the just placed saddle. He coughed before pushing at one of the men. "Do it again!" The man's form tensed and Kahil prayed he did not act recklessly even though he wasn't sure he would be so calm if it were him. To his credit the man redid the saddle without a word. The man coughed again before turning his nasty eye to the captain who was loading the last of the arrows into a box.

"You!" The captain froze.

"Pack up the last of this and get your people to the river to wash off. Your smell is offending our brothers." The captain briefly made eye contact with Kahil before he nodded and moved the box onto the wagon.

Kahil made eyes at Iaki who nodded as well. Kahil felt a strong surge of excitement. 'Finally,' he thought.

Most of the others stayed behind as over twenty of them led the Senoian men into the woods toward the river. Only a handful of Katsuo men, including the one Kahil had his eye on, were with them.

The Senoian men got to the river only to turn and stare at them. Katsuo's target let out a disgusted and gleeful chuckle.

"I suppose you know you are no longer needed. Good. We can give you the undeserved honor of a dignified death." He laughed with his comrades, not noticing the serious faces of everyone else, or how they all had their attention on them. The men drew their swords and Kahil and the others did the same. As Katsuo's men stepped forward Kahil hung back. A whistle echoed in the sky. Shouts and cries could be heard back where they had just been. Katsuo's men looked back in concern. As they did, the Senoian men ran up behind them and attacked. The few weapons they'd been able to secretly give them were being put to use as some men held their enemies down while the others stabbed them over and over. The leader spun around in shock. He looked back at Kahil who finally was able to smile. The man paled before sneering and taking out his sword. Another fit of coughs fell from his lips. Kahil stepped forward, eager. The captain moved faster than either of them and had a dagger in the man's back before they could even move toward each other. The man grunted and the captain pushed him down until he fell to his knees.

"Treasonous dogs!" He spat, still holding his sword. Kahil went to finish him off but the captain waved him off as more coughs came out of him. The captain pointed at the bandage on his hand.

"Your life has already been claimed by my lady," he said. The man looked at his hand and back to him in confusion, until more coughs exploded out of him this time with traces of blood and black bile.

The man's eyes widened in fear. He attempted to pull himself up with his sword only to collapse onto the ground. The captain walked away from him. The others were piling up the bodies and heading back to help in what was sure to be a one-sided fight.

"Should we-," 'leave him alive' was what Kahil was going to say until he got a good look at the still breathing and writhing man. He couldn't stop coughing it seemed and more blood poured out of him.

"He will not survive," the captain said confidently. Kahil stared in awe. He'd heard about the Gi poison but had never seen it work before. Lady Gi must've had just as much hatred toward this man as he did.

When Jae-Hwa first heard the shouts, she thought the men were celebrating their chance to finally rejoin their brethren. But the screams were too loud, too panicked. She hesitated to even peek out, knowing the guards would force her back in. She tried looking through her window but there was no one in the back courtyard. However, past the walls she thought she could see smoke in the distance.

When they began shouting in the halls, she decided she had to take a look. She slowly pulled the door open. When she saw no one there, she yanked it open the rest of the way. Down the hall she could see the guards talking in a panic while some ran past. The ones talking tried to get the runners to come back but they didn't. After a few more seconds of deliberation the men also ran off. Jae-Hwa stuck close to the walls as she slowly moved to the entryway. A few of the female servants were cowering in the corner staring at the open door leading outside. She rushed over to them.

"My lady," one said as she approached.

"What's happening?" Jae-Hwa asked.

"We do not know. It started a while ago. More and more of the soldiers started leaving."

"I heard one of them say they were under attack in the city."

Jae-Hwa didn't want to get her hopes up. She cautiously approached the door. The only guards she could see were heading out the gate. However, after a few seconds a group of them ran back in and rushed to close the gate behind them. They looked to be having difficulty doing so. Soon, they were pushed back with such force several went to the ground. Men came spilling through the now open gate. Jae-Hwa had to squint to be sure but felt genuine joy for the first time in months as she saw the Senoia armor. They made quick work of the few men ignoring their pleas of mercy. She stepped out ignoring the calls of the female servant to come back. The soldiers immediately scattered in different directions as they searched for any more enemies. Captain Chung-Su ordered them not to show mercy before noticing her. Jae-Hwa almost fell to her knees in relief. He practically jogged over to her as she moved toward him as well. He stopped just as they were only a couple of feet apart.

"My lady," he addressed her. "The city has been retaken." Jae-Hwa wondered if she heard right or if she was dreaming.

"How?" Was all she could manage to ask. Chung-Su smiled in a way she'd never seen before.

"Our king lives," he told her. Jae-Hwa shut her eyes feeling like those were the most beautiful words she'd ever heard.

CHAPTER 61

Serenity entered the room, where Amoli lay. She had yet to wake. She came to talk to her every chance she got. When she had to be away, she made sure someone would do so in her stead. She was skinnier. Serenity felt like she became smaller every time she saw her. Serenity took the brush from the table and began running it through Amoli's dark wavy hair.

"Amir would kill me if I let your hair turn to a matted mess," she told her unconscious form. "He loves your hair, you know? He was always moving his fingers whenever you were near him like he was thinking about touching it. It was cute," she mused.

"He'll be back soon, I promise. Then he can be back on hair duty. You know me. I barely want to deal with my own hair," she joked.

"I know, you probably wanted me to bring Blessing. She's with Uncle Jung-Soo and her father at the moment." Serenity didn't want Blessing to keep seeing Amoli like this. She kept that to herself. It was starting to upset the young girl when she tried to get her to play with her and she didn't respond. It would break Serenity's heart.

After she was done, she set the brush back down and just gazed at her friend. "I really miss you," she said softly. "We all do." A couple of times she caught Jung-Soo in here just sitting by the bed. "I would really love it if you woke up now. But I can understand if you want to wait until you have a better view."

"Don't worry. We'll be back in our home soon. But don't get used to being back. You have a wedding to plan and a life to enjoy. That's the only way I'm allowing you to leave me, understand," she threatened half-heartedly. "You can't go like this. You won't go like this," she declared out loud. She took her hand in hers and began to pray as she always did for her friend to recover.

When she was done, she kissed her hand and set it down.

"She will wake," Jung-Soo's voice came through the room, scaring her. She turned to him. "She's strong. Stronger than she realizes." Before Serenity could ask about Blessing he said, "she's with her grandmother." Satisfied, she turned back to Amoli. Jung-Soo went to stand on the other side of her.

"I just want to be able to thank her."

"I think she'll take your survival as the greatest gift she could receive." The way his voice actually showed emotion made her look at him. Like always, that stony mask was present but she knew what she'd heard. They had never spoken about it, that horrible day. Serenity didn't like to think about it at all. Once she was away from Katsuo, she focused solely on the fact that she was alive, never wanting to dwell on how close she'd come to never seeing any of them again. Kang-Dae told her how Jung-Soo had been adamant she was dead. She vaguely remembered hearing someone call her name during the attack but had thought it was some auditory hallucination. She'd imagine it would be traumatizing for any regular person to see. Even though Jung-Soo was anything but regular it must've affected him greatly. This would be the second time he witnessed her "death." Knowing Jung-Soo, he'd put the undeserved blame on himself.

"If you were meant to save me, you would have," she told him. Jung-Soo's brow twitched but he kept his eyes on Amoli.

"I should've gotten there sooner. It's always been my job to protect you."

"No. It was Arezoo's and she did a damn fine job doing it. So don't walk around here thinking I wasn't saved. Don't tarnish her memory like that. And don't tarnish yourself in that way. I'm here, right in front of you. That's enough." Jung-Soo's head dropped. Serenity might've seen a tear fall but she didn't acknowledge it, not wanting to make him any more uncomfortable than he already was.

"You know only a few years ago you didn't even know me," she mused. "I think the first thing I ever said to you was sorry."

"And then you kicked me," he said with his head still bowed.

Serenity grinned. "I don't remember that part," she lied. "But you must have deserved it," His shoulders moved as a light chuckle escaped him.

"She was my first friend here. It took a little longer for you to warm up to me."

"I wonder why," he said sarcastically, finally raising his head.

"But when you did, I had the greatest friends in this world. I wouldn't trade those days for anything." She grabbed Amoli's hand once more and held it over her stomach. She opened and closed her hand over hers while raising her brows at Jung-Soo. He took the hint and reached out and covered both their hands with his.

Serenity felt it first, the twitch. It was Amoli's hand beneath hers, so she would. She stared at their joined hands with her brows knitted and her eyes narrowed. She looked over at Amoli's face. Beneath her closed lids there was slight movement. She looked to Jung-Soo to check if he saw what she saw. Judging from his perplexed look she figured he had not. She leaned over her.

"Amoli," she spoke gently. More eye movement. Jung-Soo stood, having seen it that time.

Serenity gently ran her thumb over her brow and called out to her once more. Her lips slightly moved next.

"We're here, we're right here. Follow my voice, come on," encouraged Serenity. As Amoli's eyes began to flutter, Serenity's excitement grew. By the time her eyes actually opened, she was practically bouncing in joy.

"Amoli?" She stared upward. Her eyes were glassy. It was unclear how aware she was that she was even awake. Serenity didn't want to overwhelm her so she gave her a few seconds to hopefully begin to regain her senses. Her eyes shifted over to her left first. Jung-Soo let out a small sound of disbelief and happiness.

"You're awake," he said. She blinked a couple of times and looked over at Serenity who was unable to keep the wide smile off her face.

"Hi."

After a couple more slow blinks, her eyes only widened slightly.

"My-," she began to speak. Her voice was so hoarse it was hard to understand her. After a couple more tries, she managed to get out, "My queen."

"Hey!"

Jung-Soo was already on the other side of the room pouring a cup of water. "Where- where-."

"In the Rocky fortress," Serenity told her, not wanting her to talk any more than necessary. "Jung-Soo got you here after the attack."

Her eyes began searching around frantically.

"Amir's okay. He's safe," she assured her. Amoli began to relax.

"Ba...by."

"She's fine. Perfect, Thanks to you." Serenity leaned down and kissed her forehead in gratitude. Jung-Soo brought over the water and carefully helped her take a small sip. Serenity didn't need a dream to tell her this was confirmation. Things were going to turn out fine.

CHAPTER 62

The sun was high in the sky by the time a small group came down the road. The noblemen on horseback were being guided by over two dozen armed men. Kang-Dae stood in the middle of the road with Serenity by his side as they approached. The bored but unbothered expression on Lord Goi angered Kang-Dae from his position which was why it was a genuine pleasure to watch it fall as soon as he spotted him.

"My king, my queen!" He exclaimed. His entire party came to a halt. Kang-Dae saw how the soldiers surrounding Goi took defensive stances.

"I wish I could say it was as much of a surprise to you to meet here as it was to me," Kang-Dae said to him.

"My king?" Goi questioned, trying to appear ignorant.

"We haven't had the pleasure of your company for months. Every summons was met with excuse after excuse."

"But one call from our enemy and you came running," finished Serenity.

"Please don't misunderstand me," the man pleaded. But Kang-Dae couldn't help noticing he had yet to dismount from his horse or that his men had yet to relax in their stances.

"I merely came to put an end to vicious rumors of your demise," he lied unconvincingly. "I've even brought my men to take up arms with you."

Kang-Dae's eyes hardened to the pitiful showing.

"I suppose your other 200 men are behind these?"

"I couldn't leave my city unprotected," Goi tried to deflect.

"I'm sure, with the amount of help you've given Katsuo's forces you must be spread very thin," remarked Serenity.

"You disparage me, my queen." he sputtered.

"Apologies. You only loaned him a small portion of your men. With the larger forces you were expecting that Katsuo promised you never showing up, it must have really put you in a bad position."

"It is a mystery as to what could have happened to them," Kang-Dae said musingly. Serenity shrugged dramatically.

Goi became quiet trying to figure out how to talk his way out.

"I am expected. If I do not show he will know something has happened."

Serenity turned her ear up to him, pretending she was giving him her full attention to see what else he could possibly say. Kang-Dae, already tired of his lies, just glared.

"And then what? What will he do?" She inquired.

"What do you think he can do?" added Kang-Dae.

"I had to do what I could to protect my people," he claimed pathetically.

"And how safe are they now?" challenged Serenity. "Forced from their homes, food taken from their hands to give to his men and yours. People starving in your streets while they cater to the enemy," Serenity listed off, her voice rising with each sin. She slowly approached him. His men, taking their cowardly cue from Goi halfheartedly attempted to block her from going further. With ease she pushed past the two in front, stepping up to the horse.

"A title and an estate. Was that all it took? "Duke" Goi." The man blanched.

"How did you-."

"She *is* my seer," Kang-Dae interrupted dryly.

"It's not just me. I can help you draw out the others," he offered. Kang-Dae tossed him the pendant he was holding. Goi caught it and paled, noticing who it belonged to and the small trace of blood on it.

"You came a bit late," Serenity told him.

"Baek and Fei were quick to name you as well," Kang-Dae informed him.

Sensing he was completely found out the man clumsily tried to pull out his sword. The arrow hit him in his shoulder before he could even get the blade out. Goi tumbled off his horse with a high-pitched cry. His men looked around nervously drawing their own weapons but it was clear they had no real fight in them.

Jung-Soo came out of the trees with the other men. Seeing the numbers the Goi men quickly tossed down their weapons and pled for mercy. Most claimed they could only obey to keep their families safe. Kang-Dae approached Goi who attempted to crawl away. With a kick he ended up on his back. "Have mercy?" The man begged, tears pouring from his eyes down his snot covered face.

"I will give you mercy, the only mercy I have in me to give to you." Kang-Dae bent down to get closer. "Your people will not only survive. Despite what you have done to them they will thrive. Your family will survive, not to suffer for the cowardly and selfish actions of their lord. These men, your men will be sent back to their families and homes never to take up arms again but able to spend their final days in peace. This knowledge I give you as a mercy. So you may take comfort in the fact that through your failure, those around you will live on and with the sacrifice of your life that this was so. Go in peace to the underworld knowing this," he finished standing up straight bringing his sword out.

"No pleas-," his final words ended with one strike to his heart.

Kang-Dae left the dead man and found Serenity helping collect the weapons of the surrendering soldiers. With a frown he pulled her up.

"Let the men do that," he scolded, not wanting to see her put anymore unnecessary strain on herself. It was hard enough allowing her to convince him to let her come. Their promise to stay together was a plea he could not deny. Serenity rolled her eyes but didn't argue.

"That's the last of them, right?" she asked. Kang-Dae nodded. All the traitors and collaborators outside the capital had been dealt with. Any others were already with Katsuo, most likely taking residence in the palace. His jaw clenched at the thought.

"Let's return!" Kang-Dae shouted. Just in case Katsuo decided to come looking for his "allies" he didn't want to be out here. Serenity sighed in relief. Kang-Dae knew she was as eager to get back to their daughter as he was. He wrapped an arm around her and led her into the woods to make the journey back.

CHAPTER 63

Katsuo hummed as he poured himself a cup of wine. He felt his mood shifting. He'd received a message earlier that evening from Senoia informing him of their departure. Not only that, they were able to give him the good news that more people back home had fled to his cause and they would also be coming. It was happening. He felt himself smiling. It may not look exactly how he pictured it but this was it. He was uniting people, bringing them together under his rule. The world would be better for it. Once he took care of Xian opposition, he could take care of who was left, those who could live in his peaceful kingdom, and then return home. Once the East and West kings saw his triumph and his power, they would have to stand down. With all the armies united no one would dare destroy what they built again. He would even offer the Assani a chance to join them. One chance only. If they refused him, his great army would wipe them off the continent, finally claiming the whole land for the Anoeka. He'd give his mother the title and respect she deserved. As for Akimitsu, he would make it up to him. Once he made sure he could never come for his crown he would give him a place of his own to rule over. Something small, of course, but something to make up for all his mistakes. Everyone else back home, who'd doubted him, opposed him, stole from him, would be treated as his enemies. Traitors like that had no place in the peaceful world he would build. Loyalty would be an unnegotiable quality for every citizen. That brought his thoughts back to the two women who'd brought him to this point.

He had promised Jae-Hwa he would make her his queen but to hold onto his power he needed someone powerful at his side. He was no longer sure she could be that person for him. His dream walker was that and more. Her Assani appearance may complicate things but if the people see him accepting her and know how she helped him fulfill his prophecy they would accept her. Maybe he could marry them both. Take his dream walker as his concubine. The people may be more accepting of that. The thought whispered in the back of his mind that he was doing what he despised his father for. He'd almost destroyed their family. Katsuo would be better. He already was.

Her child could not join them of course. He could have it sent away to be raised by good people. That way, she'd grow up never knowing who she was and never would grow aspirations for the crown. He would explain to his dream walker that it was for the best. The old king's seed could not be around him while he ruled. It would cause too much trouble. He knows what Sho would suggest but he could not order such a thing twice in his lifetime. No matter whose child it was. He took a sip enjoying the sweetness of the wine. Soon he would have everything he needed to bring things to an end. His body hummed with excitement. King of the new world, King Katsuo.

"My king," his general approached, a paper in hand, as he kneeled.

"What is it?" Katsuo asked, staring at the map of all of Xian that he'd had painted. He had spent hours staring at what he had taken for himself. "Have the lords come?" He had been waiting for the Xian lords to make their appearance for days now. He was told they were on their way weeks ago. It was only a matter of time before all of Xian realized who was truly in charge.

"One of our scouts came back with this. They say they have been posted throughout several western cities."

Katsuo turned from his map and took the paper. Katsuo could have screamed when he saw the contents.

'Long Live King Kang-Dae and Queen Serenity of Xian, the undefeated and undying leaders of Xian!' He crumpled the paper until it was but a fraction of its size and tossed it into the fire.

"Who is responsible?!" He demanded.

"We cannot be sure, my king. They are too numerous and widespread to determine its origins."

Was this what kept the lords from naming him their king? Had foolish hope in their weak king stopped them from embracing the truth? Katsuo paced the room unsure of how to put a stop to it. How did he crush hope? He had to show the people it was false. He had to come out as the true victor and ruler. He needed to make it so there would be no doubt to the people that he was the last king standing. The world needed to see him put down the Xian worm for good. No more waiting, no more fruitless attacks, and searches. He needed to bring the enemy to him before the people of Xian so they could see for themselves as he put an end to the idea and life of the former king.

CHAPTER 64

Ami stared at the door, as he had for the last few minutes trying to make himself go in. When Kang-Dae asked him to join them to help strategize and plan the next steps, he'd been more than a little shocked. When he agreed to come and help, he figured he would be more in the background following whatever orders the Xian king gave him. He never expected to be included as any type of leader or authority figure. He had never been involved in these types of meetings back in Anoeka. His mother had "graciously" allowed him to sit them out claiming she could handle it on his behalf until he could understand how things worked. Even though he'd been there for months and wore the crown for months he still had yet to learn anything about how things worked. She only brought him out for formal briefings with the assembly and to participate in their monthly meetings with the people for partitions.

"Good morning, Ami," Kang-Dae's voice brought the young boy out of his thoughts.

"Morning, my-, King Kang-Dae," he corrected himself, still not used to having to address him in such a way. Kang-Dae gave him a friendly pat on his shoulder.

"Shall we?" he asked, gesturing to the door. Ami couldn't answer and still did not want to move.

"I don't have to be in there," he finally spoke. "There's important work you all have to do. I can go help the others prepare."

Kang-Dae tilted his head and gave him an odd look. "You belong in that room," he told him.

Ami shook his head.

"I don't. I don't know anything about wars or ruling," he admitted. "I'm just a kid with a crown."

Kang-Dae led him away from the door to the corner of the hall.

"Ami, you may be young but that does not excuse you from your responsibilities."

It was the exact opposite of what his mother would tell him. 'You're too young to understand.' 'Once you're older I will teach you.' 'Children do not need to involve themselves in the problems of government.' All things she'd said to him in private while openly telling others how he had come up with some plan or edict that she was presenting to them.

"Whether you wanted to or not, you have become a leader for your people. They depend on you to do what is best for them. They can only respect you if you show you are worthy of their respect. And you, Ami, are worthy of it. You need to believe that or you have already lost."

Ami tried to take in his words but it was difficult with all the other things that had been seeded inside him. "You cannot allow others to do things in your stead. It is not they who will be looked at if things do not go the way the people want, it will be you. If you must take their blame, you should take the responsibility." Ami slowly nodded understanding what he was trying to tell him.

"But what if they will not listen to me?" He asked genuinely, wanting an answer to a scenario that had been in his mind for months.

"They may not want to. But you must make your voice heard. If they demand you take the throne then they must accept your rule. Power seeks the hands of those who believe they have it the most. If you believe you have none, others will believe it as well." Kang-Dae gave him another pat and led him back to the room. Ami was still nervous and unsure but he had a lot more to consider.

***

Amir was nervous at first, seeing the Anoekan dressed men at the base of the mountain but recalled the king's message about their help and pressed through without incident after revealing his identity. He wanted to go straight to Amoli and check on her but knew he had to brief his king on everything. Tae-Soo thankfully offered to do it alongside Queen Prija. After thanking them both he almost ran through the fortress to her. He expected to see her in the state he left her, there was the anxious feeling in his gut that made him wonder if the worst had happened while he was away. It had been on his mind every day that he was gone. He feared coming back to an empty room. What he had not expected was to hear laughter and voices chattering warmly as he approached. He definitely did not anticipate seeing a perfectly alert and awake Amoli sitting up leaning against the wall with the queen laughing at her side while Jung-Soo stood by smirking in the corner. Amoli's smile faltered only a bit before it returned even brighter than before. Amir rushed over to her, almost knocking the queen over. He would apologize for it later on. He grasped Amoli's hand in his and kissed it enthusiastically. He touched her hair. "I am alright," she told him. Her voice was the sweetest thing he'd ever heard. He was almost brought to tears just from those words alone. He hadn't even noticed the queen and general leaving the room to give them privacy. It was much needed as he found himself taking her face in his hand and bringing her lips to meet his in a soft but firm kiss. He was as gentle as he could be considering her state but he did not think it could be helped. He'd come so close to losing her.

"I'm sorry I wasn't here-," he started to apologize but to his surprise, she cut him off with a kiss of her own, letting her lips linger on his. The moment was almost too perfect, he feared it was just another dream of his.

"I love you," she told him. The words seeped into his heart down to his very soul. He kissed the top of her head and took her in his arms.

"I love you."

***

When Serenity saw Queen Prija for the first time since she'd left her island, she still had not quite figured out how to greet her. They were both queens and now she was technically on their turf. A slight nod of the head seemed to suffice for the queen so Serenity did the same. "Thank you for coming," she told her.

"It is a duty and an honor to be here to see the end of such a tyrant."

"We do not have much time. Katsuo will be making his way here soon. Everything must be done before his arrival!" announced Kang-Dae. The words were like a fire that got everyone moving.

"What can I do?" offered Prija. Serenity was so appreciative of the offer.

"We still have some things to pack up in the storerooms if you'd like to help me?"

"Of course." The two queens went off to make themselves useful as Kang-Dae looked on, impressed by the women.

"Are all the weapons accounted for?" he asked Jung-Soo who nodded.

"Bring the men inside. We'll work in shifts. Make sure the Anoekans know their part in this," he said looking down at Ami.

"Yes, si-, my Ki-, King Kang-Dae" he managed to stutter out before almost running away.

"You believe we can do this?" Jung-Soo asked, keeping his voice low. They looked around at the men, women and even children hustling and moving like they all had purpose. They sought to pull off something people would speak about for generations to come. Even if they failed, this would be the moment they would tell stories about, of that Kang-Dae was sure.

"I believe it's already done, so yes," answered Kang-Dae.

CHAPTER 65

Katsuo sat on his horse staring up at the fortress. He would not hold back this time. He would make sure everyone inside would meet him or perish. He thought to take some inspiration from his enemy and bring their strongholds down from beneath them. He had men knowledgeable in such things advise him the best places to strike. He forced his men to work night and day on strong explosives that were more consistent to the ones they had back home. They had to sacrifice a lot of their powder to do so, even digging up what they'd used to fortify themselves within the palace, but it would be worth it. Once it was over they would receive more from Anoeka as a gift to apologize for ever doubting his destiny.

The first round hit the fortress right beneath the base sending chunks of rock tumbling down the side. He quickly ordered them to fire again in the same spot. The second hit sent a wide crack up the first story wall. Katsuo smiled at that. He ordered another hit. They weren't firing down at them. Katsuo knew they must be in a panic and were trying to get the people out. He had men all around the mountain to catch them when they did. He brought every soldier at his disposal. He didn't care about protecting the palace. All his enemies were here and soon they wouldn't be here either. The wall cracked and a large piece fell. A few of his men got caught in the rubble but it was okay. Their sacrifice would be honored at his coronation. The entire first balcony came down next. Luckily, his men managed to dodge the fallout this time around.

He looked around to his men on the side waiting to hear they'd spotted the fleeing people but the men just shook their heads. Katsuo frowned and took his horse around to the men on the other side. Like the others, they reported no movement. Katsuo kept moving, ignoring the sounds of destruction happening around him. He almost went around the entire mountain but the story remained the same. Had they elected to just stay and die inside? He didn't take the king as that much of a coward.

Feeling things were off he ordered the attack to halt. He ordered his men to begin checking the mountain and the surrounding forest to be sure they had not let anyone get by them. Hours of searching and nothing, not even a piece of clothing.

A horn in the distance made his blood run cold. It was coming from the palace, a Xian horn. Katsuo ordered his men to return as fast as they could. It took hours, his horse and his men were exhausted by the time the palace was back in their sights. Just as they pulled up toward the main gate, Katsuo and his men were forced to halt at the rows and rows of Xian soldiers standing before them. His men all pulled their weapons, ready to fight. On the walls, more Xians could be seen, their arrows ready to fire. Katsuo felt like he was trapped in a nightmare. He couldn't believe this was real.

"My king," his general whispered. "We must go." Katsuo couldn't move or respond. He kept waiting to wake up. This could not be happening, not again. He could not have had a taste of victory, only for the throne to be snatched from him once more.

No, he would not have it.

"We will return to the city," he told the general. They could regroup and await his forces there. Once they came, he would have them raid all the surrounding towns and cities. Take all the land and force them into a corner. They may believe they have won by returning but they would die in the palace. He would make sure of it. They retreated row by row keeping the enemy from firing on their backs.

CHAPTER 66

The state of the once lively and beautiful city filled Kang-Dae with anger and resentment. They walked the streets taking in all the damage. Hearing the shaky breath Serenity released he knew she was feeling the same. He reached for her hand and squeezed. He'd grown up running through these streets. He had hundreds of memories coming down with his mother as they wore plain clothes to blend in with the people as they shopped and pretended they were a normal family, free from the burdens of palace life. They were memories he planned to recreate with his own family. The smell of burnt wood permeated the air no matter where they walked. The empty and destroyed market filled him with another level of anger.

Once Kahil and the other Anoekans returned from their "propaganda" parade as Serenity called it, where they'd spread the word of their survival for all to hear, they had everyone slowly and quietly escorted out of the fortress. They sent all the civilians to the new fort, where they would be safe from what was to come. They'd removed any and everything worth taking and made the journey through the woods to the city where they knew none of Katsuo's men would be, having already done all the damage they could do.

"Check for any civilians," he ordered the men near him. They immediately went out to search. They made their way into the business district. Most of the stores and restaurants had been raided, but they were otherwise still standing.

As Kang-Dae continued, he had to stop when he noticed Serenity was no longer moving. He looked at her to see she was focused on something else. Noticing exactly what she was looking at, his heart dropped. He was about to say something but she let go of his hand and rushed inside the building. Kang-Dae followed closely behind. The building had not been as lucky as some of the others. Though they had never finished setting up the school, what had been left was destroyed. Desks were scattered, and some were broken. A fire had eaten at two of the four walls. Serenity looked around in silence, face blank. Until she suddenly fell to her knees. Kang-Dae was next to her in seconds, taking her in his arms. She had been so strong for so long, probably even before she made it back to him. He wasn't surprised to see her break, even over something others would think is a small thing compared to everything else. But Kang-Dae knew it wasn't the building she was mourning. It was the time they lost, the people, the things. He knew she truly believed they could not have prevented this, but it did not hurt any less and for the first time she was allowing herself to feel that loss. He would let her, and help her through it as she did him. She cried and he supported her, away from everyone and everything else. It was just them so he let her go as long as she needed.

They stayed on that floor for a few more minutes until she slowly pulled herself back together. She took a large breath, sniffled, wiped her face, and began to stand. He helped her up. He couldn't help but notice and admire her strength as her face took on the regal and determined expression it had before as if the last few minutes had never happened. Unable to help himself, he grabbed both sides of her face and kissed her. It was short but meaningful.

They made their way back outside into the streets as the men searched. They came to another smaller street with a few businesses and more homes. It looked more untouched than the rest probably because of its tucked away location.

Movement in his peripheral had him pulling Serenity behind him. The other men made a protective circle around them. A woman with a small child made her way out of one of the shops. Everyone around them relaxed and one of the men went out to help her. She wore tattered clothing and the daughter clung to her leg. Kang-Dae and Serenity approached them.

"Are you alright?" She asked. The woman looked at Serenity in shock, then her eyes went to Kang-Dae and the soldiers.

"OH!" She cried falling to her knees. "My king, my queen," she wept. Serenity helped her back up, hushing her with kind words.

"We thought we would be at the mercy of that invader. He said you were dead," she continued to cry.

Kang-Dae was about to assure her when more movement and sounds broke out around them. Little by little more people came pouring out of the various buildings. They all looked to be in the same state of fear, lack and hunger.

"My King"

"My Queen."

Choruses of formal greetings echoed in the streets as more and more people came out to meet them. Serenity's hands covered her mouth as her watery eyes looked around at them all. Within the hour hundreds had emerged to lay their eyes on the resurrected king and queen. They gave out everything they had from water to grain. Kang-Dae ordered his men to set up perimeters and fortify the walls. Their city had already seen great loss and cruelty. They would make sure Katsuo would not get the chance to harm anyone or anything in their land again. Knowing their time was limited they decided against having the people escorted to the fort with the others. Instead, he ordered several troops to take them to the homes still standing in the highest point of the city and keep them protected. The men got to work preparing the city for Katsuo's retribution.

CHAPTER 67

He began to feel something wasn't right
even before the city came into view. Katsuo brought
his horse to a stop as he stared up at the large gates,
gates his men had left in shambles on their last visit.
He ordered his men to open them as he looked on.
The men behind him were ready with their arrows
just in case. The gates opened with ease which
prompted Katsuo to believe that he was being
paranoid due to everything that had happened. He
sent in one troop first, to check around. He kept
sight of them the whole time as they went up the
street. Having seen nothing, they shouted it was
clear, so Katsuo and the rest of his men entered the
gates.

Katsuo rode slowly through the streets,
which were quiet. It was as he expected but he felt a
bit unsettled by it for some reason. Nothing seemed
different from how they left it. Not a soul could be
heard or seen. He had assumed many had fled
hoping to seek refuge in nearby villages. This

would work, he thought to himself. Even if he lost the palace, the capital was just as much the heart of Xian. If he claimed this city, it would be even more impactful than some palace. The thought did not bring him the assurance or relief it was meant to. They pulled up, moving to the center of the city.

***

Serenity stayed crouched in front of the window next to Nasreen. The men had already given the signal that Katsuo was on his way half an hour ago. She knew he must be in the city by now. Her heart was going a mile a minute but she managed to keep her cool demeanor. She would not be watching this battle from a distance or from a safe place. She would be there right in the middle because it was where she was needed. She may not know all the steps to how things would work out but she knew that much. She had her part in this fight and she meant to play it. It was quiet on the streets below, giving the illusion of desertedness. If Katsuo looked for any feet on the ground, he would not find any, they'd made sure of it. Nasreen gripped her crossbow tightly. Kang-Dae had been kind enough to give Serenity his special bow that had been modeled after the one he was gifted by her brother. It was much easier for her to control than the others. A small shift behind her reminded her of the others also lying in wait.

Kang-Dae and Jung-Soo were in their position, keeping their horses steady. Kang-Dae glanced at the buildings at his side. The streets were narrower here. They'd chosen their location because of it. All the other ways leading their way had been blocked with soldiers hidden, waiting for the enemies to approach, to send them running or to their deaths.

"How long will you stay, once this is over?" he asked Jung-Soo casually like they were not minutes away from the greatest fight of their lives.

Jung-Soo mulled over his question just as casually.

"Long enough to make sure you don't lose your throne again," he joked.

"When will you tell her?" He asked and Jung-Soo knew who and what he was referring to. Neither of them had had the courage to break the news to Serenity that Rielle was not only in this world but was being "held" in another land.

"When will you?" he challenged back.

"I told you to take her home. I was very clear on my instructions," Kang-Dae defended himself.

"She's more stubborn than your wife. How was I to manage that?"

Kang-Dae laughed.

"Perhaps you need to become better equipped to handle such a woman," he informed and lightly teased. Jung-Soo scoffed.

"Not necessary," he claimed, looking back for any sign of the enemy.

"If you believe so."

"I do," he declared, making Kang-Dae chuckle more.

"You ready?" Kang-Dae asked him, in a more serious tone. Jung-Soo nodded.

"I have no fear of death you know," he said.

"You think we will not survive?"

Jung-Soo shook his head. "No, I know you will." Kang-Dae looked over to him.

"The moment I saw her again I knew I would never in my life doubt that you two were fated to rule this land."

Kang-Dae stared at his friend thoughtfully before turning back to the streets ahead.

CHAPTER 68

Katsuo's dark feeling had only increased as they moved further into the city. Two miles in and they still had yet to encounter anything that should concern him. But that feeling still would not go. The men in front turned the corner as there was a dead end ahead of them. He slowed his pace just a bit. The men around him did the same to stay with him. He was starting to rethink taking refuge here. Maybe they should continue on. Spread themselves back out into the land. Take over a city at a time until it was all in his grasp.

They made it to the turn and as soon as they entered the street, he, and everyone else paused. There was nothing ahead. The streets were just as empty as before, only now it was alarming, as there was not one sign of the men who went before them. Ahead there was nothing but lines of properties going almost half a mile. They couldn't have made a turn in such a short amount of time. If they could have, they definitely would have waited for them or given them a heads up.

"Turn back. Turn back!" He whisper/yelled at the men. They started the awkward and difficult process of trying to turn their horses when the first boom sounded. In the very back of the line he could hear men shouting and horses screaming.

"Turn ba-!" another roar interrupted his orders. This time he saw the flash of light and the aftereffects of some of the blast including smoke and a man being thrown several feet from his horse. The horses surged forward regardless of their riders' commands trying to escape. They were pushed into the narrow street unable to turn or back up. As more blasts and screams were being heard from behind, Katsuo didn't know which way was worse. All weapons were drawn at this point. Katsuo kept his hands on the reins fully prepared to race down out of the area as fast as he could. Their pace was faster but still cautious. Heads spun in every direction, trying to spot any of their enemies. The sounds in the back had begun to slow. Was that because they had them exactly where they wanted? Katsuo wondered. As they reached the middle of the street his man on his side pointed out the splatter of red in the dirt. Once he saw it, he noticed the same type of splatter covering some of the walls around them. The drag marks in the ground only made the hair stand up on the back of his neck. Katsuo had seen enough.

"Move!" He shouted to his men as he took the reins and snapped them hard. The horse took off. Katsuo could hear the others behind him trying to keep up. At the moment, Katsuo had no thoughts of anyone or anything but getting out of the street. He could vaguely hear the sounds of men shouting from behind him. He may have even heard a few fall from their horses. He did not dare look back, not wanting to slow for anything. As his horse made it out, he was forced to stop. Three street paths lay ahead of him but only one was clear. The other two were blocked with piles and piles of broken wood, furniture, and other miscellaneous things. Katsuo didn't have time to think things out fully but he knew he did not want to go down the clear path. It was a trap for sure. He went toward the left hoping to push through the trash. As soon as he approached a group of flaming arrows landed only mere inches from his horse's feet. When the arrow shot past him into an unfortunate soldier behind him, he forced his horse to change directions toward the middle street. Almost on cue, more arrows flew. Katsuo had to duck to keep from getting hit. As he backed away the rubble in both streets was now aflame. Feeling the heat from the rising fire Katsuo turned toward the last street with a snarl. He raced once more hoping to speed past whatever horrors lay ahead.

CHAPTER 69

Kang-Dae and Jung-Soo steadied themselves as a large group of soldiers approached. At the head of them were two Xian lords.

"My king," Lord Chu spoke first. "We offer our assistance in this fight."

"Do you?" Kang-Dae scoffed while Jung-Soo's eyes narrowed.

"Of course. It's why we've come."

Kang-Dae smirked. He had expected this. Once the palace was lost and Katsuo's luck seemed to have run out, the ones who'd taken up with him would try to weasel their way back into his good graces. Not just predictable but foreseen. They figured with their knowledge of the city they would make it to him first.

"If that is the case. Throw down your arms," Jung-Soo ordered.

"My king," the other lord spoke. "We would be helpless and useless to you in this fight."

"You are already useless to me," countered Kang-Dae. The men looked taken back.

"Today is the day we purge all dangerous and useless things from our land."

The arrow could've come from anywhere. They were hidden everywhere. But the coloring of it and the angle made him guess it had come from Serenity's group. The other lord paled, watching his friend clutch at his pierced armor. He slumped over on his horse. The men behind them tried to draw but it was too late. A hail of well-shot and precise arrows hit them all. The arrows didn't stop until all of the men were no longer moving. Kang-Dae and Jung-Soo looked on, never having to even unsheathe a sword. Jung-Soo whistled and a group of soldiers came out and quickly dragged the men into the adjacent buildings. If not for the few splashes of blood and the now riderless horses no one would know there had been any type of confrontation. Kang-Dae went up to the remaining horses and tapped them on the rear, sending them running off.

***

Katsuo exited the street without any trouble as did his men. It confused and frustrated him. If they had been so adamant for them to go this way, why wouldn't they have attacked? It didn't make sense to him. He kept looking around waiting for some sort of attack or an indication of one.

"My king," he could hear the general next to him call, but he didn't care about what he wanted. Their enemies were everywhere. They could pop out at any moment. "My king," he tried again. There was only one street to go down. Once again it was completely clear. Katsuo stared at it. That's where the real trap is, he thought.

"Set fire to those buildings," he ordered, pointing down the street.

"My king, that's our only way out," the general reasoned. Katsuo glared at him. "We can't go back," the man continued. "We'll be truly trapped."

Katsuo shook his head trying to shake off his reasoning. No, this would save them. He was sure. But maybe it wouldn't. Maybe this was exactly what that false king wanted him to do. What if he was playing exactly into his hands?

"My king?" the general tried again. Katsuo's focus was inside his mind. He was in debate with himself. He couldn't hear the man's urging. He could barely see where he currently was anymore. Things were beginning to look so much like the streets of Anoeka. Home, his home. This was home, he had to fight for it. Fight off the invading force who tried to take it from him. Katsuo's eyes narrowed and he looked determinedly down the street. Without a word to any of his men, he led his horse inside.

"Tell the men behind to burn whatever they can behind us." He ordered coldly. They could always rebuild. They've done it before. They went through the street without looking back.

***

The Duke of Illeanda had not sported armor in years. He had never had the need to. When Katsuo had invaded his city, he had wanted to but it had been too late. Now he wore his colors proudly as his men trailed behind Katsuo's forces. Far enough back they would not be detected. After receiving the king's summons, he left half his men to defend his home and took time preparing to join him with the other half. The memory of their occupancy was still fresh in all his people's minds. If there was even a chance it could happen again, he needed to be a part of the effort to stop it. For the children, for his men, for his citizens. He quietly gestured for his men to stop once they came upon the open street where Katsuo and his men had just gone down. Only a few trailed behind. He was about to wait it out and let them go until he saw what they were doing. They had torches in hand, preparing to light a fire.

"Woo!" He whispered loudly. The commander came up beside him. Seeing what was happening he didn't hesitate to pull out his bow. The duke and the captain beside him did the same. Stealthily, without shaking or a tremor, they released at the same time and the men went down together. Two engrossed in their work the final two had not noticed their fallen brothers. They had no clue what happened when the arrows pierced their backs. Like they had been doing, his men moved quickly, clearing up the mess they made. They hoped to keep the damage to the city as minimal as possible. He would not stand by and allow Katsuo to do as he wished here. Like his home, he meant for the capital to stand.

CHAPTER 70

'Another empty street,' Katsuo snarled in frustration. He stopped his men. Against his general's advice, he dismounted from his horse. Katsuo would not play into the enemy's hands any longer. They had embedded themselves in his home and he would root them out like he had before.

"You and your troop continue on. If you run into an ambush, send a signal up."

"My king?" the general questioned.

"Second and third with me!" Katsuo shouted.

Instead of going toward the street, he went inside one of the larger buildings. His men followed close behind. Katsuo climbed the stairs and searched each room until he found what he was looking for. In the room on the side, there was a window facing the side of the next building. He opened the window and looked out. The gap wasn't too big, but he'd have preferred it to be shorter.

Nevertheless, without warning or speaking to his men he took several large steps back, took a breath, and rushed at the window full speed. He heard the men calling for him to stop but he was already in the air hurtling toward the closed window of the next building. He landed with a roll. The impact knocking the wind from him and keeping him stunned for a few seconds before he could move. He was a bit sore but other than that, sustained no other injuries. He stood and looked out toward his men still staring wide eyed from the other building. He waved them over and turned to go search out another window.

***

Serenity was feeling restless. She hadn't looked out in a couple of minutes. The wait was getting to her. It had been over an hour since the last group had come by. They had yet to hear any signs of battle. She hoped their strategy was working and that was why they were being made to wait. After all, they could plan it all out but the timing was something they could not control. She had to stop herself multiple times from going out to check on Kang-Dae. She knew he was alright but she just wanted to see him.

"Something is wrong," Nasreen spoke out, voicing Serenity's fears.

"We don't know that," Serenity tried to rationalize. "They could be here any minute."

Nasreen let out an impatient sigh looking out the window and moving her head from side to side. She must not have seen what she wanted because she returned to her position after a couple of seconds. "They may have gotten through one of the barricades and found another way through the city," Nasreen surmised. Serenity thought that was possible but they were prepared for that. If they had managed to make it into one of the blocked off streets the men stationed there should have been enough to turn them back. That could account for the waiting game they were in at the moment. "Perhaps we should send a group to check."

Kahil shuffled over to them, keeping his body low. "I can take a few men out, just to take a look," he offered.

Serenity bit her lip as she contemplated it. It might be good just to get an update on the situation. But she shook her head. They needed to stick to the plan. "We need to keep our positions," she stated, fully believing it was the best course of action. Nasreen did not look as sure but conceded to her. Kahil nodded and gave a quick peek out the window before returning to his position.

Kang-Dae leaned against the statue in the center. He was starting to feel the sweat rolling down his back beneath his armor. Jung-Soo kept his stance, seemingly unbothered by the heat or the wait. Katsuo should be here soon, he hoped. He'd hate to go searching for him purely out of boredom and impatience.

The sound of horses trotting gave him relief as he stood to his feet to join Jung-Soo. The person on the horse leading the group was not Katsuo,

Kang-Dae noticed and was immediately deflated. He didn't recognize him so he figured he was just a leader in Katsuo's force. Kang-Dae didn't have the drive to face off against Katsuo's middlemen any longer and was quick to give the signal to attack. The men, though surprised, did have enough sense to get their shields out in time, at least, some of them did. The man on the horse managed to dive down fast enough to avoid the arrows. He hid behind his horse as his men covered him and themselves with shields.

A whistle sounded in the air and Kang-Dae watched as something flew up above the buildings, leaving a trail of smoke in its wake. Whatever it was, quickly burst into a flurry of smoke that became a small cloud of black that could be seen for miles. Kang-Dae took out his sword ready to take out this enemy before whoever saw that signal came to aid them.

CHAPTER 71

Serenity had moved out of the way to let the more experienced archers take their chances at the group. Once they hid behind their shields, she found it impossible to get a good shot. She continued to look though, keeping Kang-Dae in her sights as he went into the fray. Her heart rate jumped watching him pull on one of the shields along with one of the soldiers holding it, sending him sprawling. Kang-Dae wasted no time swinging into the opening. She couldn't see it clearly but from the spray of blood she could tell he had gotten at least one of them. The archers in her group kept any of the braver men who meant to attack Kang-Dae and Jung-Soo away from them. She wanted to give the men the go ahead to go out and help them but they still had not seen Katsuo. They were meant to stay hidden until he showed his face. Serenity continued to watch, even though she was impressed by her husband and friend's skill, she was still nervous seeing multiple enemies try and fail at getting to them. The group was tougher than the others, she could tell.

Whatever opening they managed to make would quickly be reformed by the enemy, even at the expense of their lives. A clattering above them drew her attention from the window.

Kang-Dae was getting frustrated. Though he and Jung-Soo had managed to take out half a dozen of them they had yet to make a big enough impact to take them out completely. A sharp pain on his side made him hiss. The arrow that had just barely scraped him, bounced off the statue behind them. Jung-Soo had his dagger in hand before Kang-Dae could retaliate and sent it perfectly through the same opening the arrow had come from. The shout that followed let him know the target had been reached. Kang-Dae contemplated pulling back a little to give them the space and the false assurance they could emerge from their cocoon. Movement had him looking towards one of the shops to the side. At first, he thought it was a trick of his eye but he saw it again. A blur of movement from one building to the next. He brought Jung-Soo behind the statue for cover so he could continue to look and show Jung-

Soo as well. To their dismay they realized it was Katsuo's men making their way into the buildings where their people were hidden. Where Serenity was hidden. They both raced out to warn them but a couple of arrows had him going back pulling Jung-Soo with him behind the statue. The group had managed to regroup enough to put them in the line of fire.

"They're coming in through the window!" Kang-Dae shouted, praying they could hear him.

Serenity only heard the word "window" from Kang-Dae as the noises from above were too much. Shuffling of heavy footsteps and the sound of fighting let her know the enemy had infiltrated. Kahil ordered the men to take aim at the steps just as a couple of feet became visible. Not knowing if it were the enemy or their men trying to escape, they waited until bits of their armor came into view. The second they saw the Anoekan colors they let loose. The men came tumbling down the rest of the way. While Kahil and the others reloaded, more footsteps pounded overhead and this time a group of five made their way down. The men had their arrows up and fired as soon as they could. Kahil jumped on top of Serenity taking her to the ground with a grunt just as the arrows flew towards her. He apologized as he let her up. Serenity was about to thank him when she saw the arrow in his back. "Kahil," she cried. Kahil smiled it off. He reached behind himself and pulled it out.

"I'll be fine my queen," he said with confidence as he tossed the arrow.

Another group came down. A few of their men managed to get the arrows raised in time to take out most of them. But as they went to reload once more, an even larger group came right behind. Only a couple in the front were hit and then they were filing into the small space engaging with their people. Kahil pulled Serenity up and went to fight, after pushing her toward Nasreen. Nasreen pushed Serenity behind her as the men came at them. Serenity grabbed a sword from the ground and took on the defensive stance Arezoo had taught her. Nasreen took out the first one to approach with a swipe to the belly. Someone came at Serenity from the side. She managed to block his high swing with much effort. He was using his strength to try and force his sword into her. She dropped her foot on his as hard as she could, making him grunt, throwing off his balance. She quickly moved to her right. Without her support, he fell forward. Serenity wasted no time impaling him through the back.

More and more men came pouring down the stairs.

"My queen you must go!" Kahil called out while engaged with two different men. Serenity went to go help him but was pulled back by Nasreen. Chaos all around them, Serenity looked behind her at the window figuring it was their only way out. She was about to pull Nasreen with her and froze at the sight of Katsuo coming down the stairs. He walked with no urgency, almost lazily. He had an unearned confidence in his stride that both unnerved and angered Serenity.

Kang-Dae was still stuck behind the statue. "Tae-Soo!" Jung-Soo called out. Kang-Dae didn't fault him for breaking their plan to hold out until Katsuo appeared. They needed help. He couldn't see what was going on in the shop but the sounds he heard were putting the worst images in his mind. Within seconds, Tae-Soo and his troop ran out from their position across the street with a war cry that echoed throughout the sky. They bombarded the shielded men, pushing in, breaking their lines.

Kang-Dae ran toward Serenity's position with Jung-Soo right next to him. They made it to the building just as Serenity came crawling out of the window. Kang-Dae raced over and grabbed onto her, lifting her over the rest of the way. She clung to his back.

"He's here," she whispered. Kang-Dae stiffened then nodded. Jung-Soo was helping Nasreen out as well, while more of their men started slowly making their way out the shop. He could hear the faint sound of Kahil yelling for them to get out from inside. Kang-Dae pulled Serenity away back toward the center. By now all of Tae-Soo's men were heavily engaged with the others, their shield wall demolished. From behind them he could hear more men approaching. He looked up hoping it was just the Duke but was disappointed to see another group of Anoekans along with Xians heading for them. Men loyal to their now dead lords no doubt. The battle in front of them raged essentially blocking them in. That became even more true as the enemy started following his men out of the shops. He didn't see Kahil among the retreated, filling him with fear over the man's fate. He looked Serenity in her eyes. "Stay here," he told her. She nodded. He gave a look to Nasreen who understood she was still on duty to protect her with her life. Together, Kang-Dae and Jung-Soo rushed into the battle ahead.

CHAPTER 72

Kang-Dae sliced upwards at the back of one man. He pushed into the two Anoekan men in front of him, sending them right into the swords of the Xians' they were facing. Jung-Soo swung high, severing most of the Anoekans neck who'd foolishly tried to challenge him. Kang-Dae picked up a fallen shield and rushed at the two men aiming their crossbows at his men. Once they saw him coming towards them, they fruitlessly sent off two arrows that only hit the center of the shield. He rammed into the one on the left and he went flying. He then swung the shield into the face of the one on the right, causing a spray of blood to come spitting from his mouth. The man he sent flying got up quicker than he expected and was running at him with a dagger. Kang-Dae held his ground preparing for the impact but was shocked when an arrow stopped the man mid-run. He looked back to see Serenity aiming with the crossbow he gifted her in his direction. He would definitely thank her for that later. So emboldened by her he still had a smile on his face as he cut down the other charging archer.

Serenity tried to keep her aim toward the outside for easier targets not trusting her skills enough to attempt the large pile of men engaged in heated battle. After she took out the one who tried to come for her husband, she managed to get at least two more. Nasreen stayed close, only engaging in a fight if it came for them.

"My queen," she said, pulling on her shoulder. Serenity looked up to see the enemy force behind them getting closer. She let Nasreen pull them to the other side of the statue. They were still stuck between two forces, but were a much harder target. At least on this side, they were doing well. That's what she thought, until more men came charging out of the shop.

"Kill them!" She turned to see Katsuo storming out, sword raised. The coming force began to charge and Serenity was fearful that they would overrun any second.

As the men began charging, Serenity watched as some started to fall. At first, she thought maybe they had just tripped but the harder she looked into the crowd, she was able to make out that some of the men inside were turning on those right next to them.

Ami had been told he should stay behind with his guard. Captains, generals, all claimed they could go into this fight without him and it would be safer if he stayed behind. Ami thought back to Kang-Dae's words to him and decided he could not do that. If he were forced to be king, he would be a king, just like Kang-Dae. And Kang-Dae would be out there with his men. Still, he felt Kang-Dae had been trying to protect him in his own way by ordering him and his soldiers to stay back and keep the rear protected. They sat waiting for a long while before they saw any hint of the enemy. Luckily, due to their similar armor they never considered them a threat. Ami, with his smaller statute, stayed buried in the middle between his guards, where he could hardly see. He could hear the general speaking to the men, cleverly hiding their intentions under a lie about being sent to enter the city from the north to cut off any possible enemies. They claimed to have arrived from the west to surround anyone who may be lying in wait for them. The general masterfully talked the men into combining their forces to really "overwhelm" the enemy and take them out in one great attack. Most of the men stayed within their formation with a few making their way into the enemy's troop. They marched through the city searching for their fellow soldiers when they saw the signal, and changed directions heading towards it. Once they arrived at the scene of chaos Katsuo's men started to charge into the fight. The eastern Anoekans along with his men made their move discreetly at first. Ami could see some of them actively tripping some of the runners only to jam their staffs swiftly and smoothly into them while they were down. Their fellow soldiers were so consumed with their charge they didn't notice as they ran past or actively trampled over their comrades. As more went down and they began to notice, discretion was forgotten. The general ordered an all-out attack and the Anoekans faced off against the Anoekans.

Serenity let out a short laugh at the sight of the confused faces of Katsuo's men as they were attacked by those they thought were on their side. The chaos of that attack completely stopped them from continuing their charge. She searched out Katsuo to see if he noticed the state of his forces and blanched as he was making his way toward Kang-Dae whose back was to him.

CHAPTER 73

Kang-Dae tossed a soldier over his shoulder right into the pile of dead men. He could hear the chaos coming from behind him but believed the Anoekans, their allies, had it handled. He wanted to decimate this force before him and then Katsuo.

"Kang-Dae!" Serenity's piercing scream had him tensing and he knew he had only a second. Trusting his gut, he moved left, barely missing the blade that came down right where he had been standing. He spun with his sword at the ready, finally coming face to face with Katsuo. Serenity had told him he'd been scarred. Seeing it for himself gave him no small amount of satisfaction. The furious look on his face only brought Kang-Dae more joy.

"What have you done?!" Katsuo spat, swinging at him again. Kang-Dae used his sword to bat his away.

Kang-Dae circled around him, the two never took their eyes off one another. "Are you disappointed?" He teased, unable to help himself. Katsuo's eyes narrowed. "All your planning, your great victory, only to end up right back here."

Katsuo charged forward with his sword above. Kang-Dae moved to his left only for Katsuo to meet him with his sword swinging low. Kang-Dae barely managed to jump out of the way, Katsuo's sword scraping against his armor. Katsuo didn't let up on his assault, spinning into another upward swing that Kang-Dae managed to avoid by leaning back. Katsuo growled, running on rage and hate. Kang-Dae could see it in his eyes. He was like a wounded animal. He had become even more dangerous than when he faced him last.

Serenity tried to aim for Katsuo from her position but didn't dare fire. She would never take the chance she'd hit Kang-Dae, plus there was that knowledge in the back of her mind that Katsuo's life would not and could not be hers to take. She could only watch helplessly as he continued to attempt to brutally attack her husband. Around them the Xians and allied Anoekans were still engaging with the enemy, still trying to overtake them. In the distance, she could see the Duke of Illeanda coming towards them.

Ami ordered his guard to get him closer to the battle ahead. The men were still engaged all around them making it difficult. There was some space as some of Katsuo's men had fled from this battle into the other trying to turn the tide. More than a few times they were attacked, but thankfully his guard was skilled enough to push them back as they moved out of one fight into another.

Kang-Dae and Katsuo's swords locked together. A battle of strength engaged between the two. Kang-Dae gritted his teeth as he pushed back against Katsuo with all his strength. The two were stuck in a fruitless fight as one would push the other back only a couple inches only for the other to quickly regain their strength and push the other back just as far. When it became too much, too futile, the two simultaneously jumped back. They were both panting, and red in the face.

Behind Katsuo his men were jumping on a Xian soldier. Behind Kang-Dae two Anoekans fell to three Xian soldiers. None of this was noticed by either man whose sole focus was each other. Kang-Dae spun his sword in his hand and Katsuo pointed his straight at him. The two ran at each other with a shout, swords clashing.

Serenity heard Nasreen cry out and looked up. Her eyes widened seeing the arrow going through her hand. Nasreen wasted no time breaking half the thing off and snatching it through the rest of the way with a small whimper. Serenity pulled off her scarf and wrapped it. Both fights were getting closer and closer to them about to box them in. Serenity grabbed Nasreen's uninjured hand and prepared to sprint toward the buildings where it was mostly clear. Just as they were about to go, a couple of fighting men blocked their path, forcing them to go around, sending them deeper into the fight. Nasreen managed to push off a soldier who'd bumped into Serenity. She hadn't known whose side he was on but Nasreen didn't seem to care as she forced him into a crowd where he was immediately jumped on. They weaved through men, avoiding swinging staffs and swords as best they could. A curved blade would have almost taken Serenity's head if she hadn't ducked in time. They made it to the wall of the building where there was only a few feet of clearance from the fighting. It was a brief moment to catch a breath but definitely not an opportunity to let their guard down.

Kang-Dae reared his head back and slammed it into Katsuo, forcing him stumbling back only a couple of feet. He took the chance to come at him swinging at his midsection. Katsuo raised his armored arm to block the blow and slammed the back of his elbow into Kang-Dae's face. Kang-Dae felt momentarily stunned, his vision went white for a split second and his sword fell from his hand. He regained his composure just in time to see Katsuo preparing to run him through.

He went to the right, letting Katsuo's sword go through his arms, before grabbing hold of Katsuo's hands that were wrapped around the hilt. They tugged and pulled each one determined to take control of the weapon. Kang-Dae suddenly threw his body back sending them both backwards onto the hard ground. More prepared for the sudden drop Kang-Dae regained his composure a second sooner than Katsuo and elbowed him in the stomach. The would-be conqueror choked and coughed. Not finished, he returned Katsuo's earlier jab and went for his nose as well. Some of Katsuo's blood hit his own face at the impact. Kang-Dae rolled away and quickly gathered his fallen sword.

Katsuo struggled to get up, still gagging and wiping at the blood flowing down his face. Kang-Dae's armor must have cut a gash in his forehead because blood rolled over his eyes as well.

Kang-Dae stood and went over, with his sword raised. He slammed it down but it only hit dirt as Katsuo dove out the way, slicing the blade of his sword into Kang-Dae's thigh. It took everything for Kang-Dae not to fall over. He shifted most of his weight to his other leg as Katsuo climbed to his feet. Wounded and fatigued the men stared at the other, neither ready nor willing to allow the other to win. Both were unaware that at that moment they were thinking the same thing. Even if they died, they would take the other with them.

CHAPTER 74

The battles, along with the crowds around them were diminishing. Dead Anoekans and Xians littered the streets. Those remaining were starting to lose their strength. The hits became weaker and the damage was less. Some fights ended with surrender rather than death, with Katsuo's men on the losing end. As things began to quiet, attention became drawn to the two kings locked in battle. Serenity stepped closer, heart pounding seeing the state of Kang-Dae. He looked tired, and he was limping. Still, he met Katsuo head on as he charged. Katsuo wobbled in his run just a little and he managed to go past him like he couldn't see where he was. Kang-Dae grabbed him by the arm and bent it back until it snapped and Katsuo howled.

Serenity winced. Someone grabbed her hand. At first, she thought it was Nasreen offering support but the hand squeezed hers with such force she had to look. She saw Ami next to her, his eyes were locked on his brother and her husband. She squeezed back.

Katsuo shook his head and hair in frustration letting out a snarl. He wiped his eyes once more to remove the blood obscuring his vision. Katsuo could see it even if he chose not to acknowledge it. His men were falling and he was slowly becoming surrounded by enemies. He would not let that stop him from killing the one in front of him. None of it would matter if he could just show them all, he was the stronger one, he had been chosen. Once he did it would stop and they would bow to him. 'No, they won't,' the sober voice in his head piped up. 'However this ends you won't live.' He tried to shake the voice away. It used to be so quiet, now it was clear and overriding the other. The sword was too heavy in his hand for some reason. He tossed it aside and pulled out his dagger, his father's dagger, the one he had planned to gift to Ami when he became old enough. He had wanted to teach him how to use it.

Katsuo couldn't feel his face anymore. His arm was throbbing painfully. He held the dagger in front of him and beckoned the king with his fingers. "If you want my kingdom, you have to take it from me," he rasped.

"It was never and will never be yours. You are not a king. You're a lost fool led astray by those with selfish ambitions. You let them convince you that you rule because you were born to it but no one ever taught you to earn it," Kang-Dae proclaimed with a tired sigh. "I didn't earn that throne with my birth. I earned it with every swing of this sword. I earn it with every enemy I cut down. I earn it with the safety of my people. If the throne is to be taken from me by you, you better have earned it." Kang-Dae emphasized his point by raising his sword ready for him to do just that.

Every word spoken from his mouth was a hit to Katsuo's pride and his heart. 'You will be the great king who unites the world.'

Katsuo looked around. Xians from all throughout the land, the people of Kah Mah, Anoekans from all corners of the country stood by watching what was to transpire, united….against him. He let out a mirthless laugh.

"This can end here," the king said. He hated his voice so much. He should take his head just to shut him up forever, he thought.

"Brother." This voice was less detestable and more familiar. He turned toward it and saw Akimitsu standing with his dream walker. He had a hard time making out his face but he had a feeling he was crying. He saw the Anoekans at his side, guards of the royal family. Guards of the king.

"So, you've taken my throne after all, little brother," he said with a slight chuckle, hugging his broken arm. Akimitsu didn't respond or look away which made him proud in a way. 'Kill him,' Sho's voice spoke in his mind. Katsuo fingered the dagger in his hand. 'Kill them all.'

Kang-Dae watched Katsuo. The fight in him had dimmed significantly even as he held onto his weapon. Perhaps the defeat had finally gotten through to him. But there was an internal war raging inside from the way his eyes would shift from murderous to tired.

Kang-Dae's grip on his sword never relaxed. When Katsuo, with his tired eyes, suddenly ran at him, silently, no shouting, no words of death, Kang-Dae was still able to raise it up high enough. He held out his hand to push against Katsuo's shoulder to try and keep him at bay. As Katsuo's dagger sunk into his armor, Kang-Dae's sword went through Katsuo.

Serenity gasped and her hands went over her mouth seeing Katsuo thrust his knife into Kang-Dae. Katsuo's body blocked her view, she couldn't see how bad it was. No one could move or breathe in that moment. No one knew what would happen next. The two kings stayed entangled for what seemed like an eternity.

Kang-Dae stared into the sad and defeated eyes of a broken man. Blood dribbled from the corner of his mouth. His grip on the dagger stuck in Kang-Dae's side slackened, and he began to slump. Kang-Dae released his sword as he fell to his knees. He looked up at Kang-Dae looking truly pitiful for the first time. The corner of his mouth quipped up just a little before he fell over to his side.

Serenity ran up to Kang-Dae stepping around the fallen Katsuo. Kang-Dae was pulling out the dagger. She froze to see the small amount of blood on it. Kang-Dae tossed it down and reached for her.

"My armor took the brunt of it," he assured her. Serenity went to inspect it but he pulled her up to him in the fiercest hug.

"Long live the King and Queen!" Tae-Soo shouted from the crowd. Cheers and roars broke out all around. What was left of the enemy stayed silent, kneeling in surrender. Kang-Dae wiped at Serenity's happy and relieved tears. The crowd closed in on them, making their joy known. Some of the hiding citizens began to appear, brought out by the cheers. Upon seeing the body of Katsuo, they too celebrated amongst themselves.

Ami approached cautiously with his guard at his back. The poor boy looked like he was numb.

"King Kang Dae," he spoke, his voice breaking slightly. "May we take his body back with us? For my mother?" He asked, staring into Kang-Dae's face, eyes red. Kang-Dae nodded.

"You may."

The men around him moved quickly. Gently picking up the limp body and carrying it off. The cheers only grew louder as they passed with the body. Ami didn't appear to have any reaction to any of it. Serenity wanted to hug him but didn't want to do it in front of the other Anoekans. Instead, she settled for bowing her head slightly to the teen, hoping to convey her support and sympathies. Ami returned the bow, and went to follow after his men and his brother.

"The Anoekans will take care of the rest of his men," Jung-Soo informed them. "Queen Priya and the Duke managed to wipe out the remaining Xian traitors within his ranks. The capital is once again within your control."

Serenity could burst into tears at the news.

"Thank you General," she said with a smile that he surprisingly returned.

Kang-Dae looked down at her while she looked up at him.

"Let's go home."

CHAPTER 75

Blessing seemed to recognize they were home when they entered through the gates. She perked up after being drowsy from just waking from her slumber. It brought a smile to Serenity's face to see her eyes light up as she looked around in excitement. They entered through the west gate not wanting to face the destruction on the northern side. Luckily, they'd left a lot of the section intact. Kang-Dae assured her that the soldiers they sent ahead to drive Katsuo away had done their best to remove as much trace of Katsuo as possible before their return. So far it looked as though they'd done well. Kang-Dae led her by the waist through the familiar paths toward the back of the hall where they resided. They didn't go toward their room though but she hadn't expected to. She wasn't ready to see the state of it yet. Instead, they moved towards Kang-Dae's old room before his ascension. As soon as they stepped inside, a feeling of relief went through her seeing that it had been left untouched. She placed Blessing on the floor as she started bouncing, wanting to get down. The toddler crawled over to the rug in the middle of the floor.

"It will take some time for them to rebuild," he told her. She knew he was speaking of their room.

"Maybe we can take this as a chance to build something new," she suggested. Kang-Dae's brow lifted.

"Oh?"

She reached for his hand and took him over to the bed where they both sat. Serenity hadn't voiced it aloud but going back to the hall, where she'd lost Arezoo and so many others was not something she was looking forward to.

"This place has looked the same since the day it was built, right?" Kang-Dae thought for a second and he nodded.

"It has."

"We wanted to bring some change. Let's build a new home. A place just for us." She had dreamed of having a house in Xian for a while but never brought it up thinking it was impractical. But now seemed like the time to make things new.

"We wouldn't have to leave the palace, just build a place in the back, where we can just be Kang-Dae and Serenity. Where we can raise our kids. We can do that right?"

"Kids?" He immediately repeated.

"Was that the only thing you heard?" She tried and failed to hold in her laughter. Kang-Dae kissed her cheek.

"We can do that." She beamed and leaned into him. Blessing busied herself with the fur rug, running her tiny hand up and down it while pressing her face into it.

***

Jung-Soo held Blessing as his horse was being packed and saddled. She clung to his neck tightly as if she knew she would not see him for a while. Kang-Dae stood by him while Serenity fretted over whether he had everything. Once they had been able to settle back into their home, Jung-Soo finally broke the news to Serenity about Rielle's whereabouts. She of course almost left right in that moment to retrieve her friend before Jung-Soo and Kang-Dae calmed her. Jung-Soo informed her of his plans and intentions to bring her back and told her she didn't have to worry. She got a strange look on her face for a moment like she was remembering something before she said, "You're right. I don't." Jung-Soo felt like there was something he was missing, but chose not to press just glad she had accepted everything.

Amoli was being walked out by Amir. Jung-Soo gave a disappointed look. "I told you not to come," Amir just shrugged as he brought her over. She was moving better since they'd been back but he didn't want her to over-exhaust herself.

"I can do this much," she explained. Kahil was carrying a chair behind them which put him at ease. Amir helped her into it.

"All set?" Amir asked. Jung-Soo nodded.

"How long will it take you?"

Jung-Soo cocked his head. "With the ship Queen Prija gifted me it should not be a very long journey to Assani. With the seas clear of Anoekans there shouldn't be any obstacles in my way."

If anyone caught that he hadn't technically answered the question no one mentioned it. In truth, he did not know when or even if he would return. He would send Rielle back, that, he would make sure he did. What happened to him afterward, he didn't know. He never told them about the deal he made. He wanted to keep them from worrying and avoid the lecture for agreeing to something without knowing what it would entail.

The peek of the rising sun covered the courtyard highlighting the working builders. They were making great headway. Most of the debris had been removed. What was left of the demolished buildings had been completely ripped away leaving empty spaces. Jung-Soo, feeling it was time to go, gently but forcibly pulled Blessing from around him and handed her to her father. She whined the entire exchange only calming when he gave her to Amoli who was reaching out for her.

"Have a safe journey," Amir told him with a smile. Jung-Soo nodded his thanks. Amoli smiled up at him as she bounced the baby over her shoulder.

"We will await your return. I expect you to be at my wedding," she grinned and Amir placed a loving hand on her other shoulder.

Kang-Dae slapped his back and held onto his shoulder. "Be quick."

Serenity stepped over and Jung-Soo felt a sudden need to avoid looking in her eyes, fearing she would find the truth, but he remained still. She hugged him and leaned up to whisper in his ear. "Your turn." He pulled back, brows furrowed not understanding what she could mean. Serenity didn't repeat or clarify her words, only giving him a mischievous and knowing smile. "When you two get back here we'll really celebrate." She announced before shuffling back to Kang-Dae. Jung-Soo wanted to press. He even opened his mouth to ask but quickly closed it. She would never tell him he realized, looking at the gleam in her eye. Frustrating as it was, it also filled him with a large amount of hope. She believed it would work out, so he knew it would.

He climbed on his horse and Tae-Soo did the same. No matter how many times Jung-Soo told him to stay, the insolent soldier refused to obey and now he was forced to have him as his traveling companion. Serenity waved enthusiastically; Blessing even copied her mother's actions amusingly while the rest just smiled. Jung-Soo gave them one final look before turning his horse and setting off on his own unknown journey.

CHAPTER 76

Three months later

Serenity and Kang-Dae stood outside the foundation of their coming home. They held hands as they prayed over it that week. It was a tradition Serenity started on her own a couple of weeks into building and Kang-Dae had decided to join her. She wanted to speak out loud everything she sought for the home and what it would be as it was being built. Blessing walked around their legs in her own world. As they ended the prayer with a simultaneous "amen" they pulled away but still hung onto the other's hand. Serenity stared at the property imagining how it would look once finished. They were tucked away, half a mile from any other halls or buildings within the palace. There were trees and a small pond. When Serenity found the area, she immediately knew it was the perfect spot.

"I was told you made some more requests about the space," Kang-Dae brought up, trying to be nonchalant.

"Mmm-hmm," she hummed while keeping up with Blessing who was waddling toward the pond.

"They wouldn't tell me any more than that."

Serenity pretended to ignore him, squatting down to keep Blessing from going into the water. "I know we discussed wanting rooms for Mi-Sung and anyone else who may appear."

"Yep."

Kang-Dae squatted next to her and leaned in close. "You seem to have a specific idea of how many rooms they needed to build."

Again, she said nothing. Blessing reached her hand in the water, splashing and laughing. Serenity kept her secure between her knees. "Do you know how many rooms we need?" He finally came out and asked. Serenity smiled to herself before turning to him.

"Maybe."

Kang-Dae's eyes sparkled and he fought a grin. "Are you going to tell me?"

"Nope." Kang-Dae frowned, but it only lasted a second before a wide grin spread on his face.

"I guess I can wait until they've finished." Serenity shrugged.

"Rooms can always be added later," she said with a smirk. She stood grabbing Blessing's hand and walking toward the path back to their hall. Kang-Dae frowned once more, realizing she was right.

Serenity paused and spoke over her shoulder, "I did ask them to try and have the nursery done before the new year's festival." She headed back down the path while Blessing babbled a song. Kang-Dae's brows furrowed as he took in her words. His eyes widened and he spun a little too fast, almost falling into the pond.

"Truly?!" He called after her but she didn't pause in her stride, only letting out tiny giggles. Kang-Dae scrambled to his feet to chase after her.

Even More Months later…

Kang-Dae helped Serenity into the chair. "I'm fine," she said, waving him off.

Her mother clicked her tongue as she placed a tray of ham on the table.

"Can't believe you came over here like that just for some food."

"I'm not even in my third trimester. And it's Thanksgiving," Serenity said, eyeing the feast in front of her.

"You should know better," Patrica scolded Kang-Dae.

"I am sorry Mother but she would not be dissuaded." Kang-Dae rubbed at Serenity's protruding belly before going to help set out the food.

"I got it, just take care of that foolish one in there," Patrica fussed, going back into the kitchen.

"Love you, Mommy!" Serenity called out as her mom scoffed. Kang-Dae chuckled at his wife as he took a seat next to her. He looked outside the dining room.

His brother-in-law, Levi, and his father-in-law were watching television as the kids played at their feet. Blessing laughed at one of her cousins' funny faces. This time his sister-in-law came out of the kitchen with a bowl of rolls. Serenity quickly snatched one up before it could hit the table.

Denise just laughed. "I won't tell ma," she told her.

"Thank you," Serenity whispered back.

"She better not be eating out there!" Patricia called out. Serenity froze and hid the roll under the table.

"I'm not," she lied.

"Kang-Dae, is she eating?" Serenity looked up at him, her face at first pleading with him before shifting into a more threatening expression, one that made him swallow.

"I do not see her eating mother," he said, being as truthful as he could without invoking his wife's wrath. Serenity, satisfied, smiled, and sneakily took a bite of the roll.

Once all the food had been brought out Patricia called everyone into the dining room. Blessing made her way over to Kang-Dae who quickly scooped her up. The boys stood together eyeing the food. His father-in-law took his place at the front of the table and Patricia stood next to him. The family all took hands as they prayed over the food, a concept Kang-Dae had gotten used to over the years.

Afterward, everyone sat down, the kids over at the "kids table" and the adults around the larger one. Kang-Dae helped Serenity fill her plate knowing exactly what she wanted. Though he had been truthful with Patricia that he had tried to convince Serenity not to travel he was grateful she had been stubborn. He cherished these moments with the family he did not get to see often and he knew Serenity did as well. He watched as Serenity leaned into her mom's caress as she brushed her cheek. His father-in-law raised a glass at him and he reciprocated. Levi rolled his eyes at the attention Serenity was getting and she stuck her tongue out at him. These were the moments when they were not king nor seer. They were just a husband and wife with a family. Serenity had been right when she told him that was just as important as everything else. Though they had made their house their own little sanctuary, it was times like these, away from the palace, away from everything, that he felt it most. Blessing laughed at the boys as they discreetly tossed food at each other. Levi caught on and scolded them but their smiles remained. He remembered how hurt he had been when Serenity fought so hard to get back here. He understood all too well now what she was fighting for because now he had it, and he would never let this go.

EPILOGUE

15 Years later…

Mi-Sung Blessing Kwon stared at the portrait above the throne in the main hall. Seeing her parents looking so young with her as a baby sitting between them filled her with unexplainable peace. The hall was empty. The last meeting had been a couple of days earlier. Her father allowed her to sit in on it after she asked him for the tenth time.

"Boo!" Blessing nearly jumped out of her skin as she spun with a small scream right into her laughing brother who steadied her. Frowning, Blessing pushed at his shoulder.

"Stop that," she fussed trying to calm her heart. Hye-Jin continued laughing, bent over only showing the top of his loose curly hair. Blessing rolled her eyes at his antics but waited till he gathered himself. It took longer than she thought it should for him to finally stand up, while he dramatically wiped at nonexistent tears. He was taller than her by a couple of inches despite being younger.

"That's for making me come get you," he said, rolling his neck in a similar manner to their mom. Blessing refused to laugh at the impression, still upset at his trick.

"Come get me for what?" she asked looking back over at the portrait.

"You're supposed to be home, it's almost time to eat." Blessing let out a silent oops once she realized. She must have lost track of time.

"Why are you always staring at that? We have pictures at home." Hye-Jin asked. Their parents had dozens of pictures hung up around their house. Pictures of them and their family back where their mom was from. There was even a couple with her grandmother and grandma together. Grandmother had wanted to see her mom's world at least once so her mother took her. Her mom said it was better to keep the photos in their home to keep anyone from getting suspicious. Hye-Jin preferred the photos to the paintings but Blessing liked them.

"It reminds me of when I was once an only child and happy," she joked. Hye-Jin scoffed.

He tugged at her arm pulling her out into the hall past another portrait with just the two of them sitting in their grandmother's lap. "Come on, let's go," he said.

She wrenched her arm away. "I'm coming. We still have time." Hye-Jin looked away.

"What?"

"We have to find Grace," Blessing gave him a look.

"Who's we? It was your turn to watch her," she reminded him.

"She got away," he admitted sheepishly. Blessing rolled her eyes again.

"You know she's probably playing with the twins."

"I looked already." Blessing shook her head in disapproval and headed out of the hall.

"Are you going to help me?"

"Uh-uhn."

"Mi-Sung!" He whined in a high-pitched tone. Blessing groaned and turned around.

"Fine."

Hye-Jin smiled like their dad and ran over. They both made it out of the hall when Blessing paused. Hye-Jin kept walking.

"Favor," she called out, using his nickname.

"What?" he answered, not stopping.

"Look!" He frowned before looking at what she was pointing out only to let out a sigh.

On top of the statue, on the side of the steps leading into the hall, a small, skinny, smiling girl stared down at them.

"Get down!" Hye-Jin scolded. Grace giggled as she effortlessly slid down like she wasn't in a dress. Blessing held out her hand and the young girl took it. She pushed some of Grace's wild curls off her sweaty forehead. She had obviously been playing hard.

"Where were you?" Blessing asked her.

"Following Faaaavor," she said in a singsong voice. Blessing looked over at her brother with her brow raised.

"Really?"

"It's not my fault. Mom keeps saying she's like a cat." Blessing wrapped her hand around Grace's and started walking with Hye-Jin following behind. The three headed toward their house, their parents, and their home.

That is the end for Serenity and Kang-Dae, my lovelies! Thank you for joining them on this journey. And thank you for your continued support. Just in case you feel let down about some of your other characters' endings don't fret. The end of one story only leads to the beginning of another.

For example...

Coming Soon

The General's Healer

Unopened Scars

Jung-Soo has a promise to keep and he intends to do so. Never one to back down from duty or a fight, Jung-Soo is asked to enter into the unknown to fulfill a debt. He knows there's no guarantee he will return but he won't be dissuaded, not by his king, his men, not even an out-of-place healer from another world whose purpose seems to be to vex Jung-Soo in every way. Already in an unfamiliar land, Jung-Soo must go even further, further than he or any Xianian has ever gone.

Despite what he ordered, Rielle refuses to leave the stubborn general on his own. Even though she is already far from home, she is more than willing to go further to keep that infuriating general from disappearing from her life without a trace.

Duty, stubbornness, and unspoken affection force the two on a journey neither could have anticipated.

Made in the USA
Middletown, DE
06 March 2025